Marcus Dods

Erasmus and other essays

Marcus Dods

Erasmus and other essays

ISBN/EAN: 9783743382008

Manufactured in Europe, USA, Canada, Australia, Japa

Cover: Foto ©Andreas Hilbeck / pixelio.de

Manufactured and distributed by brebook publishing software (www.brebook.com)

Marcus Dods

Erasmus and other essays

ERASMUS

AND OTHER ESSAYS

BY

MARCUS DODS, D.D.

PROFESSOR OF EXEGETICAL THEOLOGY, NEW COLLEGE, EDINBURGH

SECOND EDITION

London:

HODDER AND STOUGHTON,

27, PATERNOSTER ROW.

MDCCCXCII.

PREFATORY NOTE

OF the Essays collected in this volume, those on "Confucius" and on "Christianity and Civilisation" have been already published in *Good Words*; the address on "Preaching" was separately issued by Messrs. Maclehose of Glasgow; the Essay on "Marcus Aurelius" was printed in the *Madras Christian College Magazine*; and the remaining papers were contributed to the *British and Foreign Evangelical Review*. To the Editors and Publishers concerned I am indebted for permission to republish. Some of the papers are rather out of date, and had I been writing them now, I should probably have expressed myself differently on one or two points, but I have judged it better on the whole to reprint without alteration.

M. D.

EDINBURGH, *October* 1891.

CONTENTS

VII

VIII

IX

I

ERASMUS[1]

WHOEVER has looked upon the portrait of Erasmus — that portrait which he himself was so reluctant to sit for[2]—must have wished to acquaint himself with the soul that dwelt behind those brightly intelligent but melancholy and sceptical eyes. Whoever has considered that large eloquent mouth, whose proportions are preserved by the finely-cut curve which denotes scholarly taste, and whose massiveness is relieved by the humorous, ironical smile which plays about the upturned corners of the lips, must have

[1] 1. *The Oxford Reformers John Colet, Erasmus, and Thomas More.* Being a History of their Fellow-work. By Frederic Seebohm. Second Edition. London, 1869. 2. *Erasmus : his Life and Character, as shown in his Correspondence and Works.* By Robert Blackley Drummond, B.A. 2 vols. London, 1873.

[2] " Vix extortum est amicorum precibus, ut se pingi pateretur."— *Vita Erasmi—prefixed to the Colloquies.*

said to himself, There is a man who has known and thought much, but who has strength enough to be free and airy in his movements with all his burden of knowledge,—a man who has seen strange and sad experiences in this world, but who has spirit enough to be gay, nay, to be hopeful and tender throughout,—a man who must have been the best of company while living, and who must have dropped from these lips pregnant sayings which cannot die. It is one of the great faces of the world, to be ranked with that of Dante, or of Newman; though distinctly memorable from the first glance we get of it, it draws one back again to look at it, as if there were a meaning we had not taken up, or perhaps a capability which even all the difficulty of threescore years and ten had not developed.[1] And it is not the face alone which attracts us. The most superficial facts of his life show us that it must be one of the most significant ever lived. The man who laid the egg which Luther only hatched;

[1] In the nearly magnificent but queer Valhalla at Ratisbon, in which the busts seem to have been made to order rapidly and in large numbers, at so much per hero, neither inartistic dulness nor payment by the piece has availed to chisel that face into insipidity. But it is doubtful whether it was judicious to place amid all the solemn dignitaries, a face whose curl of the lip seems to be pouring perennial satire on the whole affair.

the man who in that time of fierce strife, when all Europe was divided into two parties diametrically antagonistic, ' refused to join either party, though wooed by both as essential to their complete success,—this man deserves to have his biography written and read. And yet, like Alexander at the tomb of Achilles, he may still weep for a biographer; or possibly it may give his restless shade a more congenial satisfaction to observe the baffled efforts of his would-be biographers, as one after another they attempt to weave into a consistent character his quite transparent and yet never sharply defined aims and leanings, or to form a readable narrative out of the perplexingly superabundant material which lies to the hand of any one who undertakes the work.

In saying that Erasmus has not yet found an adequate biographer, we do not mean to speak slightingly of the many well-equipped writers who have thrown light upon his character and career, and least of all, of the two authors whose works are named at the head of this article. Indeed, of Mr. Seebohm's volume we feel disposed to speak in terms which would at once be set down as exaggeration. And it is of little moment how we speak of it, for already it has been accepted as a standard work on a period which deserves the most careful study. Of Mr. Seebohm's leading aim or conclusion, viz. that the theology of Jerome and the Oxford Reformers, is preferable to that of Augustine and Luther, we may have more to say in the sequel; but however much we may dissent from his conclusions, we heartily admire his accurate research, and the masterly finish with which he has arranged and presented his material. His work has obviously been a labour of love, and it is not too high praise to say that he writes in a spirit worthy of two of the noblest Englishmen, Colet and More, whether he has imbibed this spirit from so long cultivating their society, or whether his own native love of what is true and pure and of good report has led him to live with these congenial spirits. We have not happened to see any other production of Mr. Seebohm's pen, but this volume alone gives him a place among our most accomplished writers in the historico-biographical department. It is this style of controversy we welcome; a careful and truth-seeking investigation into what men really thought and said, together with an earnest but dispassionate statement of the author's own views, if he thinks fit to give us them.

In this quality of uttering his own opinion, without spitefully abusing that of his neighbour,

Mr. Drummond somewhat fails. There is a want of dignity about his attacks on evangelical religion which is beneath the historian; and there is a manifest bias in his reading of some of Erasmus's opinions, which will, we fear, cause the public to think his work rather a plea for looseness of opinion than an impartial narrative. His book is to a great extent a polemic; and a polemic against polemics. He is haunted throughout by the "evangelicals," and too frequently, to the reader's surprise, turns aside from his proper course to make a rush at them. We do not, of course, object to his interspersing his narrative with reflections of his own. We welcome reflections which reveal the springs of character or the pregnancy of a situation; reflections such as that master of critical biography, John Morley, knows so well how to insert.[1] We welcome the sudden flashes which George Eliot shoots through a whole region of life, leaving it for ever more comprehensible or more entertaining to us. But when a writer interrupts his narrative with passages which suggest that he is writing with a strong theological bias and with a controversial aim, it is inevitable that he loses as a

---

[1] It must be owned, however, that Mr. Morley sometimes very seriously offends in the same way as Mr. Drummond.

biographer more than he gains as a controversialist. Mr. Drummond sometimes writes well, with information and force, on controverted topics; there are passages in these volumes which must have shown extremely well in the *Theological Review*, where they first appeared, but his biography of Erasmus would have been better received, would have been read with greater pleasure and trust, and would have lived longer, had he exercised some self-restraint, and withheld from his book applications of his subject to modern circumstances, and indignant pleadings for his own school of theology. He may suppose, and justly, that to mend his own times is a higher task than to write a good biography. But as the dramatist who understands his art does not give us an interlude of sermon between the acts to enforce the moral of his piece; as the novelist who writes to reform a grievance or to shame out of countenance a social abuse, misses his end, just in so far as his teaching is separate from his story; so the greatest possible amount of light would have been shed on our times, and the greatest possible conviction produced in our minds, by the simple exhibition of Erasmus's own character and views. Nevertheless, Mr. Drummond's book is valuable. To those who have tried to use Jortin's chaotic mine, we may best describe Mr. Drummond's volumes as an arranged Jortin. The earlier writer had probably greater learning, and certainly had a keener edge on his mind; but any one who wishes to form an opinion of Erasmus, will find ample material for doing so in Mr. Drummond's book. He will find in it a careful collection of facts, an accurate and spirited translation of the most important of Erasmus's letters, a skilful analysis of his best known writings, and sufficient allusion to those which are less read. It is a work of great diligence, and will be really useful as a guide to the study of Erasmus's own writings. No one can read it without feeling that he is in the company of a modest, unostentatious, painstaking, competent writer, who has the rare virtue of taking his own measure, and understanding what he is most likely to do well. There are a few writers who, as they move, shed a blaze of light into every surrounding region. We do not mean to claim for Mr. Drummond a place among these; but we should deem it only justice, were his book acknowledged as a successful attempt to shed light upon a single and very important line of fact. And it is, at all events, the most satisfactory life of Erasmus which our language can boast.

Of other lives of Erasmus, a very judicious estimate will be found in Milman's well known and delightful essay, into which there is condensed an amount of information which few men could have afforded so prodigally to lavish on a Review article. But probably the most living portrait of Erasmus is that which has been drawn, since Milman's article was written, by the accomplished and perfervid historian of the era of England's rejuvenescence. In one point certainly Mr. Froude excels the other writers who have chosen Erasmus for their theme. He has abundant sense of humour. His wit indeed is earnest and fierce, but he quite understands, if he somewhat underrates, the more genial and less bloodthirsty satire of the author of the *Praise of Folly*. Besides, he has a native genius for apprehending the characters of the past, if not with perfect accuracy, yet with a vividness of imagination which enables him to present them quite definitely before our eyes. And therefore it is Froude's Erasmus which lives in one's mind; and, correct the picture as we may, it is still the stronger colouring of that consummate artist that shines through our feeble re-touchings.

We fear that, like Erasmus himself, his true biographer has passed to that land in which earthly careers are read, not in the printed page of laborious investigation and doubtful criticism, but in results manifest to all at a glance, in fixed features of character which reflect an infallible judgment on the essence of what was done and thought here upon earth. A very few years ago the most ardent students of Erasmus felt that in the hands of James Hamilton his life and labours were safe, and looked eagerly for the completion of a work whose first portions gave promise of a complete and perfect biography. Here was the needed culture, diligence, humour, sympathy with the subject. Here was the eye, candid and truthful, open to see what was without, and not the mere reflection of what was within; here was the spirited, graphic style, which could engage the reader's interest and rise level with his theme. To many, as probably to Hamilton himself, it seemed that this was a subject instinctively chosen, as likely to elicit from him the fullest power he could exert; but by choosing a task which it will take years to finish, a man does not always secure that he shall live out these needed years.

We are not now to attempt to tell again the story of Erasmus's life, nor to re-mould material which has already passed through the hands of accomplished writers. As we have already said, there are few lives regarding which there is more abundant or more accessible information. The romantic but sad story of his parents and of his birth has been told by Charles Reade, in his somewhat highly-coloured but entertaining and useful novel, *The Cloister and the Hearth.* In Erasmus's own letter to Grunnius,—a letter vitalised by indignation,—we have a moving sketch of his youthful difficulties and troubles, of the unscrupulous arts used to entrap him into the monastic life, and of his unfitness for such a life by reason of his delicate constitution, which disabled him from enduring the smell of fish without a headache, and from getting to sleep again after rising for service during the night.[1] In the *Colloquies,*[2] he makes use of his own college experiences to expose some of the grievances under which students at that time laboured, and which, as he tells us, drove some to madness, and doomed others to leprosy or blindness for life. We see him in the College Montaigu (*Vinegar College,* from the sour or acid theological disputa-

---

[1] "Habebat adolescens peculiare incommodum, quod illi a teneris annis in hanc usque aetatem haeret. Non nisi profunda vespera potest obdormiscere, et a semel interrupto somno non redormiscit, nisi post horas aliquot."—*Ad Grun.*

[2] Ichthyophagia.

tion that was carried on in it till the very walls reeked with theology ; so he says) rising from a filthy bed, coughing out of his throat the damp which had distilled from the mouldy walls, and shivering out in the darkness and frost to break the ice from the well and draw the fetid water, scarcely distinguishable from the pestilential sewers that flowed or stagnated close by. By means of his letters it is easy to trace him indomitably fighting his way out of ignorance, poverty, obscurity, now keeping pupils in Paris, now teaching Greek at Cambridge, writing dedications, begging with more or less shamefacedness, declining the invitations of popes and princes but accepting their gifts, publishing books at almost every printing office in Europe, everywhere making some friends and many enemies, always learning and always making startling use of his learning, until he stood the recognised first scholar of the world. By means of his letters—a collection full of interesting reading, bringing one into pleasant connection with all the leading men of the age, and putting the reader into, as nearly as possible, a contemporary's point of view—we insensibly gather an impression of Erasmus and of his influence, as with him we impatiently revisit what he refused to call his fatherland, and preferred contemptuously to nickname his "beer and butter land"; or go with him to Rome, and mark the disappointment and contempt of the ecclesiastics that mingled with his admiration of the literary collections, and broke through his desire to stand well with all dignitaries; or dwell pleasantly with him in his most congenial residence at Basle, doing as much work in one day as most men did in two,[1] and yet finding time to stroll about in Froben's garden, or spend the afternoon writing in his summer-house; or come back again and again to England, drawn mainly by his love of Colet, "the best beloved of his age,"[2] attracted, too, by the culture of More, Linacre, Grocyn, Fisher, Warham, and others whom he is never weary of extolling, and bearing, no doubt, also a not unpleasing remembrance of the women who, probably for the first time, showed him the possibility of combining a perfect purity of thought with the most encouraging frankness of manner, always leaving our island

---

[1] "Plus operis abs te uno factum die, quam quantum abs quovis alio biduana opera exigi consuevisset." — *Scaliger's remark about Erasmus's work at Venice for the Aldine press,* quoted in Drummond, i. 172.

[2] Seebohm (p. 505) tells us that his coffin bore an inscription which contains these words, "ob vitae integritatem et divinum concionandi munus, omnium sui temporis fuit charissimus."

with regret, and prepared to defend everything in it but its houses;[1] thus we wander with him, sharing the hardships and the triumphs and pleasures of a literary life in the beginning of the sixteenth century, until the clouds gather, though not with so heavy a gloom as Froude depicts, and the air, which had rung with the voices and been brightened by the kind faces of many friends, becomes silent and chill, and the last touching signature is written, "Eras. Rot. aegrâ manu."

And the impression which is thus conveyed to the mind, is that of a man not of the very first order, either intellectually or morally. It has been observed by one who sows truth and error in about equal quantities, that "our fatuous persistency in reducing man to the spiritual, blinds the biographer to the circumstance, that the history of a life is the history of a body no less than that of a soul; many a piece of conduct that divides the world into two factions of moral

---

[1] See the letter in which he complains, like any sanitary commissioner, of the inconvenient internal arrangements and unwholesome situation of English houses. "The floors are commonly of clay, strewed with rushes, which are only lifted at long intervals, and under which lies unmolested, an ancient collection of beer, grease, bones, spittle, and every nameless abomination."

assailants and moral vindicators, provoking a thousand ingenuities of ethical or psychological analysis, ought really to have been nothing more than an item in a page of a pathologist's case-book." Certainly in any endeavour to estimate the character of Erasmus, we must take into account his nervous temperament. It was this which made him so keenly sensitive to physical pain, so averse either to its infliction or endurance. It was this which made him at once intensely alive to the current of public affairs, and shy of the responsibility and danger which beset a leader of opinion. It was this which fitted him for society and enabled him to find his best and most pleasurable stimulus in the friendship of good men, but this also which prevented him from showing any of the deeper qualities which friendship elicits. Kindly, charitable, ever genial, he was a bright, cheerful, entertaining companion, but always, as one of his enemies said, "homo pro se." Often displaying a quick resentment, and sometimes as abusive in his language as Calvin, he was never vindictive. He was almost too ready to be reconciled to those who had injured him; in this, as in all matters, shrinking from disagreeable personal collisions, and from everything which would perturb him. He would involve himself with no party ; he would identify himself with no movement which he could not himself control, with no opinions which might demand from him unwelcome action.

It is a mistake, however, to suppose that this was due to timidity ; and it is a greater mistake to appeal to Erasmus's fear of death as a proof of this timidity. No one accuses Samuel Johnson of timidity, because we find him exclaiming, " O my friend, the approach of death is very dreadful. I am afraid to think on that which I know I cannot avoid." And they who are fond of quoting passages, which show that Erasmus partook of this common shrinking from dissolution, should have had the decency to remark also, that when death did approach, this fear and horror entirely disappeared. When he lay ill at Louvain, when doctor after doctor had turned from his bed in despair, and when the monks of Cologne were already shouting (in Latin worthy of the taste and feeling which prompted the triumph), that he had died "sine lux, sine crux, sine Deus," his mind was calm and hopeful.[1]   " When the disease

---

[1] Romanists have for one reason or other altered their views of Erasmus, for we find one of their living writers making the audacious assertion, that he died "with the names of Jesus and Mary on his lips."

was at its height, I neither felt distressed with desire of life, nor did I tremble at the fear of death. All my hope was in Christ alone, and I prayed for nothing to Him except that He would do what He thought best for me. Formerly, when a youth, I remember I used to tremble at the very name of death." So he writes in a letter to one of his most intimate friends.

Indeed, no one can read even a little of Erasmus's writings, without being amazed at his boldness. Read, *e.g.*, the description he gives in his *Adages*[1] of the royal bird—

"Let any physiognomist worth anything at all consider the look and features of an eagle—those rapacious and wicked eyes, that threatening curve of the beak, those cruel jaws, that stern front—will he not at once recognise the image of a king? a magnificent and majestic king? Add to this a dark ill-omened colour, an unpleasing, dreadful, appalling voice, and that threatening scream at which every kind of animal trembles. Every one will acknowledge this type who has learnt how terrible are the threats of princes, even uttered in jest. At this scream of the eagle the people tremble, the senate yields, the nobility cringes, the judges concur, the divines are dumb, the lawyers assent, the laws and constitutions give way, neither right nor religion, neither justice

---

[1] Under the proverb "Scarabaeus Aquilam quaerit."—See Seebohm, 310.

nor humanity avail. And thus, while there are so many birds of sweet and melodious song, the unpleasant and unmusical scream of the eagle alone has more power than all the rest. Of all birds the eagle alone has seemed to wise men the type of royalty—not beautiful, not musical, not fit for food; but carnivorous, greedy, hateful to all, the curse of all, and, with its great powers of doing harm, surpassing them in its desire of doing it."

Pretty well this, for the beginning of the sixteenth century, and for one who received pensions or gifts from nearly all the kings and princes in Europe.

If further proof of the boldness of Erasmus be needed, it is to be found in his unsparing denunciation of the corrupt practices of the Roman Court, and especially of what Ranke terms "the ruling passion" of Pope Julius II.,—namely, his innate love of war and conquest. In the *Praise of Folly*, Erasmus drew a picture of Julius which no one could mistake; "The decrepid old man, assuming all the vigour of youth, sparing no cost, shrinking from no toil, stopped by nothing, if only he can turn law, religion, peace, and all human affairs upside down." The whole passage is important as bringing out very unmistakably the point and vehemence with which Erasmus assailed the real evils of the Church of his own day—

"Of spiritual weapons, indeed," he says, "the popes are mighty liberal, of interdicts, suspensions, denunciations, greater and lesser excommunications, and bulls that fright those they are thundered against ; and these most holy fathers never issue them more frequently than against those who feloniously and maliciously attempt to lessen St. Peter's patrimony. For although in the gospel that apostle is said to have declared 'we have left all and followed Thee,' yet these popes speak of 'St. Peter's patrimony' as consisting of lands, towns, tributes, customs, lordships ; for which, when their zeal for Christ is stirred, they fight with fire and sword at the expense of much Christian blood, thinking that in so doing they are apostolical defenders of Christ's spouse, the Church, from her enemies. As though indeed there were any enemies of the Church more pernicious than impious popes, who give dispensations for the *not preaching* of Christ ; evacuate the main design of our redemption by their pecuniary sales ; adulterate the gospel by their forced interpretations and undermining traditions ; and lastly, by their lusts and wickedness, grieve the Holy Spirit, and make the Saviour's wounds bleed afresh. Further, as the Christian Church was founded in blood, and confirmed by blood, and advanced by blood, now in like manner, as though Christ were *dead*, and could no longer defend His own, they take to the sword. And though war be a thing so savage, that it becomes wild beasts rather than men, so frantic that the poets feigned it to be the work of the Furies, so pestilent that it blights at once all morality, so unjust that it can be best waged by the worst of ruffians, so impious that it has nothing in common with Christ, yet to the neglect of everything else they devote themselves to war alone."

Surely he who wrote this was not ambitious of a cardinal's hat, nor very careful about giving offence to the most formidable power then on earth. But we shall be better able to estimate his strength of character and his relation to the Church of Rome, after we have briefly reviewed his literary labours, and recognised what it was that he himself reckoned the proper work of his life.

His diligence in his proper vocation as a literary man has rarely been equalled, never surpassed, not even by the most "adamantine" of scholars, such as Heyne. For a combination of rapidity and brilliance of execution, his work may be compared to that of his almost compatriot, Rubens. The one artist "careers over the canvas," earning his hundred florins a day, and leaving from a few strokes of his brush a lasting joy to men. The other writes his forty letters a day, collates manuscripts which are maddeningly corrupt, edits the most voluminous writers of antiquity, does not always earn as many florins as he could wish, but wins the hearty admiration and gratitude of all lovers of genial humour, pungent wit, and lively learning. Unconquerable as Richard Baxter, he worked on through the attacks of one of the most painful of diseases, and managed to produce sallies of merriment where other men would have fancied themselves legitimately excused from all but groans. Indefatigable as the elder Pliny, and infinitely less pedantic, he used every available moment for study, and was yet always ready to turn an epigram for a friend, and never denied himself the pleasures of social intercourse. He once challenged Froben to print as fast as he could write. He could compose in the midst of the greatest noise, and his great satire, *The Praise of Folly*, is evidence that the work he produced on horseback was of better quality than some which we are told proceeded from that stimulating seat.

Too frequently great scholars have wasted their energies on subjects of no general utility or even interest. But one is struck, in reading over the long catalogue of Erasmus's literary labours, with the sagacity which, at the very revival of letters, guided him to discern what stood highest in literature. He stands between the ancient and modern world, as a kind of gentleman-usher, selecting with unerring instinct such writers as were worthy of immortality, redeeming them from the obscurity to which a non-reading world had consigned them, and introducing them, as free from soil as he could make them, to the world which dates from the invention of printing. A number of the classics, which have ever since remained the favourites, he either edited or translated, or both. In summing up the character of Erasmus, Mr. Drummond makes the somewhat unintelligible statement, that " original genius, or creative power of any kind, cannot be ascribed to him, nor was the time ripe for the appearance of any such qualities, when the apparatus of literary workmanship had still to be got into order " (ii. 346). Creative genius has not been wont to wait for the elaboration of any particular apparatus. But certainly, when we consider the difficulties which a scholar in those days had to overcome, the want of previous editions, the corrupt state of the manuscripts, the absence of grammars and dictionaries, and of trustworthy geographical and historical information, it is impossible to overrate the perseverance, if not the genius, which compensated for the lack of these aids. The picture of a scholar's life which is graphically sketched in the letters of Erasmus, is very different from that which floats in the imagination of the youthful student of modern times, and invites him to a life of quiet if not of ease, to a comfortable competence if not to wealth. Tischendorf and Curzon are the modern scholars, whose adventurous labours in some respects most fitly compare with those of Erasmus. His frequent changes of residence were due not solely to the restlessness of his disposition, but mainly to his desire to consult manuscripts which lay scattered in distant libraries, and to find printers capable of executing his work. He was thus compelled again and again to traverse Europe in days when travelling was both tedious and dangerous. At one time we find him laid up at Ghent with a sprain in his back, caused by the shying of his hack; again a dolorous lament comes from the banks of the Rhine in flood, and where he says he was kept swimming rather than riding. In one respect his fate was the same as that of more recent travellers, his passages from England to the continent prostrated him with sea-sickness. The channel had, besides, associations in his mind which might well have debarred him from ever revisiting our island. On one occasion he was stripped, by the custom-house officers of the niggardly Henry VII., of the hard-earned English gold with which he was expecting to pay his way through the succeeding year. On another occasion, after embarking, he discovered that his luggage containing his Jerome and the collation of New Testament MSS., was not on board—one of those skilfully-contrived accidents which are still, we fear, sometimes practised upon travellers for the sake of extorting the *trinkgeld* which is readily given in the moment of relief that follows the long anxiety. But his bitterest complaints are of the bad wines and stifling filthy inns of some parts of Germany. Every reader of the *Colloquies* remembers the passage in which he describes the sufferings of a guest in one of these inns; a passage we would quote, were it not so painfully graphic, that we fear our readers would sicken with the loathsome steam which rises from the damp and dirty travellers gathered round the stove, or finally turn from a page which thrusts sights so disgusting before their eyes.

It was no ordinary zeal which carried the delicate and sensitive scholar through scenes such as these, but there was no sacrifice he was not prepared to make in the cause. "If any new Greek book comes to hand," we find him writing, "I would rather pawn my coat than not obtain it; especially if it be religious, such as a psalter or a gospel"—*especially if it be religious*, for those quite misunderstand Erasmus, who do not know, or refuse to believe, that his main object and chief endeavour, was to Christianise rather than even to educate Europe. "If we are genuine Christians," he says, "nothing ought to seem erudite, elegant, or admirable to us which is not redolent of Christ, wherever the subject admits of this." And again, "The highest object of the revival of philosophical studies will be to become acquainted with simple and pure Christianity in the Bible." His preference for religious writings was sufficiently proved by his enormous labours in patristic literature. He edited the whole works of his favourite Jerome, of Cyprian, Augustine, Hilary, Irenaeus, Ambrose, with portions of the works of Chrysostom, Athanasius, Basil, Epiphanius, and Lactantius. To read these works would in these degenerate days constitute any one a learned man, and it is opppressive to think of the labour involved in preparing so many ponderous folios for the printer, even though he had correctors of the press so accurate as his friends Lystrius and Beatus Rhenanus. Once or twice he broke down under the labour, but this was the sacrifice he thought himself justified in making to the Fathers, the true and legitimate worship of the saints. "We kiss the old shoes and dirty handkerchiefs of the saints," he says in his preface to Jerome, "and we neglect their books, which are the more holy and valuable relics. We lock up their shirts and clothes in jewelled cabinets; but as to their writings on which they spent so much pains, and which are still extant for our benefit, we abandon them to mouldiness and vermin."

It was this masculine sense and discernment which lifted Erasmus above the inveterate superstitions and follies of the time, and which also saved him from the vices peculiar to scholars. A mind that steeps itself in classical literature, sometimes gains refinement at the expense of robustness. In our own day, certainly, some of our most distinguished scholars have also been among the most vigorous thinkers, and have been no less remarkable for practical sagacity than for delicacy of taste; but this is probably due rather to the tendency of the times than to the inherent influence of classical studies. It may have been due to the character of the times that Erasmus did not degenerate into a mere bookworm, or student, or litterateur; though the times did not save his friends Budaeus and Reuchlin from that fate. But the nature of Erasmus retained throughout a manly vigour, which forced him to take a part in the stirring events of his times, and taught him to use his learning merely as a weapon in the fierce conflict which he himself had in great part stirred. His *Adages*, of which one large edition

after another was rapidly sold out, as no books
of the size are now sold out, was not more
remarkable for the unrivalled research it displayed,
than for the fearless and pointed invective and
satire which it levelled against existing abuses
and stupidities. So it was with all his writings;
they were all of the nature of artillery, not of
fireworks; while the reader is admiring the flash,
he finds himself already hit. Each of his writings
has its motive in the real world around him, and
all of them are alive with the characters he was
daily seeing.

We must therefore ascribe it in great measure
to Erasmus that the Renaissance was even as
Christian as it was. For, as Hallam tells us,
"the object of the Italian scholars was, to write
pure Latin, to glean little morsels of Roman
literature, to talk a heathenish philosophy in
private, *and leave the world to its own abuses.*"
This school would use no word which was not
found in the writings of Cicero, and would resort
to the most circuitous circumlocution, or paganise
the most sacred subjects and names, rather than
depart from this rule.[1] This trifling seemed to

---

[1] Bembo is said to have kept forty portfolios, through all of
which each sheet of his writings had to pass, being examined
and corrected at every stage. See Hallam.

Erasmus both silly from a literary point of view, and dangerous to Christianity. And it was against this coterie of exclusive and semi-pagan purists, that he issued his effective *Ciceronianus*. In his brochure he holds up to ridicule the weak pedants who tabulated every word, phrase, and cadence to be found in the works of the master, and who, after reading no books but those of Cicero for seven years, can only feebly and stiffly imitate the graceful language of their model. Erasmus convincingly proves that this is not the path to eminence in literature, and shows that it is a thorough understanding of the subject treated, and an interest in it, which give a forceful and copious style as they give a naturalness and warmth of sentiment, which captivate the reader. There is much in the *Ciceronianus* which is capable of universal application. He distinguishes between the slavish imitation which reproduces what is obsolete, and the intelligent revival of the ancient severity of taste. He proclaims the folly of putting new wine into old bottles; and dis-criminates between the adoption of antiquated forms and the application to modern uses of the ancient enlightenment and knowledge. In a word, he distinguishes—and when will men learn the distinction?—between that imitation which consists in a superstitious clinging to old forms and traditional customs, regardless of their inapplicability to modern society, and that imitation which adopts the ancient spirit, and lets it freely produce such forms as may suit the changing times.

But while Erasmus exposes the literary mistake with overwhelming force and abundant humour, one sees that he has a much more serious aim than the exposure of a mere piece of silly pedantry. Erasmus thoroughly understood these Italian scholars, and knew that they preferred the culture of heathenism to the self-repressing ethics of the cross. If Christianity was not recognised as a force of sufficient power to produce a new vocabulary, it was because it was misunderstood or purposely held in the background. And if the ideal which these men of culture proposed was to be sought, Christianity must be held in the background, or appear only as the disfigured and dishonoured servant of culture. Erasmus saw that there might be a revival of paganism more dangerous than that attempted by Julian, and no one did so much as he to avert this danger. Not only in the *Ciceronianus*, but in many other writings, and especially in his letters, he expresses the fear that the revival of classical literature might veil a revival of pagan sentiment, and professes that for his own part, he would rather be a Christian with the barbarians, than a pagan with the Ciceronians. This, coming from a man who knew Horace and Terence by heart, who had acknowledged that in reading Cicero he could not but sometimes kiss the page, and pay tribute to the heavenly inspiration that had filled the writer; this coming from the man who was acknowledged by all but Scaliger as the foremost scholar in Europe, could not be without a very powerful effect. Let those who are accustomed to think of Erasmus as himself but a half-hearted Christian, consider whether there was any other man then living, whose decision as to the relative positions of culture and Christianity, would have had the same weight in Europe, and whether he does not deserve our gratitude for so boldly and decidedly throwing himself into what might other-wise have been the losing side. For to ascribe his alienation from the Italian scholars to mere personal vindictiveness is absurd. It is true he had been nicknamed *Errasmus* by those who thought it a feather in their cap to find him out in small *errors*, as he had been called *Porrophagus*, on account of his extreme fondness for the word *porro*. It is true also that he was unduly sensitive to such kinds of annoyance, but his other writings,

and especially his letters to his dear friend Colet,
put it beyond a doubt, that he did not prize
culture for its own sake, but mainly as the best
means of introducing a purer Christianity.

This is very clearly brought out by his connection with Dean Colet, in the founding of St.
Paul's school in 1510, which, taken all in all,
forms one of the most pleasing passages in the
history of education. We see the two great men,
the one the foremost scholar, the other probably
the purest minded and bravest man then alive,
filled with mutual esteem and affection, correspond-
ing and taking counsel together, and finally devoting their means and their labour to the education
of 153 boys. No sooner did Dean Colet receive
his patrimony, than he devoted it to this object,
ordaining that "the children should be taught
good literature, both Latin and Greek, specially
Christian authors who wrote their wisdom in
clean and chaste Latin, whether in prose or verse;
for my intent is by this school, specially to increase
knowledge, and worshipping of God and our Lord
Jesus Christ, and good Christian life and manners
in the children." One can scarcely mistake the
spirit of the man who concludes the preface to
the Latin grammar he wrote for his school in
these terms—

"I pray God all may be to His honour, and to the erudition and profit of children, my countrymen Londoners specially, whom, digesting this little work, I had always before mine eyes, considering more what was for *them* than to show any great cunning. . . . Wherefore I pray you, all little babes, all little children, learn gladly this little treatise, and commend it gladly to your memories, trusting of this beginning that ye shall proceed and grow to perfect literature, and come at the last to be great clerks. *And lift up your little white hands* for me, which prayeth for you to God, to whom be all honour, and imperial majesty and glory.   Amen."[1]

Erasmus was not only thoroughly at one with his friend regarding the propriety of using Christian authors in preference to the impure writings of heathen classics, but evinced his tender regard for children, by writing against the practice of flogging,[2] by composing schoolbooks, and by doing his utmost to secure the right kind of teachers.   In an amusing letter to Colet, dated from Cambridge (where Erasmus had been appointed Margaret Professor of Divinity), he tells of the ill success of his application to some of the college dons for their help in the matter.   One of

---

[1] Seebohm's *Oxford Reformers*, 213.

[2] Flogging for the mere purpose of breaking the will was denounced also by Anselm, in most reasonable and instructive terms. See Church's *Anselm*, p. 82.

them sneeringly asked "Who would put up with the life of a schoolmaster, who could get his living in any other way?" When Erasmus modestly urged that he considered the education of youth the most honourable of all callings, and that no man could serve God better than by bringing children to Christ, the Cambridge doctor turned up his nose in contempt, and replied, "Whoever wishes to give himself up entirely to the service of Christ, let him enter a monastery." Erasmus ventured to ask whether St. Paul did not make true religion consist rather in charity and doing as much good as possible to our neighbours; but this remark was treated as a mere proof of his ignorance. "Behold, we must leave all; in that is perfection." "*He* can scarcely be said to leave all," replied Erasmus, "who, when he has a chance of doing good to others, refuses the task because it is too humble in the eyes of the world."[1]

Of Erasmus's writings, the two which produced

---

[1] Further insight into Erasmus's regard for children is to be gained from a perusal of the pretty colloquy, entitled *Pietas Puerilis*, from which one suggestive quotation must suffice. "*Er.*—Aiunt vulgo, pueros angelicos in Satanam verti, ubi consenuerint. *Ga.*—Sed ego proverbium isthac ab autore Satana natum arbitror. Imo vix existimo, senem esse vere pium, nisi qui a teneris annis assueverit. Nihil felicius discitur, quam quod ab ipsa statim pueritia discitur."

the greatest sensation, and exercised the mightiest
influence, were the *Colloquies* and *The Praise of
Folly.* Clever and easy, like everything he wrote,
full of learned allusion, and yet hitting straight
at the faults of his own age, the *Colloquies* also
reveal considerable dramatic power. The spark-
ling dialogues are maintained by characters who
live in our memory as substantially and familiarly
as those of Shakespeare or Scott. The dialogues
are not launched with the exquisite grace of the
Platonic masterpieces, but they are vigorous from
first to last, and are probably as lively reading as
any that remains to us from that period. What
was said of one of our greatest talkers, may be
said of the writer of the *Colloquies*, that " he
winds into his subject like a serpent." There is
no appearance of effort; he seems to carry a light
which makes obvious to him what other men
have groped after. He finds natural utterance
for what all other men have been trying to say.
Under the smile that ripples everywhere on his
page, and that now and again breaks into uncon-
trollable laughter, he is still profoundly in earnest,
and each sentence is alive with a real purpose.
We may read many Histories of the Reformation,
and derive from them all less real knowledge of
the church and society which needed reforming,

than we gain from a pleasant hour or two with the *Colloquies*.

But his most pungent and popular satire was the *Praise of Folly*—a satire so popular, that during his own lifetime no fewer than twenty-seven editions[1] were called for, and so pungent, that an ecclesiastic in Constance hung up the author's portrait in his room, that he might have the satisfaction of daily spitting in the face of the man who had so galled his order. The origin of this piece was very simple. On his journey from Italy to England, his thoughts naturally turned to the cultivated men whose society he hoped shortly to enjoy there, and it occurred to him as an odd coincidence, that the word *more* should in Greek signify a fool, and should at the same time be the surname of the wisest and wittiest man of his acquaintance. This seems to have led him to think of the large number of persons who were fools, not in name, but in reality; and while passing these in review, he perceives how truly Folly is queen over a large part of human affairs. Arriving in England, too much knocked up to apply himself to more serious studies, he beguiled the days in the absence of his congenial host, Sir

---

[1] The first of these appeared in 1511, and consisted of 1800 copies; other editions were very much larger.

Thomas More, by writing down the thoughts that had occurred to him on his journey. "It was not done with any grave design, or any view of publication; but he knew his friend More was fond of a joke, and he wanted something to do, to take his attention from the weariness of the pain he was suffering. So he worked away at his manuscript." [1] In one week the whole was completed.

The plan of the work gives the author the widest range for his satire. Folly is introduced in her cap and bells, declaiming to her ass-eared votaries, and extolling herself as the mistress of human affairs. Under this slight mask Erasmus passes in review all the varieties of fools and follies in the world; the dicing, hunting, antiquarian, saint-worshipping fools, are all sketched in a few sharp lines. He hits off the pretenders who after long patching at a speech call it extempore, and swear they wrote it in a hurry; those who interlard their sentences with Greek they cannot construe; those who nod and smile when they hear anything unusual, that they may be thought to apprehend that of which perhaps they do not understand a word. Taking a wider sweep, Folly claims that she gives all the stimulus to great action, for is it not Folly that blinds

[1] Seebohm.

men to the emptiness of the world's rewards, and
leads them to distinguish themselves that they
may have a statue in the market-place? Consider,
too, the miseries and indignities of human life,
miseries so great that we cannot but commend
the Pythagorean cock, which had passed through
life as a man, a woman, a fish, a horse, and a
frog, and after this large experience, declared
that man was the most wretched and deplorable
of all creatures. What but Folly can blind men
to these miseries? Is not Folly therefore an
essential of our nature?

"We may as well," says Folly, "call a horse un-
happy, because he was never taught grammar, or an
ox miserable because he was never taught to fence, as
call a man unfortunate for being a fool, for this is
what nature and providence have ordained him to be.
. . . Self - confidence is a folly, and yet take away
this one property of a fool, and the orator shall become as dumb and silent as the pulpit he stands in ;
the musician shall hang up his untouched instrument
on the wall ; the completest actors shall be hissed off
the stage ; the painter shall himself vanish into an
imaginary landscape ; and the physician shall want
food more than his patients do medicine. In short,
without self-love, instead of beautiful you shall think
yourself an old hag of fourscore ; instead of eloquent,
a mere stammerer ; instead of well-bred and gentle-
manly, a downright clown ; it being so necessary that

every one should think well of himself before he looks
for the good opinion of others. Happiness is nothing
else than a contentment to be just what we are, and
this is effected by self-love, which so flushes men with
a good conceit of their own, that no one thinks ill of
his shape, of his wit, of his education, of his country,
so that the half-drowned Hollander would not exchange his country for the sunny plains of Italy, nor
the Scythian quit his desert to become an inhabitant
of the Fortunate Islands. . . . Upon this account it is
that the English challenge the prerogative of having
the handsomest women, of being the most accomplished in music, and of keeping the best tables; the
Scotch brag of their gentility, and pretend that the
genius of their soil inclines them to be good disputants; the French think themselves remarkable for
their good breeding," and so on.

The satire of Erasmus belongs rather to the
school of Lucian and Goldsmith than to that of
Juvenal and Swift. At least there is in the
Colloquies and the *Praise of Folly* the same playful raillery and the same keen exposure of vice
and ignorance which delight the reader of the
Dialogues or the *Citizen of the World*. Certainly
we miss the turns of deep pathos and the touches
of tender humanity, which have made all men
love the thriftless, scrambling, generous Irish-
man; but we happily miss also the fixed scorn
that disfigures the pages of Swift, and the some-

what overdone and self-conscious indignation which, while it gives brilliance to the style, lessens the moral power of Juvenal's satire. Erasmus depends upon ridicule as exclusively as Horace. He excites contempt, not indignation, against the objects of his satire. He laughs ill-doers out of countenance, and leaves it to others to use the lash. Neither is he a buffoon who makes fun of everything, nor a mocker who sneers at what is good as well as at what is corrupt; but he is discriminating, and merits the praise which has been accorded with less justice to another, that "no satirist has to answer for fewer attacks on what is valuable."

Satirists have been accused of affecting alarm at the consequences of their own freedom. One of our keenest classical critics, G. A. Simcox, has exposed the "comic mixture of vanity and cowardice," in Persius protesting against a persecution he had done nothing to provoke, and anticipating a martyrdom he was never to undergo.[1] Horace records how he took advice of his friend Trebatius, the lawyer, regarding those who threatened him with an action at law, because he was "nimis acer, et ultra legem" in his satire.

[1] Simcox's *Juvenal*, Introduction, p. xviii.

Voltaire seems to have considered Erasmus guilty of the same species of timidity, for he introduces him (in his dialogue between Lucian, Erasmus, and Rabelais), excusing himself for not taking the same liberties as Lucian, on the following ground: "Vous n'aviez affaire qu'à des dieux qu'on jouait sur le théâtre, et à des philosophes qui avaient encore moins de crédit que les dieux; mais, moi, j'étais entouré de fanatiques, et j'avais besoin d'une grande circonspection pour n'être pas brulé par les uns ou assassiné par les autres."[1]   But Erasmus was never seriously disturbed by the violent threats of his enemies, though undoubtedly he was at times in danger. He rather, indeed, makes a jest of the danger, saying that it is hazardous to satirise the divines, "for they are a sort of men very hot and passionate, and should I provoke them, I doubt they would set upon me and force me to recant."   But while he was not deterred from writing by fear of actual violence, he was more annoyed than he need have been by the violent language the monks used against him.   He had none of the self-reliant vigour of our own burly moralist, who could say, "Who the plague is hurt with all this nonsense? and how is a man the worse, I wonder,

---

[1] *Œuvres de Voltaire*, ed. 1827, vol. ii. p. 1932.

in his health, purse, or character, for being called Holofernes?" So hurt was he by an attack made upon him from a pulpit in Louvaine, that he demanded a meeting with his assailant, Nicolas Egmondanus, prior of the Dominicans. Of this meeting he writes a very amusing account to Sir Thomas More.[1] For want of space we must refer those of our readers who wish to see this, to Drummond's *Erasmus* (ii. 52), or to Froude's Essays on Erasmus and Luther.

The history of Erasmus's *magnum opus*, his edition of the Greek Testament, or *Novum Instrumentum*, is tolerably well known. It has been told by Mill,[2] who, though not uniformly accurate, has done more than any other critic in collating the different editions of the work, and affords material for more recent writers on "Introduction." Wetstein, while acknowledging the services rendered by Mill, gives an independent and interesting account[3] of Erasmus's, as indeed of all the editions preceding his own. The useful manuals of Scrivener and Tregelles have made the leading facts familiar to readers of such literature, and have given fair estimates of the importance of the work. But by non-professional readers,

---

[1] *Ep.* p. 721. [2] *Nov. Test.* Proleg. 1116-1141.
[3] *Ibid.* Proleg. p. 120.

and those who are not in search of mere technical details, the well-informed and thoughtful narrative of Mr. Seebohm will be most highly relished.

Probably a little too much has been made of Erasmus's own expression regarding the rapidity with which this volume was compiled, that it was "praecipitatum verius quam editum." It is with surprise we find so careful a writer as Mr. Scrivener using the following language: "It is almost painful to be obliged to remember that a portion of ten months at the utmost, could have been devoted by Erasmus to the text, the Latin version, and the notes";[1] and even Wetstein is too absolute in his assertion, "Quod nimis festinanter tale ac tantum negotium susceptum gesserit." It is of course natural that Mill, who had given thirty years of toil to his own edition, and Wetstein, who had from his boyhood chosen the editing of the Greek Testament as the great work of his life, should feel hurt at any one who did the same work in a slim and insufficient manner. But though Erasmus did not give himself so early and so undividedly to this same work, there is abundant evidence, that from the time of his acquaintance with Colet, he meant that all his other studies should subserve the

[1] Scrivener's *Introduction*, 296.

work of making the Bible known and understood. Thus we find him, in 1504 or 1505, writing, " I cannot tell you, dearest Colet, how, by hook and by crook, I struggle to devote myself to the study of sacred literature,—how I regret everything which either delays me or detains me from it." Then, after relating how he had attempted something on Paul's epistles, and had found his Greek defective, and had in consequence devoted himself for the three past years to the study of that language, he goes on thus :

" Although, however, I may for a while be engaged upon an humble task, yet whilst thus working in the garden of the Greeks, I am gathering much fruit by the way for the time to come, which may hereafter be of use to me in sacred studies. For I have learned this by experience, that without Greek one can do nothing in any branch of study ; for it is one thing to conjecture, and quite another thing to judge,—one thing to see with other people's eyes, and quite another thing to believe what you see with your own." [1]

Seven years after this, in July 1512, he writes to Colet again, that he has completed his collation of the Greek Testament, and in the remarkable letter which he wrote to Servatius two years later,[2]

---

[1] The above is Seebohm's translation.
[2] Dated from Hammes Castle, 9th July 1514.

he claims to have corrected the text of the whole
New Testament, and to have made annotations,
"not without theological value," on more than
one thousand places. "I have also commenced
commentaries on St. Paul's epistles, which I shall
finish when the others are published; for I have
made up my mind to work at sacred literature to
the day of my death." The knowledge of this
fact, that at least ten years had been spent in
preparatory labour, must considerably modify our
opinion of the haste with which the work was
executed. It is obvious that he already had his
material pretty well in shape, and that the idea
of this publication did not come upon him
suddenly. That the work was sent through the
press far too hurriedly, every one will admit.

If any one repeats the question of Wetstein,
"Quomodo ipsam festinationem excusavit, aut
quis ipsum eo adegit ut festinaret?" the answer
is best given by those very citations which Wetstein himself makes from the letters of Erasmus.
On the 17th April 1515, Beatus Rhenanus writes
to him on behalf of the great printer Frobenius,
and invites him to issue his Greek Testament
from the Basle press: "Petit Frobenius, Novum
abs te Testamentum habere, pro quo tantum se
daturum pollicetur, quantum alius quisquam."

And on the 30th of the same month, the application is renewed. It is generally understood, that the urgency of Froben was prompted by his desire to anticipate the publication of the Complutensian edition; a desire in which he was gratified, for though the Complutensian New Testament was *printed* early in the year 1514, the publication of it was delayed till 1522. It was this rivalry which occasioned one of those memorable passages in literary history, which, though every one knows, every one likes to recall. When Stunica found that the edition on which he had laboured under Cardinal Ximenes was anticipated, he attempted to depreciate the work of Erasmus, but was rebuked by his chief, in words which are as immortal as the Polyglot: "I would that all might thus prophesy; produce what is better, if thou canst; do not condemn the industry of another."

During the summer of 1515, Erasmus repaired to Basle. The printing, however, cannot have begun before September, as the letters of Erasmus show that in that month it was still undecided whether the Latin version should be printed in parallel columns with the Greek (as eventually it was, and in very beautiful type), or in a separate volume. In the beginning of March 1516, the volume made its appearance, a marvel of rapid work ; for although Erasmus lightened the labour, by simply correcting one of the Greek codices,[1] and sending it to the printers as copy, and although he received not only the scholarly aid which the printing office of Froben could always supply, but also that of Oecolampadius, as his corrector of the press,[2] it is to be considered that, during this same winter, he was engaged in several other heavy literary undertakings. Unfortunately the results of this rapid printing are too apparent. Mill speaks of the "menda, quibus scatet, typographica"; Scrivener says, that in this respect it is "the most faulty book" he knows; and Wetstein gives examples which certainly reflect no credit on the carefulness of Oecolampadius. It appears, also, that the best MS. of the Gospels within his reach was overlooked by him. This

[1] The MS. thus used is that known as Cod. Basil. B., vi. 25. It belongs to the fifteenth century, and had been bought, Wetstein tells us, by the preaching friars of Basle, for two Rhenish florins ; and "dear enough at the money, in Michaelis's judgment." It contains the four Gospels. Wetstein gives specimens of the corrections made by Erasmus on the margin.— *Nov. Test.* Proleg. p. 44.

[2] The words of Froben's prefatory note are worth quoting : "Nec meis laboribus peperci nec pecuniis. Quin et precibus et praemiis egi, ut castigatores adessent complures, haud vulgari doctrina praediti, et in primis Joannes Oecolampadius Vinimontanus, praeter integritatis ac pietatis commendationem, insignis etiam theologus, triumque linguarum egregie peritus, ipso quoque Erasmo in hanc partem advigilante."

was the MS. known as E Codex Basiliensis, and which had been given in 1431 to a religious house in Basle, by Cardinal John de Ragusio. Its antiquity was much overrated by Mill, whose knowledge of it was second-hand (and who also erroneously thought that Erasmus had made use of it), but Wetstein refers it to the ninth century, while Scrivener concludes that it was written about the middle of the eighth century. Of the five MSS. which he did make use of, none belonged to an earlier period than the tenth century.[1] And where his MSS. altogether failed him, he did not scruple to create a Greek text, by translating from the Vulgate.[2]

Still, with all its imperfections, this edition effected the purpose of Erasmus, which was to begin the great work of discovering and circulating the true text of Scripture. He recognised the superior value of ancient MSS.; he led the way in boldly adhering to MS. authority in critical passages, such as 1 John v. 7; and thus, and by his own Latin version, he exploded the authority of the Vulgate. Even the Complutensian

---

[1] For a full account of these MSS., see either Wetstein's *Prolegomena*, or Scrivener's *Introduction*.

[2] This was scarcely so reprehensible as his practice of amending his Greek MSS. from the Vulgate, where he *thought* them defective. He thus introduced the thirty-seventh verse of

editors shared in the vulgar veneration for this version, as may be seen from the language they use regarding their arrangement of the Old Testament page. In this page in their edition, the Vulgate occupies the central column, the Hebrew and the Septuagint being on either side; this they compare to the position of Christ as crucified between two thieves,—"the unbelieving synagogue of the Jews, and the schismatical Greek Church." We admire the intelligence and courage of Erasmus the more, when we find another scholar writing thus: "What if it be contended that the sense, as rendered by the Latin version, differs in truth from the Greek text? Then, indeed, adieu to the Greek. I adhere to the Latin, because I cannot bring my mind to believe that the Greek are more correct than the Latin codices."[1]

Acts xiii., and in the ninth chapter he inserted the clauses of the fifth and sixth verses, which are recognised as spurious, but which have nevertheless maintained their place in the Textus Receptus through all these years. It is extraordinary how quickly a kind of sacredness attached to the printed text of the New Testament ; so that, as Tregelles observes, "the readings originally edited on most insufficient MS. authority, were supposed to possess some prescriptive right, just as if (to use Dr. Bentley's phrase) an apostle had been the compositor."

[1] The results which flowed from the exclusive use of the Vulgate, are illustrated by the well-known incident in the Convocation of 1512, when an old divine urged as proof that heretics should be put to death the command of Paul to Titus

No one can read the "Paraclesis," which Erasmus prefixed to his Greek Testament, or the annotations he appended to it, or the address to the pious reader which prefaces his "Paraphrases," without recognising that he was not more interested in his work as a scholar than as a Christian, and that if he expected that the literary success of his book would be great, his hope was that it would bring Christ and His people into a more real contact and communion. None of his writings are more worthy of a perusal, or speak more directly and forcibly than these. They are the utterances of a mind that has long been full of the subject, illustration follows on illustration, argument on argument, to persuade men to the study of the New Testament, and especially of the gospels :

"No anxious preparatory learning," he says, "is needful. Only bring a pious and open heart. The sun itself is not more common and open to all than the teaching of Christ. For I utterly dissent from those who are unwilling that the sacred Scriptures should be read by the unlearned, translated into their vulgar tongue, as though Christ had taught such subtleties that they can scarcely be understood even

---

(iii. 10), "Haereticum hominem devita," which he understood to signify "de vita tollere."

by a few theologians, or as though the strength of the Christian religion consisted in men's ignorance of it. The mysteries of kings it may be safer to conceal, but Christ wished His mysteries to be published as openly as possible. I wish that even the weakest woman should read the Gospel—should read the epistles of Paul. And I wish these were translated into all languages, so that they might be read and understood, not only by Scots and Irishmen, but also by Turks and Saracens. To make them understood, is surely the first step. It may be that they might be ridiculed by many, but some would take them to heart. I long that the husbandman should sing portions of them to himself as he follows the plough, that the weaver should hum them to the tune of his shuttle, that the traveller should beguile with these stories the tedium of his journey." And again : " If the footprints of Christ be anywhere shown to us, we kneel and adore. Why do we not rather venerate the living and breathing picture of Him in these books ? If the vesture of Christ be exhibited, where will we not go to kiss it ? Yet were His whole wardrobe exhibited, nothing could represent Christ more vividly and truly than these evangelical writings. Statues of wood and stone we decorate with gold and gems for the sake of Christ. They only profess to give us the form of His body ; these books present us with a living image of His most holy mind. Were we to have seen Him with our own eyes, we should not have so intimate a knowledge as they give of Christ, speaking, healing, dying, rising again, as it were in our own actual presence."

There cannot be two opinions, then, about Erasmus's services in the revival of letters and in the Reformation. His intelligence, his judgment, his industry, his influence, were surpassed by no one of his contemporaries. He was constantly writing, and all that he wrote was eagerly read. It was Goldsmith's characteristic complaint, "Whenever I write anything, I think the public *make a point* to know nothing about it." Erasmus could complain of no such neglect. Few authors have found in their own lifetime so large an audience, or have seen such manifest results of their writings. While Calvin was learning to prattle in the patois of Picardy, while Tyndale was hanging about Oxford, uncertain as to his future, while even Luther was as yet but groping for light, Erasmus was collating manuscripts of the New Testament, advocating its translation into all vernaculars, and writing annotations to explain its sense to the people. He had already spoken so plainly to two popes about the necessity of reform, and had published, in his own telling and popular style, an exposure of Romish corruptions so formidable, that his writings were placed on the *Index.* No one can read his *Colloquies,* no one can remember that they were the most popular reading of all classes in Europe at that time, without believing that to the author of this book the Reformation, in great part, owed its success. Once for all by this and other daring publications, the fear and superstitious reverence which had been the bulwark of the religious orders were broken through and abolished, and the difference between true godliness and a religion of ceremonial was brought clearly and indelibly before the mind of the people.

But no testimony to the important part played by Erasmus is so convincing as the fact, that no sooner did Luther begin his work, than Erasmus was at once charged with having suggested to the Reformer his leading ideas, and with being the real author of all the disturbances in the Church. So constantly was this charge repeated, that the letters of Erasmus are full of remonstrances against the injustice of those who made it. Thus he writes to Cardinal Wolsey:

"As to Luther, he is altogether unknown to me, and I have read nothing of his but two or three pages, not because I despise him, but because my own studies and occupations did not give me leisure; and yet, as I hear, there are persons who affirm that I helped him. If he hath written well, the praise belongs not to me; and if he hath written ill, I ought not to bear the blame, since in all his works there is not a line that came from me. His life and conversation are universally commended ; and it is no small prejudice in his favour that his morals are unblamable, and that calumny itself can fasten no reproach upon him. If I had really been at leisure to peruse his writings, I am not so conceited of my own abilities as to pass a judgment on the performances of so considerable a divine ; though wise children in this knowing age will pronounce that this is erroneous, and that heretical."

Such is his uniform, constantly reiterated reply, when besought or commanded to prove his orthodoxy by attacking Luther :

"I would not hesitate," he says, "to die without confession, were I as free from all vices as I am uncontaminated by Lutheranism." Again : "I have cursorily turned over some pages of his writings, and have recognised in him gifts well fitted to serve the cause of religion, if he employed his abilities to the glory of the Saviour. As many atrocious crimes were charged upon him, and some of them manifest lies, I wished that if he were at fault in some things, he should be amended, not made away with" [handed over, as he elsewhere says, not to the hangman, but to the theologians]. "If this be favouring Luther, I frankly own that I favour him, and so doth the pope, and so do you all, if you be true divines, and, indeed, if you be true Christians." [1]

Here, then, it will be observed, is the first

____

[1] Most of these passages, and many others, will be found in Jortin.

reason for Erasmus being neutral. He was busy with his own work—work which he conceived to be too important to admit of his forsaking it to entangle himself in party strife. He had useful work of his own to do, and he was provoked that he should be summoned from the work he had chosen, to work which he detested. A very slight acquaintance with his letters, however, shows that there was another reason for his not joining the Reformers:

"I have refused the bribes which men in power have offered me, that I should write against Luther; and I would rather lose what I have than write to please any one contrary to my own conviction. It is no vulgar crime to betray the Gospel of Christ for money. But I have declined to give my name to Luther's party, both for many other reasons, and also because there occur in his books some passages I do not understand, and some which I cannot approve of; and especially because I have become aware, that in his party there are men whose character and efforts are very far from being in accordance with the spirit of the Gospel."

To Melanchthon he complains of Luther's violence, and asks how many of the princes and ecclesiastics against whom he has written, have been turned by his words to the pursuit of holiness. He believed that milder measures should first have been tried; physicians do not resort to severe measures till milder treatment has failed. He refuses to listen to those who plead that such a course was useless, and bids them remember the Greek proverb, that it is better to let an evil alone than to apply unsuitable remedies. To what extent he was right we can never know. Whether it was a wholly baseless hope, to expect that men like himself, Warham, Colet, More, and Vitrarius, might effect much in the way of reform within the Church, we cannot say. But that it was natural for Erasmus, who lived among these men, and knew the healthiness and power of their influence, to expect that something might result from their protests, no one can deny. Neither can any one be surprised that the author whose works were the most popular of the day, and who saw that his popularity rested mainly on the circumstance that he pleaded for reform, should have been led to believe that such reform might be gained. We believe the hope was vain. We believe that the death of More, and the petty persecution which drove Colet into retirement, must have taught even Erasmus that no reform from within the Church could be looked for. But before he learned this, he was hopelessly separated from the Lutherans.

There was still another reason which perhaps operated most powerfully of all in holding Erasmus aloof from the Reformers. He has been claimed as the precursor of the modern spirit, the Broad Churchman of the sixteenth century, the apostle of free thought. It is quite a study to observe how Mr. Drummond is divided in his mind, not knowing whether to claim Erasmus as a pronounced Arian, or as the herald of deliverance from all dogmatism. If Mr. Drummond had been wise, he would not have hesitated to relinquish the former in favour of the latter claim. But there seems to be an idea abroad, that so long as dogmatism is not orthodox, it is not dogmatism. To be a Trinitarian is dogmatic; to be an Arian is to be imbued with "the modern spirit." And so Mr. Drummond thinks he may safely claim Erasmus both as an Arian and as a man who had no theological opinions whatever. We must pause for a moment to protest against his insinuation that Erasmus leant towards Arianism. The passages which he cites (ii. 162), in proof of this, are from the colloquy entitled "Inquisitio de Fide," and are in the following words: "The Son also is God, but of God the Father. But the Father alone is of none, *and obtains the principal place among the divine persons.*"

The other passage is an answer to the question, "Why is the Father alone called God in the Apostles' Creed?" and is as follows:

"Because He is simply the author of all things that are, and the fountain of all Deity. For nothing can be named whose origin does not flow from the Father; and to Him even the Son and the Holy Spirit owe their Divinity. Accordingly the chief authorship, that is, the principle of origination, resides in the Father alone, because He alone is of none. Nevertheless, the creed may be thus understood, that the name of God is not personal but generical, and is afterwards distributed by the terms Father, Son, and Holy Spirit, in one God; which word expressive of nature, comprehends the Father, the Son, and the Holy Spirit, that is, three persons."

Now, if this be the Arianism of the *Theological Review*, we are sincerely glad to hear it. But we should like to know from whom Mr. Drummond has taken his notions of Trinitarian doctrine; for on turning to Waterland (vol. ii. 401), we find him professing precisely what Mr. Drummond considers to border on Arianism:

"Supremacy of order," he says, "consists in this: that the Father has His perfection, dominion, etc., from none; but the Son *from the Father*. All that the Son has is referred up to the Father, and not *vice versâ*. This kind of supremacy is of the Father alone;

and the Son's subordination thus understood, is very consistent with His equality of nature, dominion, perfection, and glory, according to all antiquity."

And when Waterland is asked (ii. 97), why the creeds style the Father the one only God, his answer is identical with that of Erasmus. "The Father is, as it were, the top of unity, the head and fountain of all." Or if we turn to the other great writer, whom every student of Trinitarian doctrine might be expected to consult, we find that Bull lays down this thesis regarding the subordination of the Son to the Father:

"Filium eandem quidem naturam divinam cum Patre communem habere, sed a Patre communicatam; ita scilicet ut Pater solus naturam illam divinam a se habeat, sive a nullo alio; Filius autem a Patre; proinde Pater divinitatis, quae in Filio est, fons, origo, ac principium sit." [1]

But even had Erasmus enounced and defended Arian propositions, the fact would have been of no significance, because he lost no opportunity of showing that doctrinal theology had no interest to him. He was willing to accept as his creed whatever the Church enjoined. "I know not what weight the authority of the Church has with other men," so he writes to his friend

[1] Bull's *Def. Fid. Nic.* p. 3.

Pirckheimer (p. 960), "but with me its weight is such that I could think with Arians and Pelagians, if the Church had given its approbation to their doctrine." It is not of such stuff that theologians are made. The natural tendency of his mind was not towards abstract thought; and this natural incapacity for philosophy and theology was converted into a hearty contempt and dislike by the dry, barren, hair-splitting, merely verbal teaching, which was current in his college-days. He left college, not caring to make up his mind about the more abstruse doctrines, conscious that he could never very decidedly take up one position rather than another regarding them, and fearing that, if he should adopt any definite opinion, it might turn out to be heretical. In this state of mind he met Colet, who was then passing through an intellectual conversion, common enough in this century, but extraordinary and most significant in the end of the fifteenth. By this conversion Colet was passing over from reliance on the mass of theological dogmas, which the schoolmen and fathers had built up, to reliance on the simple historical facts recorded in the Gospels, and to the natural expressions of the Apostolic letters, which brought him, "not to an endless web of propositions, to the acceptance of which he must school his mind, but to a Person Whom to love, in Whom to trust, and for Whom to work."[1] He had found sure standing ground in the Incarnation and Life of Christ, in the few facts on which our religion rests, and which have made salvation for us; and standing here, he could patiently wait till the mists which rolled everywhere around him, should lift and show him what yet he saw not. He became, in short, a Broad Churchman of the best type. Firmly believing the Gospel history, deeply imbued with the spirit of Christ and the apostles, he declined to turn attention to doctrine, except in so far as the reception of hope in God and the practice of a pure and high morality involved the belief of those few fundamental doctrines which are implicated in the facts of the Incarnation and Death of Christ.

The influence exerted by Colet on Erasmus, may best be gathered from the following colloquy, entitled " Pietas Puerilis," in which Erasmus and Gaspar talk over some of the matters which concern the lads, and among these the choice of a profession :

---

[1] The whole account of Colet's mental growth, and indeed of the entire movement, as given by Seebohm, is extremely interesting and valuable.

"*Erasmus.* Many nowadays abstain from theology, because they fear that they may waver in the catholic faith, seeing as they do that there is nothing which is not called in question. *Gaspar.* For my part I believe firmly what I read in Holy Scriptures and the Apostles' Creed, I don't trouble my head about anything else [nec ultra scrutor]. I leave the rest to be discussed and defined by theologians if they please. And if the Christian people use any custom which does not manifestly conflict with Scripture, I observe it, that I may not stumble any one. *Er.* What Thales taught you this philosophy? *Ga.* When a boy I lived in the house of John Colet. He imbued me with these precepts."

It was only by slow steps that Erasmus came round to Colet's position; but in 1522 (and not then for the first time) we find him saying:

"You will not be damned for not knowing whether the Spirit proceeds from one origin only, or from both the Father and the Son; but nothing will avail to save you, if you have not cultivated the fruits of the Spirit, love, joy, peace, goodness, temperance, meekness, purity, truth. Not that I think all investigation of supra-mundane things is to be condemned, but only that he who undertakes this task, should be by nature fitted for it, and should avoid rashness in defining, and an opinionative dogmatism, and above all, that lust of victory, which is the bane of all concord."

This occurs in the preface to Hilary;[1] the

[1] Ep. 1631. [The present writer's references to the letters are to the London edition, 1642.]

whole of which should be studied, as containing the ablest defence of a brief creed, and a very temperate and well-toned discussion of the natural history and proper sphere of minute doctrinal definitions. And when we speak of Erasmus as conceiving a disgust for theology, it must be borne in mind, that the theology which was chiefly pressed upon his attention was the theology of scholasticism, which was certainly open to all the charges he brought against it. Not the science in itself, but the mode of teaching it, was what he condemned—a mode of teaching which, in his own words, "stripped this queen of sciences of all her beauty, and exhibited that theology which was once most venerable and full of majesty, now almost dumb, poor, and in rags." He resented precisely what all right-thinking theologians have resented, that their science should be identified with questions such as these :

"Whether God could have taken upon Himself the nature of a woman, a devil, an ass, a gourd, or a stone? *What* Peter would have consecrated if he had consecrated the Eucharist at the moment that the body of Christ was hanging on the cross?" [1]

---

[1] *Praise of Folly.*

And the kind of subtlety of definition he complained of was this:

"The apostles spoke of 'grace,' but they never distinguished between 'gratiam gratis datam,' and 'gratiam gratificantem.' They preached charity, but did not distinguish between charity 'infused' and 'acquired,' nor did they explain whether it was an accident or a substance, created or uncreated. They abhorred sin, but I am a fool if they could define scientifically what we call sin, unless, indeed, they were inspired by the spirit of the Scotists." [1]

It is a great matter when men condescend upon instances, and do not content themselves with general statements which may mean a great deal or nothing at all. If all men who cry out against doctrinal theology would follow the example of Erasmus, and say definitely what they allude to and have in their mind when they so speak, some of the popular illusions of our time might be dissipated. Erasmus knew his own mind; he had not attained to that sentimental laudation of the spirit of doubt which characterises our own day, nor had he learned to prize investigation more highly than the truth it discovers. He declined to express an opinion on many points of theology, but he was too clear-headed a man to

[1] *Praise of Folly,* Seebohm, 197.

esteem doubt more highly than ascertained truth. He had not imbibed "our lofty new idea of rational freedom as freedom from conviction, and of emancipation of understanding as emancipation from the duty of settling whether important propositions are true or false."

But to return. What Erasmus said of himself was perfectly true. He was not a theologian; and he could not become one. A theologian *nascitur non fit.* And to invite him to write controversial pieces, or to take a lead in ecclesiastical movements was a mistake; as it is a mistake now to judge him by the lives of other men, and condemn him because he was himself, and not Luther or Zwingle. As Mr. Drummond very justly remarks, "In order to do justice to Erasmus, we must not contrast him with Luther, but rather consider what his own work was, and how far he would have improved its prospects of success by declaring for Luther." He served his generation with formidable weapons and an untiring industry, and were it possible to distribute to every man who had a part in the Reformation his own share of merit, it may well be questioned whether any one would have a larger share than Erasmus. But his work was not the formation of doctrinal opinion or belief. His best friends must be rather ashamed of the weakness of this side of his mind. The most ardent advocates of a restricted creed must believe that such few opinions as a man does profess he should honestly and consistently maintain. But Erasmus may very easily be convicted of shilly-shallying, notoriously so in regard to the sacramental doctrine of Oecolampadius. Plutarch, in his *Life of Nicias*, tells of an Athenian politician who gained for himself the nickname of *The Buskin*, having that easy adaptability to whatever might be the dominant power, which characterised our own Vicar of Bray. And the reader of Erasmus is reluctantly forced to the conclusion that his carelessness about doctrinal theology led him sometimes to utter opinions which at other times he disavowed. His error did not consist in his declining to have anything to do with subjects he disliked and for which he felt himself naturally disqualified, but it consisted in his denying his own nature, and at length taking up the pen in the very quarrels he had spent his life in denouncing. Few spectacles could have been more useful to that or any age than that of a man of his capacity and learning asserting his right to know nothing but the historical data of Christianity, and the simple lines of truth delivered in the Apostles' Creed; but

Erasmus terribly disappoints those who look for such a spectacle, when he yields to the badgering of the papists, and at last enters the lists with Luther on one of the most abstruse theologico-philosophical problems.

The question that results from the consideration of Erasmus's neutral attitude is this: Ought a man in every great conflict to take a side? To say that a man must in every such case take a side, implies that of two sides, one must be right and the other wrong, which is frequently not the case, the truth being almost equally distributed between them. But in the instance before us, it will be said, that one side was right, or so much nearer right than the other, that it was a weakness not to take a side. Certainly it would have been a weakness had Erasmus merely held aloof, to see how the strife would end, and then join the stronger party, or had he vacillated and been unable to make up his mind on the matters in dispute; but it must be borne in mind, that Erasmus had his own clearly defined view as to reforming the Church, that his method was theoretically the better of the two, that he had been working at it consistently and with all his might for thirty years; that during that time he had seen considerable results achieved, and that his expectation that a complete reform would be carried through was assuredly not unreasonable. The blame must lie, not with him, but with those who, exasperated as Erasmus thought by the violence of Luther, ultimately refused the reforms he sought. They who drove Luther out of the Church, and listened to no remonstrance from within it, are the parties responsible as well for the bloodshed, misery, and revolution which followed the Reformation, as for the ignorance and superstition which in Catholic countries have become identified with Christianity. Erasmus, as we have said, was mistaken, but his was the error of a man who thought too well of human nature. He expected inveterate abuses to be removed by those whose interest it was to maintain them. He expected that a community, which had grown to be a mighty political institution, would accept the position of the Apostolic Church, and at the voice of his persuasion, meekly return to her youthful and primitive ways. In the idea of some, it might as rationally have been expected that Napoleon, after tasting empire, should have returned to a lieutenancy of artillery. He miscalculated the strength of his weapon, and omitted to consider that the masses of the people must have an outward movement to quicken and fix their inward convictions. And above all, though it might be unwise to say that he over-rated the value of peace, yet he certainly under-rated the use of violence, and had therefore to learn the lesson which has been adequately expressed in the words of a living writer, who has profoundly studied at least one great revolution of opinion; that "those whom temperament or culture has made the partisans of calm order, cannot attune progress to the stately and harmonious march which would best please them, and which they are perhaps right in thinking would lead with most security to the goal."

II

THE CHRISTIAN ELEMENT IN PLATO[1]— ACKERMANN AND WHEWELL[2]

Our object in this article is to advert to the subject brought under the notice of English readers by this translation of the work of Ackermann. There is another work, however, now issuing from the press, the name and authorship of which will secure for it many readers. We refer to *The Platonic Dialogues for English Readers*, by William Whewell, D.D. This title means a good deal more than at first reading is suggested by it. The work is not only well written in our vernacular, which so easily and dutifully adapts itself to the exact representation of Greek thought, it is in its whole plan "for English readers." Prolix pas-

[1] *The Christian Element in Plato.* By Dr. C. Ackermann, Archdeacon at Jena. Translated by S. R. Asbury. Edinburgh : Clark. 1861.

[2] *The Platonic Dialogues for English Readers.* By Will. Whewell, D.D. 1860.

sages, of which, we must confess, there are not a few even in Plato, are abridged out of consideration for our impatiently practical ways. The remarks offered on the genuineness of the Dialogues, while they sufficiently answer the leading objections of the German commentators, do not enter into minute and finical criticisms, but judge rather by the whole production. If this suspected dialogue be not Plato's, whose is it? Where is the rest of that suit of armour of which this detached piece all but fits the Saul of philosophy? For, as Dr. Whewell says, "it seems a very wild process to assume a plurality of Platos without strong reasons." Most will heartily join with the epigram in the *Greek Anthology*, not only as regards the *Phaedo*, but many more vehemently contested dialogues :—"If Plato did not write me, then were there two Platos. I exhibit all the flowers of the Socratic discourses, yet Panaetius called me spurious. He who denied the immortality of the soul, denied the genuineness of me."

Another important principle of this translator will peculiarly commend itself to English minds. This principle we give in his own words: " In every part my rule has been to take what seemed the direct and natural import of the dialogue as its true meaning.   Some of the commentators are in the habit of extracting from Plato doctrines obliquely implied rather than directly asserted ; indeed they sometimes seem to ascribe to their Plato an irony so profound, that it makes no difference, in any special case, whether he asserts a proposition or its opposite.   I have taken a different course, and have obtained, as I think, a more consistent result."   What Plato has suffered at the hands of his disciples is incalculable.   The mistiness, the bombast, which have been issued under the professed authority of Plato, are notorious.   Some will be surprised to learn, what all who for themselves examine will discover, that Plato is never bombastic, and rarely obscure. For the most part his Socrates utters what the simplest may understand, and what the wisest cannot exhaust.

A suspicion will arise in the mind of every one who intends to spend any time in the company of Plato, whether the subjects discussed are really such as deserve the attention of busy men.   What seemed of great interest to lounging, gossiping Athenians, may possibly wear a very different aspect to those who have too little leisure to tempt them to be careless in its outlay.   A very slight knowledge of the character of Plato reassures us, and leaves us in the belief that time spent in such company cannot be misspent. It is not only the massive intellect, the soaring imagination, the vivacious fancy, the irreproachable taste which promise us noble entertainment. Nor is it, what is even more wonderful than these, the balance and harmony preserved among all his powers by his solid and clear-eyed and healthy common-sense. It is his moral greatness which ensures that we shall profit by intercourse with Plato. There is a certain contagion in his lofty and earnest purpose which kindles and elevates the soul; and as we stand by his side, can we but desire to share in his loyal defence and service of what is right and good, and to imitate his scorn and keen attack of what is empty, base, or wrong? And that man must be far sunk in scepticism indeed, who is not abashed by the humble and believing serenity of this great thinker, acknowledging that he knows nothing, but yet persuaded that there is truth, and that he himself will at length reach it. Of this, we say, a very slight acquaintance will satisfy; a little further, and we discover that the questions discussed are the very questions we ourselves are daily required to answer. How is false knowledge to be distinguished from the true ? And what hope is there that we shall be able to pass from the one to the other ? Are boys to receive a liberal or a strictly professional education ? And how may a man become good and wise, and be sure of always becoming wiser and better ? How may a man best employ himself in this life, and what may he expect when this life is done ? The man who has given such questions as these his serious consideration. will surely be better qualified to discharge his own share of duty, and to aid others with his advice. We shall be none the worse, but much the better, of standing for a little where Plato stood.

The resemblances to Christian sentiment discovered in his writings, have as frequently operated against as in favour of his influence. They are viewed by many with jealous dread, as if they were afraid that a little more searching investigation might discover that Christianity had been anticipated, and might now be superseded by Platonism. There have been at all times impatient and headstrong defenders of Christianity, men whose straightforward and direct opposition to all that is not thoroughly Christian might be laudable, were it not combined with a narrowness of view which prevents them from seeing any significant mixture of truth in an enemy's position; men, impatient of delicate discrimination, who can only say with Tertullian, "Quid simile philosophus et Christianus?" There is some excuse for the indiscriminate hostility of the earlier defenders of Christianity, to all that savoured of heathenism. Philosophy had not yet acknowledged as superior the simple "power of God unto salvation." She had not yet recognised and confined herself to her own province, and left the higher sphere to the unrivalled sway of Christianity. But it is not as a rival to our religion that we can now speak of Platonism, and it does seem a most un-Christian mode of showing our Christianity, to sneer at the efforts of those wise ancients who felt after God if haply they might find him, and on whom the day-star never rose, though their eyes, dim in death, were still turned toward the dawning. Rather should our own enjoyment of the day that God has made, lend tenderness to our admiration of those who spent their lives in unsuccessful but never-flagging toil for that of which we are born the heirs. But while there have been Tertullians to stigmatise Plato as the "condimentarius hæreticorum," the seasoning in which every duller heretic might dip his sop, there have not been wanting a Justin professing that "he delights in him"; a Clement who *need* profess nothing of the kind; an Eusebius acknowledging that he is an exceeding admirer of the man, "who alone of the heathen," as he elsewhere says, "reached the vestibule of truth, and stood upon its threshold." And, above all, there is that perennial tribute to the worth of Plato, which the warm acknowledgments of the revered Augustine continue to draw from each generation; acknowledgments which are the more commanding, because they are intelligent and discriminating, made by one who had earnestly sought for truth and peace in the writings of Plato, and whose intense and expectant search gives him some authority to declare what can and what can not be found in them. And though it might seem that our own judgment in the matter may be fully as valuable as that of one whose knowledge of Plato appears only to have been second-hand, or which at least *may* have been drawn only through the obscuring medium of commentators, yet we must consider, on the other hand, that Augustine had advantages for deciding in this matter which we can never possess. He had mainly this advantage, that he received his impressions of Plato in a mind as yet unimpressed by the truths of Scripture. We cannot but fill the expressions of Plato with the significance the same expressions would contain in Scripture, or at least we have to be continually on our guard, lest the words of Plato represent to us notions of our own, rather than introduce us to his thought. With Augustine there was no danger of finding anything liker Scripture, than was really in the mind of Plato, for as yet he was himself ignorant of the contents of Scripture. This advantage he was himself aware of, and highly prized, and, with that clear apprehension of the workings of his inner man, to which his firm persuasion of a special providence incited him, strikingly describes it.[1]

And, since it is the same element in Plato, his agreement with revealed truth, which has produced alike admiration and aversion, it becomes an interesting, and, as many now believe, by no means unimportant matter, to ascertain to what extent this agreement exists, how it may be accounted for, and what is to be made of it. Evidently very little can be made of any agree-

---

[1] "Si primo sanctis tuis literis informatus essem, et in earum familiaritate obdulcuisses mihi, et postea in illa volumina incidissem, si in adfectu, quem salubrem imbiberam, perstitissem, putarem etiam ex illis libris eum posse concipi, si eos solos quisquam didicisset." Had his judicious remark been duly pondered, some would have been saved from endeavouring to add to the wisdom and repute of Plato, at the expense of their own, by finding truths in Plato that Plato longed to find.

ment there may be, if that agreement is to be accounted for on the ground of Plato's acquaintance with the sacred writings. Unfortunately, this primary question of the sources of Plato's knowledge is involved in much difficulty. The fathers, Lactantius excepted, maintain that he profited by the Jewish Scriptures. Tertullian, indeed, in his summary way, dismisses the question with a "Quis Poetarum, quis Sophistarum, qui non omnino de prophetarum fonte potaverit?" But, wild though it may seem in the eyes of the perfervid African to split upon such a question, the ponderous learning of Witsius, Gale, Huet, Grotius, Le Clerc, Spencer, and L'Enfant, is ranged in almost equal masses on either side. The question is indeed lost in almost hopeless obscurity, an obscurity which the persevering research and wakeful criticism of modern scholars have done very little to penetrate. Some pass the subject with a sigh, while some blame others for not having already solved what they themselves can find no solution of. The first thought that occurs to an inquirer is, Would Plato not have acknowledged his obligation were he indebted to what must have so materially modified his system as the Hebrew Scriptures? Might we not expect some more definite reference

to such valuable sources of information, than is to
be found in the one or two somewhat doubtful
hints of his reverence for eastern lore? This
silence on his part is, however, possibly to be
accounted for by his circumstances, both as a
philosopher and as a man. As a philosopher, his
position precluded the necessity, and even the
possibility, of acknowledging his particular debts;
of definitely stating to whom he owed this
stimulus, and to whom that idea. For, in fact,
while he stood indebted to all who had preceded
him, this debt was not of such a nature as made
it very easy for him or very desirable to his
creditors that he should acknowledge it. His
philosophy was the result, only because it was
to a large extent a refutation of preceding
philosophies. No man can be less easily separated from his time than Plato, and yet to no man
less than to him can we apply Cicero's detraction
of Regulus, " Laus non est hominis sed temporum."
Influenced by his age, it is needless to say he
was; others suggested to him thoughts which
now appear, and very justly appear, as his own;
possibly even lines of argument may be ascribed
to him of which he saw the first indication in the
reasonings of another. There was nothing of
worth in the investigations of preceding thinkers

which Plato had not made his own, not by disguising it and presenting it in a new shape, but by himself independently rethinking it out, and giving to it its proper connection with other thoughts, till out of the whole mass there rose in his own mind a new and very different system. And was it incumbent on him to analyse this system, and, pointing to each portion, to tell us : " This struck me while listening in wonder to the first words I heard from the lips of Socrates "; " This again rose in my mind as Archytas explained to me the lofty philosophy of Pythagoras "; " Just before reaching this thought, the strong wing of Parmenides flagged " ; and " This (shall I tell you ?) is the contradictory of a proposition of Hippias ; so you will not wonder I should here have hit upon the truth ? "   In truth, such a process were impossible, the parts are inextricably interwoven, the whole mass is fused in his mind and presented really original.   Also as a man, the position of Plato forbade an open and constant reference to his authorities, if these authorities happened to be Jewish.   He had the fate of an innovator written legibly enough in the death of Socrates ; and though the suggestions of timidity seem to have found as cold a welcome with Plato as with his uncompromising master, yet it was desirable, both for himself and for the cause to which he was devoted, that some discretion should be mingled with his valour. To excite the suspicion and rouse the easily awakened jealousy of the Athenians, would by no means facilitate the introduction of new ideas, but would almost infallibly secure the silencing of their purveyor.

But while the supposition that Plato was directly indebted to the Jewish Scriptures, or indebted at the furthest to some more ancient Greek translation than any which now exists, is not contradicted by the fact of his own reticence on the subject, the question still remains, what positive support, or what necessity exists for such a supposition? Now, of positive support there is actually none; the one ascertained fact regarding the matter being, that Plato spent some years in Egypt. And why assume any more direct intercourse of Plato with revelation than is implied in this fact? For it would be running scepticism into credulity to doubt, that while prosecuting researches in that land of hoary and mysterious lore, he became acquainted with the fragments of Hebrew tradition that floated in that region. We do not suppose that he went to Egypt with expectations of finding a theology surpassing every other; but neither do we suppose that of set purpose he forbore to inquire into a religion that was known to be so peculiar as that of the Hebrews. We do not suppose that he had a rabbi to instruct him in all the learning of the exclusive people; but it would be hard to believe that the most philosophic spirit of ancient or modern times felt no interest in the hints which any Hebrew stranger might have given. That these hints were many, or to ordinary minds very significant, we can scarcely believe; for the example of Herodotus warns us not to attach too much importance to information received through the medium of Egyptian priests. But what might be insignificant to most would mean a great deal to Plato, and a hint or two received from an Egyptian, or rather from a sojourning Jew, may have, and probably did preserve Plato from some errors, and sow in his fertile mind the seeds of truth.[1] But of any actual transference of doctrines from the sacred writings of the Jews to the system of Plato we find no trace. There

---

[1] Those who wish to pursue this question further will find abundant material for so doing in Brucker's *History of Philosophy*, vol. iii. p. 332 ; also vol. i. p. 635 ; also in *J. M. Langii Dissertatio de Genealogiis*, to be found in the *Thesaurus Theologico-Philologicus*, appended to the *Critici Sacri*. In the *Egyptiaca* of Witsius there is also some information on the same topic.

was a time when the admirers of Plato would almost have undertaken to draw up out of his writings a confession which a Westminster divine might have signed. There was a time when such a sentence as the following could be penned by one of the most learned men of his day, and received with applause by others :—"This, I say, our Christian Platonist supposes to be much more wonderful, that this so great and abstruse a mystery, of three eternal hypostases in the Deity, should thus by Pagan philosophers, so long before Christianity, have been asserted as the principal and original of the whole world ; it being more, indeed, than was acknowledged by the Nicene fathers themselves."[1] As Mosheim remarks on this passage, "Many, I fear, will consider this as a great injustice done to the Nicene fathers." Brucker marvels that any one of the poorest philosophical perception could see the Trinity in the Platonic philosophy. And what is true of the doctrine of the Trinity is true also of the essential doctrines of revelation ; they do not appear as transplants in the writings of Plato. In fact it is not in certain points that the agreement of Christianity with Platonism appears so striking as in the consent of the two systems as

[1] Cudworth.

systems; a consent that might have been derived from the New Testament had Plato lived to be enlightened by it, but which could never have been attained from the Mosaic books.

And this brings us to mention with approval the work by Ackermann, on the Christian element in Plato. The chief merit of this investigator is, that he has not been satisfied with quoting from the republic a few passages reminding us of the Christian kingdom of heaven, or one or two expressions from the *Phaedo* or the *Apology* which coincide with the utterance of Christian hope, but has compared the characteristics of Plato, the essence of his system, with Christianity, Or to use his own terminology, he has not merely viewed the subject empirically, but has also developed it genetically. Proceeding with scientific calmness, he does not show us a collection of passages such as we might not notice to be out of place if we found them in our Bibles, and at once demand that we should proclaim Plato a Christian; he goes a little deeper and searches for the cause of this resemblance, the principle in Plato's system and way of thinking which secures and predicts the continual occurrence of such passages. To do him justice, let him explain himself. He says (p. 66):

"We should err if we thought that the asserted Christianity of Plato is or can be proved by such passages. They really prove nothing but the highest probability that the Christian element in Plato's philosophy will actually be found on closer examination; they are not the fruits of the examination itself, but only a layer cropping out into the daylight, which incites us to scraping and digging, by giving reason to the supposition, that if we follow its lead, we shall meet with a rich bed of ore."

And, however we may refuse to admit the conclusions at which he arrives, we cannot but approve of his method. His merit is, that he has handled the subject with scientific accuracy, and yet in so lively a manner that any one may read his book; and whoever reads it will read it with interest. It is a final book, not because his conclusions are unassailable, but because the subject is treated so fully, and yet so lucidly, that few will read it without coming to some conclusion for themselves. And praise is due to the translator for preserving the interesting and easy style of his author, and giving us really an English book, and not a hybrid, as hard to understand as the original German. We are glad, too, to find prefixed to the work a corrective of its main error, extracted from the

Lectures on Ancient Philosophy, by W. Archer Butler. We regret to find that this is needful, for in every point but the one this extract is designed to correct, Ackermann is thoroughly satisfactory. Unfortunately, this is the most important point in the book, and while it is easy for the reader to correct the author's error, the beauty, completeness, and usefulness of the work are marred. And it is with considerable regret we part company with a guide who has so intelligently pointed the way; the more so as we leave him because he stops before reaching the truth, which is as important for his own welfare as for the complete exhibition of the subject he treats. The truth he ignores is one essential to the understanding of the relative position of heathen and Christian, that Jesus Christ was the sacrifice for the sin of the world. It is inexpressibly disappointing to reach the end of a chapter entitled "Definition of the Christian Element," without finding any allusion to this cardinal truth of Christianity; the more so, as that same chapter opens with a singularly powerful and eloquent description of the misery and sinfulness of human life, and goes on to eliminate all professed saviours, showing wherein art, morality, and all else but Christ, fail to save. But in what is Christ better qualified than all else

that tries to save from sin? How is it that He
succeeds where all others fail? What, in short, is
the Christian element? "The Christian Element,"
says Ackermann, " is that which has power to save."
But what, according to him, is this saving power?
It is " the historical life-form, whose kernel, contents and soul, is the life of Christ." And how
does this operate? Ackermann continues to speak
clearly, even when wrong. He tells us that what
the life of Christ is it also produces (p. 215). He
himself lives a life free from sin, different from the
rest of the world; he does this by his uninterrupted connection with God, by his continued
subjection to him. Then this life attracts admirers, friends, at first a little company, but
gradually increasing; each receiving and giving,
" roused and filled by the Lord, each rouses others,
and communicates to them the fulness of His
inner life." We understand this because it is a
most important part of what we ourselves believe.
But what is it that begins this sanctifying love to
Christ? "The love of Christ constraineth us,"
says the apostle; and why? "because we thus
judge, that if one died for all, then were all dead:
and that He died for all, that they which live
should not henceforth live unto themselves, but
unto Him which died for them and rose again."

It is useless to be repeating that men will admire to imitation the life of Christ, a life wholly unlike their own, and grievously hard to imitate.   Men do not do so.   This is no gospel to preach to such a world as Ackermann himself represents this to be.   It does not take hold.   The truth asserts itself in *fact*; men cleave to Christ because He has redeemed them from the lowest hell—from the curse of the law.

It is not, however, our business to enter upon this point at large, but only to show how it affects Ackermann's estimate of Plato.   And, as might be expected, it operates in bringing Christianity and Platonism very near each other.   Leave out of account the defective view of sin, and of God's justice, and of the relation betwixt these two, which Plato shared with all other heathen, and you leave out of account one of the principal elements which keeps revealed religion distinct from natural religion.   We are not surprised, then, to find Ackermann speaking of Plato's Christianity in terms which want that precise accuracy which would have made his book unexceptionable, and a still more valuable contribution to our literature than it is.   He tells us that Platonism resembles Christianity in the earnest sadness with which it views the sin of the world, and in the view of sin, that it is done against God, but he does not tell us, though he enumerates the " non-Christian and un-Christian elements of Plato," that Christianity considers sin with respect to an inflexible law. And so in other instances it is easy to mark the taint of this central blemish. But of course Ackermann very clearly maintains the essential difference between Platonism and Christianity. The one does not possess that which is the very essence of the other—the saving power of the work and person of Christ. For though he does not consider that person a sacrifice, nor that work atoning (in the ordinary sense we attach to these words), he does see that salvation from sin is only attainable through Jesus Christ. He is far indeed from bringing Platonism into anything at all approaching a rivalry with Christianity ; for though he is not accurate in his statement of the mode in which Christianity achieves salvation, he is very well aware that it can never be done by Platonism. We may therefore cover his error, and yet teach all that he teaches, by stating the matter thus :—That Platonism resembles Christianity in its prevading and poignant sense of man's need of salvation from sin, and also in its belief that salvation may be attained ; that it differs from Christianity in this, that it does not know the Saviour actually provided. "The essence of Christianity consists in *saving power*; that of Platonism in *saving purpose*. In Christianity, therefore, salvation is present in deed and reality; in Platonism, only in thought, and as the end of its striving."

There is only one passage in which a higher position than the true is assigned to Plato, which seems to call for remark. At page 250 it is said "that he felt in his soul the presence of Christ in history." At first sight this seems to indicate that Plato had passed from the heathen contriving of salvation to the Jewish expecting of salvation from God. Now while nothing is more striking in Plato than his belief that God is on the side of all who strive against sin, and that man is made not to be as now the slave of sin, but to be fit for communion with God, and that this purpose of man's being will be effected; yet he expected that this would be accomplished, not by the coming of a future deliverer, but by his philosophy. To anticipate the coming of a deliverer from sin is what no power of speculation could reach, nor what any depth of faith could lead a man to, so that possibly all that Ackermann intends by this rather doubtful-sounding clause is, that Plato believed that God would at length bring good out of evil, and manifest in history, in outward acts and effects, that righteousness, and not sin, is the life designed for man. Here, indeed, God's prerogative of revealing himself asserts its unrivalled sovereignty; no power of speculation can absolutely predict historical truth, but when the manifestation of God has become historical, the poorest intellect can apprehend it. The faith of Plato needed the promise of God to withdraw him from scheming and working his own salvation, and to point his hopes to a coming Saviour. He can never step over the line made by God's word of promise, which separated Jew from Gentile. "The Jews yearned and knew what they yearned for, the nations yearned, and knew not for what"; or, as Augustine has it (*Conf.* vii. 20), "The heathen saw whither they were to go, but saw not the way." In no writings more steadily than in those of Plato, is there held before us the view of man's ultimate destiny and the vast capability of his nature; but it is simply impossible for Plato, and therefore for any other to whom the word of God has not been spoken, to know *how* this destiny is to be achieved, and this capability developed. And it is the contrast between his firm persuasion that God has not made all men in vain, and the plaintive wavering of his tone when he speaks of the mode by which the purpose of God is to be accomplished, which invests his writings with so melancholy an interest, and begets pity for the philosopher as well as admiration of the philosophy. He knew that without a divine revelation, certain knowledge on the most important points could not be attained (*Phaedo*, 85 D), and while, in lack of that revelation, he pressed the duty of persevering investigation, he yet looked forward to death as the solemn but desirable entrance into the light of the presence of "the good God." It was this same conviction, that the darkness of this life was exceptional, that ignorance of God and all the results of such ignorance was not the right, the normal condition of man; it was this which prompted him to believe in the pre-existence of souls, that he might have the consolation of believing that if light was not to be enjoyed in this present life, it shone everywhere besides, that this state was but a parenthesis of obscurity, a short Arctic night which one strange revolution had brought him into, and which another would speedily deliver him from. As Culverwell with his usual beauty expresses it, "You may see Socrates in the twilight lamenting his obscure and benighted condition, and telling you that his lamp will show him nothing but his own darkness. You may see Plato sitting down by the water of Lethe, and weeping because he could not remember his former notions." The words which are scarcely allowable to one on whom the Sun of righteousness has shed his beams find an excusable mouthpiece in Plato—

> "Behold we know not anything ;
> I can but trust that good shall fall
> At last—far off—at last, to all,
> And every winter change to spring."

We are not, then, to suppose that the resemblance between Platonism and Christianity consists merely of a larger number of those justly-conceived and well-expressed maxims regarding human life, which may be found sprinkled among the classical writers of antiquity. It is in the principles, and particularly in the purpose, of Plato's philosophy that the resemblance is found. It was a system of moral discipline, having for its object the redemption of man from the slavery of the false and the vicious, or (to use his own Scripture-like expression), the loosing of his bonds, and the turning him from shadows and from a nocturnal kind of day, to the truth and the light. It was a system which taught men to seek for a higher, more enduring, more real satisfaction of the wants and longings of their natures, than anything which was not God could give.

Ackermann says :

" The *Phaedrus*, *Gorgias*, and *Protagoras* make their appearance, like steady workmen provided with the necessary apparatus to demolish the apparitions of the Sophists, to clear the ground and dig the foundations ; the *Phaedrus* allows us at the same time to cast a glance, though but a fleeting one, at the beautiful draft of the whole ; in the *Theaetetus, Parmenides*, and *Sophist*, rise the firm buttresses and arches ; the *Cratylus* provides for the acoustic relations ; by the *Philebus* and *Banquet* the inner spaces are properly divided and ornamented ; the *Phaedo* arranges the sacrificial services ; the *Republic* collects the community into the sanctuary ; in the *Timaeus* and *Critias* the whole rises finished and concluded heavenwards,— and not till then does the beholder perceive the true meaning and idea of the whole, and see that it is, and is intended to be, nothing but a copy in miniature of the great edifice of the universe."

Now, if Christianity be so exactly what the mind of Plato would have accepted as the true religion, that already some of its fundamentals were anticipated by the inventive necessities of his own spirit, then this is strong evidence that Christianity is the religion fit for man. This certainly ought to be some evidence in its favour to those with whom Plato is as yet more than Christ. This "high priest of reason" has in fact become to many who worshipped in the temple of reason the first Christian Apologist, and led them to recognise Jesus of Nazareth as Him who can alone satisfy, and has satisfied, "the baffled aspirations of four thousand years of suffering men."

April, 1861.

III

HIPPOLYTUS'S HOMILY AGAINST NOETUS

OUR readers may have seen the celebrated painting in which Orpheus is depicted at that bitterest moment of his history, when he turned towards his all but recovered Eurydice, only to see her swept from his embrace to the implacable realms below. The sympathetic pang which they may have felt in looking at this ideal work, will be changed into a pang more sensible and immediately personal, if they engage in the attempt to reconstruct a complete likeness of Hippolytus. After countless and mazy wanderings toward the supposed place of his entombment, and after weary expenditure of the delicate manipulation of historical criticism, we turn to embrace a perfectly restored Hippolytus, when the very motion of turning seems to shake out of equilibrium the subtle elements, and down from the clear day of ascertained fact, a resistless hand drags him to the mists of the region of the shades. The silence of ancient chroniclers concerning one who was among the most stirring rulers and instructive writers of the early church, is at once remarkable and tantalising. While every one is ready to say something in his praise, no one gives us such details of his history as enable us clearly to see the man, and thoroughly to understand the grounds of his celebrity. With one he is "vir disertissimus"; with another he is "γλυκύτατος καὶ εὐνούστατος"; but all the magniloquent laudation on record, we would gladly exchange for the simple intimation of the year of his death and the place of his abode. The accuracy of the information that is occasionally dropped from early writers regarding this celebrated but little known individual, is rendered suspicious by the silence of others whom we expect to be better informed; and when we find that even in the age of Eusebius [1] it was not so much as known in what

---

[1] Eusebius has been charged with wilful suppression of facts in the case of Hippolytus. We think that this charge is sufficiently refuted by the words of Eusebius (ἑτέρας που), in speaking of the church in which he ruled, showing, as they do, that there was uncertainty in the writer's own mind. The charge, however, shows how natural it is to believe that more *must* have been known than is found recorded.

part of the world he had lived, we are thrown upon the writings of Hippolytus himself for all the information we possess regarding him. And it is satisfactory to find that these writings, and especially his recently discovered work "against all the heresies," are unusually instructive in personal detail. From these writings, and availing ourselves of the learned though not always sufficiently circumspect and deliberate labours of Bunsen, we propose to give, in as few words as possible, a sketch of Hippolytus.

Born during the reign of the last of the good emperors, Hippolytus from the first enjoyed every advantage for the education and exercise of his natural ability. The Roman world was open to him as his school, and out to that school he went, like Justin Martyr and Clement of Alexandria, determined to find some truth in the wide sea of opinion. Viewing with a wise eclecticism all wisdom as existing for his use, he went from place to place, sitting now at the feet of a teacher of Greek philosophy, and now lingering fondly in the school of the aged and attractive Irenaeus. The saying of Tertullian, "Peregrinandum nobis in literas orbis," was amply fulfilled by Hippolytus. With enough of the Roman in his nature to mingle frankly with all, and appropriate freely

" quod usquam egregium fuerit,"[1] he was so much of a Greek as to see all for his own personal development and culture. To him nothing came foreign, because all was Roman ; and as he journeyed from land to land and from one centre of influence to another, and found everywhere the same faith and worship, one Christ held to and confessed by all tongues and peoples, his cosmopolitan spirit was gradually ripened to the Christian consciousness of universal brotherhood, and what Hippolytus the Roman might have tolerated through policy or adopted through pride, Hippolytus the Christian sympathised with as human and valued with respect as belonging to Christ. And never was a man's power to sift, select, and adopt, more severely tried than in that very age, when the worn-out philosophies seemed to kindle anew and shoot up an expiring flame, when every absurd system could find willing advocates, when every fanatical leader could number his followers by thousands, and when orthodoxy was but slowly and precariously advancing towards an instructive and defensive form of sound words. Sects innumerable, maintaining every shade of error, from the most obvious misapprehensions of the truth

[1] The Roman state maxim, "Transferendo huc quod usquam egregium fuerit."—Tacit. *Annal.* xi. 24.

.to the wildest, most fantastic, and deplorable perversions of it, sprang up wherever a church was formed.   It was a time capable in the highest degree of wrecking a weak spirit or of maturing a strong one.   What strange and dreamy theories Hippolytus heard propounded by the sages of Greece, what impossible cosmogonies were given to him by the Neo-Platonists of Alexandria when he asked for science, and what mystic theosophy when he begged religious truth, it is impossible to relate ; and were it possible to relate, it would be impossible to believe.   That any one ever passed through such a pleasant but dangerous education with perfect safety, we are not prepared to assert. That when all wisdom and truth, along with all folly and error, backed by names synonymous with genius and eloquence, and by associations the most attractive and brilliant, were presented at once to an eager mind, this mind should have chosen only what was true and useful, and rejected, as if by an innate and instinctive power of repulsion, whatever was unreal and deceptive, is a conclusion certainly not warranted by any-thing we have yet learned of the youthful mind, or observed in the search after truth.   And it will scarcely be wondered at, that the young Hippolytus should not have shown a sagacity of judgment far beyond his years, and a power of rejecting error far ahead of the age on which he was thrown. But whatever confusion and mistake may have been introduced into his mind during his years of pursuit and acquisition, he returned from his travels with his critical and dialectic ability certainly whetted; with a vast store of information already laid up, and with formed habits of industry, which gave promise of still greater wealth; with a culture of mind which was rare even in an age which strove, by extra refinement and cultivation, to hide a rapidly diminishing originality and strength; with his native humour broadened, and his knowledge of man enlightened and matured by his knowledge of men; with his religious sentiments undisturbed in their practical operation, and his strict integrity and purity of character confirmed rather than relaxed by his frequent change of circumstance, and various opportunity and temptation; a man of a cheerful, active, and manly spirit, void of all bitterness and hate, but all the rather capable of vehement indignation—the man of all others fit for the place and the work in which he was to spend what he had acquired and become.

A few years before the close of the second century, Hippolytus is acknowledged by the church as a man of worth and influence, and is elected Bishop of Portus. His residence in this town, which had superseded Ostia as the harbour of Rome, proved an effectual restraint upon the usurping, heretical, and immoral tendencies of the Roman bishops. In this town .he was near enough to the great centre of action to be intimately acquainted with every turn of events, and yet was fortified, as in a citadel of his own, from all interference, and maintained here his presbytery unswayed by Roman influence, and his flock uncontaminated. From the death of Victor, in the year 198, to the termination of the government of Callistus in 222 A.D., Hippolytus was almost solely occupied in maintaining the forms of ecclesiastical government against the innovations, and the orthodox doctrine against the heresies of Rome. And had there been no such man as Hippolytus provided, a man of thorough intellectual culture and wide information, of calm and commanding spirit and sincere love of the truth, the diseased condition of the metropolitan church would undoubtedly have infected the provinces, and the submission to her proud claim of supremacy would have been anticipated by several ages.

The eloquence with which Hippolytus expounded the great doctrine of the incarnation, and inculcated the benefits resulting from it in an age when Docetism was wide spread, will appear from the following passage of his homily :

"In this person, God was manifest in the body, going forth perfect man ; for not in mere appearance (φαντασία), nor by change, but truly, did he become man.

"And so, though he were God, yet did he not refuse any conditions of the humanity he bore. He hungers, and toils, and wearies, and thirsts in his weariness ; he flees through fear, and prays out of tribulation, and he who as God has a sleepless nature, slumbers on a pillow ; he shudders at the cup of his passion, though for this end he was present in the world, and in his agony he sweats blood, and is strengthened by an angel, himself strengthening all that believe in him, and by his example he teaches us to overcome the fear of death. He who knew Judas, and what was in him, is betrayed by Judas. By Caiaphas he is dishonoured, who as God had been honoured with sacrifice and offering at the hand of Caiaphas. By Herod he is set at nought who cometh to judge all the earth ; and by Pilate he who took on him our diseases is cruelly scourged. By the soldiers he is mocked at whose word thousands of thousands, and ten thousand times ten thousand of angels and archangels stand obedient. By the Jews he who stretched out the heaven as a curtain is stretched on the accursed tree. And the Inseparable from the Father cries to the Father, and commends to him his spirit, and, bowing his head, he gives up the ghost—he who had said, and said truly, 'I have power to lay down my life, and I have power to take it again.' And because he was not subdued by death, he said, as being himself the Life, 'I lay it down of myself.' The bountiful Giver of all life has his side pierced with a spear, and the Raiser of the dead is wrapped in linen cloth, and laid in a sepulchre, and the third day is raised by the Father, though himself 'the resurrection and the life.' All these things has *he* accomplished for us, who for our sakes became as we are. For himself hath borne our griefs and carried our sorrows, and for us he was afflicted, as saith the prophet Esaias. This is he who was lauded in the hymns of the angels, seen of the shepherds, waited for by Simeon, and witnessed to by Anna. This is he who was sought after by the Magi, and discovered by the star. This is he who lingered in his Father's house, and was pointed out by John, and was witnessed to by the Father from above in these words, 'This is my beloved Son, hear ye him.' This is he who is crowned as the conqueror of the devil. This is Jesus of Nazareth, who was invited to the marriage in Cana, and changed the water into wine, and rebuked the sea when it raged under the violence of the winds, and walked upon the sea as on the dry land, and gave sight to him that was born blind, and raised up Lazarus, four days dead, and performed manifold mighty works, and forgave sins, and gave power to his disciples. Blood and water flowed from his holy side when pierced with the spear. For his sake the sun is darkened, and the day has no light, the rocks are cleft, and the veil is rent. The foundations of the earth are shaken, the graves are opened, and the dead arise, and the rulers are ashamed when they see upon the cross the controller of all nature drooping his head and yielding up the ghost. Creation sees and is troubled, and unable to approach and view his exceeding glory, shrinks into darkness. This is he who breathed the Spirit upon the disciples, and enters among them, the doors being shut ; who is taken up into the heavens, a cloud receiving him out of their sight ; who is set down at the right hand of the Father, and comes as judge of quick and dead. This is God, who for our sakes became man, and to whom the Father hath made all things subject. To him be glory and might, with the Father and the Holy Ghost, in the holy church, both now and always, even for evermore. Amen."

Hippolytus was the great champion of the truth at a very critical epoch. In Rome every heresiarch was sure of finding followers ; and wherever heresy arose, it was pretty certain ere very long to find its way to this common centre of influence, and here to make its stronghold. Valentinus and Marcion, Praxeas, Theodotus, and Noetus, were all known by sight on the streets of the city, as well as in their distant native towns. Consequently the revolution of opinion was rapid and extreme, the variety of teachers confusing in the highest degree, and many seem to have been driven, or at least strongly tempted to attach far less value to Christian truth than to diplomatic maxims, which would secure their own aggrandisement. "Omnia fui, et nihil expedit" was the sad conclusion of the contemporary emperor Severus, a conclusion which has something of the pathos of Solomon's reiterated "Vanity of vanities; all is vanity"; and many a presbyter of the church, who could mark the periods of his life by the several systems he had believed in, must have only reached at the last the same melancholy conclusion, and sighed from dying lips, "Omnia fui, et nihil expedit." In Portus, at least, so long as Hippolytus lived, there was a safe harbour, where, if the long swell of controversy still rolled in and was heard murmuring, there was, at least, a safe mooring and shelter from the violent personal assault either of tyranny or heresy. It is quite true that the catechumens at the mouth of the Tiber may not have been instructed in just those points we think most important, but had our choice been to be made of either of two infallibilities, we would not long have hesitated between the stupid, worldly, and immoral Callistus and the thoroughly Christian, if somewhat too philosophical, bishop of Portus.

To enter into the details of the protracted and

somewhat scandalous contest which the Roman bishop gave rise to, is beside our present purpose. Happily there were, towards the end of Hippolytus's life, some quiet years left, which he devoted to the more congenial labour of writing most of those " very many " books which Eusebius ascribes to him.   By means of these writings he extended his wholesome influence far and near.   His writings were in the hands of many, and his clear statements, in good scholarly Greek, made them everywhere valuable and attractive.   He has the merit also of introducing to the western church the mode of teaching by HOMILY, which had been practised with great effect at Alexandria.   Ready in everything to follow the teachers he had there become acquainted with, he instructed the assembled church at Portus upon the points of doctrine regarding which there was most doubt and discussion at the time.   How useful such addresses must have been to those who had not ability to solve difficult questions or examine the truth for themselves, nor opportunity to read the written works of other men, will be learned from the specimen given above of the homiletic style of Hippolytus.   Its distinctness of statement, its confident appeal to Scripture, and its eloquence, show us very plainly how so short a fragment has come to be so long preserved. If his homilies were often like this one, we do not wonder that Origen should sometimes have been seen among the congregation, nor that the Greek teachers in Egypt should have recommended Christians trading to the Tiber to seek the acquaintance and instructions of this widely read and judicious presbyter. It was first published in the edition of Hippolytus by Fabricius, who received from Montfaucon a copy of the Vatican MS. The Latin version of Turrianus had been previously published under the title, *Homilia de Deo trino et uno, et de mysterio Incarnationis contra haeresin Noeti.* In the Vatican MS. the title runs, *A Homily of Hippolytus against the heresy of one Noetus.* Noetus had affirmed that the Father himself was Christ, and that the Father himself was born, suffered, and died ; and Hippolytus, after stating the historical circumstances under which Noetus propounded his heresy, and the faithful exercise of discipline which ended in the casting out of the heretic from the church, proceeds with his refutation as follows :

"And this is what Christ himself said when in the gospel he confessed both his Father and his God, saying, 'I go away to my Father and your Father, and my God and your God.' If, therefore, Noetus dares to say that Christ Himself is the Father, let him tell us to what Father Christ was going away according to this saying in the gospel.   But if he thinks that we should abandon the gospel and listen to his folly, he labours in vain, 'for we ought to obey God rather than men.'

"And if he should say, 'Christ himself said, I and the Father are one,' let him attend to the expression, and consider that he did not say, 'I and the Father *am* one,' but '*are*' one.   For 'are' is not used of one, but he uses it to point out two persons and one power. he explained this himself when he said to the Father concerning his disciples, 'The glory which thou gavest me I have given them, that they may be one, even as we are one: I in them, and Thou in me; that they may be made perfect in one, that the world may know that thou hast sent me.'   What have the Noetians to say to these things?   Are all one body according to substance?   Or do we become one by the power and disposition of like-mindedness?   In the very same manner the Son ($\pi\alpha\hat{\iota}s$) who was sent proclaimed to them that were in the world, and knew him not, that he was in the Father by power and disposition.   For the Son is the mind of the Father. Those who have the mind of the Father accordingly receive Christ; but they who have not the mind of the Father reject him.   And if they cite the case of Philip, who said, 'Shew us the Father, and it sufficeth us,' and to whom our Lord answered saying, 'Have I been so long time with you, Philip, and yet hast thou not known me? he that hath seen me hath seen the Father.   Believest thou not that I am in the Father, and the Father in me?'—if they cite this as proof

that Christ calls himself the Father, let them know
that they herein adduce the most direct contradiction
to their own dogma, and convict themselves by the
very Scripture they bring forward ; for when Christ,
by very deed and word, had declared himself the Son,
they yet did not know him, and were unable to comprehend or perceive his power, and Philip, not understanding how far it was possible to see, asked that he
might look upon the Father, and so our Lord answered
him, ' He that hath seen me hath seen the Father'; that
is, if thou hast seen me, through me you may know
the Father ; for the Father is brought within easy
reach of our knowledge through the image which bears
his likeness ; but if thou hast not known the image,
that is, the Son, how think you to see the Father ?
And that these things are as we have stated them, the
context evinces, shewing that the Son, being set forth,
was sent from the Father and went to the Father.

" And many other passages, or rather, all others,
bear witness to this truth. So evidently, too, is their
testimony borne, that a man is forced, even though unwilling, to confess God the Father Almighty and Christ
Jesus the Son of God, God become man, to whom the
Father hath made subject all things save himself and
the Holy Spirit, and that these are truly three. And
if he desires further to know how the unity of God is
proved, let him know that his power is one, and that
so far as concerns his power God is one ; but so far as
concerns the incarnation, there is a threefold exhibition
(ἐπίδειξις), as shall shortly be proved when we come to
the positive side of our argument, and deliver the true
doctrine. The things which we have said are the

articles of our common faith, for there is one God in whom we must believe, but unbegotten, impassible, immortal, doing all that he willeth, as he willeth, when he willeth. What, then, will this nothing-knowing Noetus dare to reply to these things? [Νόητος μὴ νοῶν]. Since, therefore, Noetus is thus speedily confuted, let us pass to the demonstration of the truth; that, as he has endeavoured to disseminate his error, we may establish the truth against which all these so great heresies have arisen, and yet say nothing to the purpose.

"One God there is, my brethren, and the knowledge of him we receive from the Holy Scriptures, and from no other source. For, just as any person wishing to be skilled in the wisdom of this world will find no other means of attaining his desire than by studying the writings of philosophers, so as many of us as resolve to practise godliness must draw our information from no other source than from the oracles of God. Whatever, therefore, the Holy Scriptures declare, let us observe; and whatever they teach, let us understand; and as the Father wills that we believe in him, let us believe; and as he wills that the Son be honoured, let us honour him; and as he wills that the Holy Spirit be given, let us receive him,—not after our own understanding, not after our private prejudices and preconceptions, nor using violence towards the things given us of God, but as he himself intended to teach by the Holy Scriptures, so let us mark and understand."

These instructions were suddenly interrupted in the first year of Maximin the Thracian (A.D. 235).

Worthy, as his contemporaries might have said, of a more glorious death than mere decay or disease could inflict, Hippolytus won the two-fold honour of a long and useful life, and a martyr's death. When he had already spent his life in the service of his master, he was called upon to give up for his sake the remnant he yet held. Prudentius, in the verses he has written in celebration of this martyr, assures us that the heathen magistrate found in the name of Hippolytus a sufficient warrant for the manner of his death, and ordered him to be torn asunder by horses, that he might in his death resemble the chaste but slandered son of Theseus, whose name he had borne through life. This we may happily be spared believing. The numerous ·calls upon feeling which fact makes, oblige us to adopt a strict economy of emotion, and forbid that we should waste, upon what may be only fiction, the sentiments of pity or regret which are so abundantly demanded by actual events. In the case of Hippolytus, there is little need to resort to fiction, for we read that he was banished "in insulam nocivam Sardiniam"; and it is not likely that an old man, spent with anxiety, study, and manifold labours, would long resist the influence of the unwholesome climate, unusual habits of life, and harsh treatment, or

would long disappoint the intention of his perse-
cutors. "Feminis lugere honestum est, viris
meminisse."

Rather than attempt to detail the theological
opinions of Hippolytus, we would recall one or
two of the characteristics of the theology of his
time. We appreciate the service rendered by the
early theologians, and are put in a position from
which we see the whole bulk and symmetry of
their intellects only when we stand so as to see
at the same time the work they had to perform.
The men whom, for the prospects of Christianity,
it was chiefly important to win over, were those
of active and disciplined mind, who were dissatisfied with the philosophical systems in vogue, but
who could not, and would not, divest themselves
of the mental habits, nor discard all the modes of
thought to which, throughout their thinking lives,
these systems had accustomed them. The philosophical inquiries of these men were to be met by
philosophical explanations. An exposition of the
faith was called for, which should appeal to the
learned through all that was good in their previous
learning. A method and range of instruction was
required which should at once defend Christianity
from the attacks of philosophy, and should invite
the attention of all who were thirsting for the

truth. To present Christianity in such a form was a very difficult task. It required that the Christian theologian should have thorough sympathy with the intellectual culture of Greece, and yet should at the same time be wholly obedient to the teacher of Nazareth. When a modern reader finds so much philosophical terminology mingling with the words of Scripture in ancient expositions of the faith, he is to remember that, in their day, these forms of expression were intelligible and pregnant, and that throughout the educated world they were familiarly used. There were certain ideas current which, however incomprehensible or absurd to us, were not then the guilt of individuals, but the common inheritance of all thinking persons. These ideas were part of the property of every mind, and with them, whatever the mind received, had to be harmonised. Now, this was so different a juncture from that which Christian sentiments and ideas have to effect when they enter the modern mind, that we are very apt to underrate the efforts of the early theologians, not understanding the union which they had to bring about. An educated and speculative heathenism is a very different thing to deal with from that state of mind to which modern theology has to introduce itself; and few, if any, periods of the church's history have required from her leaders a more generous breadth of sympathy, or a more genuine culture, or a more judicious treatment of opinions.

Moreover, in judging of the value of early documents, we are to bear in mind that the truth delivered in Scripture was not discovered all at once, and that what is to us obvious and trite, was only slowly developed by the labour and repeated mistakes of the fathers of Christian theology. Instead, therefore, of summarily condemning as heretical every writer who does not distinctly and fully declare the truth according to our light, we are to inquire whether he spoke in denial of, or only in ignorance of, the whole truth. We are not to blame him for having come so short a distance on the road, but to consider whether his face be turned in the right direction, and what willingness and ability he manifests for prosecuting the journey. And we will also learn to distinguish between "the first principles of the oracles of God," and "the things hard to be understood." Of the latter, there is one which falls under the notice of Hippolytus in this homily; it is the doctrine of the eternal generation of the Son. The difficulties connected with this doctrine are known best by those who have longest examined it, and no one who does not expect a miraculous unanimity of consent among the fathers is astonished to discover that the church lived till the time of Origen without possessing any exact statement of this doctrine, while it abounded in statements quite inconsistent with it. The truth is, that it was the difficulties and obvious errors of Hippolytus himself that drew Origen to consider the matter, and to deliver that statement of the truth which has ever since been generally received as the orthodox doctrine. Justin Martyr, and, perhaps, Theophilus of Antioch (though even such authorities as Lumper and Dorner disagree as to his opinion), did not grasp the truth on this point, though they avoided the common error. They did not say with Tatian and Athenagoras, that the Word in the beginning of the world becomes the first-born work of the Father, but much further were they from saying with Bishop Pearson, "The essence which God always had without beginning, without beginning he did communicate, being always Father as always God." They did not with Tertullian maintain that there was a time when there was no Son ("Fuit autem tempus, cum ei filius non fuit."—*Adv. Hermog.* 3); but neither do they with Dionysius of Alexandria distinctly aver that "there never was

(a time) when God was not a Father."   Hippolytus
views the generation of the Son as dependent on
the will of the Father, and thinks of his production as merely for purposes of creation.   On
this point Hippolytus thus expresses himself:

"But as the author, and fellow-counsellor, and
maker of all that is made, he begot the Word; which
Word, retained within himself and unseen by the
created world, he makes visible; uttering the first
creating word ($\phi\omega\nu\acute{\eta}$),[1] and begetting light of light, he
sent forth the Lord to the creation; the Lord, his own
reason ($\nu o\hat{\upsilon}\varsigma$), formerly visible to himself alone, and
unseen by that which was made, he now makes
visible, that through his appearing the world might
see him and be saved.

"And in this way beside himself there existed
another.[2]   Another, I say, not meaning that there are

---

[1] In this chapter, and especially in this expression, Hippolytus evinces his belief that the prolation of the Son was
contingent upon the Father's purpose of creation.   The
similarity of this doctrine to that of Tertullian may be seen
from many passages in the tract *Adv. Praxean, e.g.* in c. 6,
he says: "Ut primum deus voluit ea, quae cum Sophiae
ratione et sermone disposuerat intra se, in substantias et
species suas edere, ipsum primum protulit sermonem habentem
in se individuas suas rationem et Sophiam, ut per ipsum fierent
universa, per quem erant cogitata atque disposita, imo et facta
jam, quantum in dei sensu."

[2] $o\mathring{\upsilon}\tau\omega\varsigma\ \pi\alpha\rho\acute{\iota}\sigma\tau\alpha\tau o\ \alpha\mathring{\upsilon}\tau\hat{\omega}\ \acute{\epsilon}\tau\epsilon\rho o\varsigma$.   This expression certainly
forces us to conclude that Hippolytus did not consider the Son
to exist *as a person* until thus sent forth by the Father to
create.   Bull feels that some defence of this passage is needed,

two Gods, but as light of light, or as water flowing
out of its fountain, or as a ray from the sun. For
there is but one power which proceedeth from the
whole (ἐκ τοῦ παντός), and the whole is the Father,
from whom proceedeth this Power, the Word. This
is the reason which came forth in the world, and was
manifested the Son of God (παῖς). All things exist by
him, and he alone is of the Father. Who then introduces a multitude of Gods increasing through the
ages ? For all, however unwilling, are shut up to thi
creed, that the whole runs up to one (τὸ πᾶν εἰς ἕνα
ἀνατρέχει). If, therefore, all things run up into one,
even according to Valentinus, and Marcion, and
Cerinthus, and all their silly talk, they are forced
unwillingly to confess that the one is the cause of all,
and thus bear their extorted testimony to the truth
that one God made all things according to his own
will. And the same gave the law and the prophets ;
and gifting them with the Holy Spirit, he caused
them so to speak that, receiving the inspiration of the

---

and says (*Defensio Fid. Nic.* 2d ed. p. 368) : "Agnosco
quidem hic ab Hippolyto generationem quandam Verbo, sive
Filio Dei tribui, quae mundi creationem proxime antecesserit.
Sed omnino nego de generatione loqui Hippolytum proprie
dicta, quae scilicet Verbi fuerit productio, quave Verbum
ipsum, cum prius non existeret, existere coeperit." This
defence is invalid. The generation here spoken of is the only
generation Hippolytus knows anything about, and is that
generation whereby the Son "becomes the first-begotten of the
Father" (v. c. 15). At all events, if he and the others who
use similar language intend to intimate that before this manifestation or prolation the Word existed as a person eternally in
the Father, they are, as Goode has convincingly shown, equally
heterodox.

Father's power, they should declare the counsel and will of the Father."

What these fathers held was not Sabellianism, for they maintained the distinction of the persons ; neither was it Arianism, for they maintained the sameness of the essence ; but neither was it the orthodox doctrine, for they held that the generation or the prolation of the Son was contingent on the purpose of God to create, and that while he was, as the word or reason of the Father, co-eternal with him, he was only subsequently to the purpose and will of the Father sent forth as a personal agent.   In fact, they felt the difficulty involved in their position.   They must have seen that it was something very like a contradiction to maintain the existence of a person possessed of the eternal divine substance, uncreated, and yet who does not come forth till a period that at least bears relation to time.   They saw that to the Son two things were to be attributed, eternal divine nature and personal genesis ; but how these two were to be reconciled, Origen was the first to see.   His philosophical mind gave the solution which does not lose the eternity in the genesis, nor the personality in the one divine essence, but seeing God the eternal Father, sees the Son as therefore eternal, though begotten, and as therefore divine, though distinct. These remarks may help to an understanding of some of the statements which occur in the homily.

January 1863.

IV

CLEMENT OF ALEXANDRIA AND HIS APOLOGETIC

No writer of antiquity has left us a more complete picture of the ancient world than Clement of Alexandria. If we were required to reproduce the philosophy, the religion, the literature, the manners of the most illustrious representatives of heathenism, and if we were confined to a single author as our source of information, the author we should choose would undoubtedly be Clement. The age he lived in was one which had little life of its own, and whose hope it was to resuscitate the past. It was a learned age and a critical age, though its learning and its criticism were alike superficial. It gathered up all the treasures of the past; and the eclectic spirit which had characterised Alexandria since its foundation, and which its position seemed to destine it to mature, was never more vigorous than when Clement took up his abode in the Greek quarter. The character of the age, and the character of the city in which he lived, were well represented in his own up-bringing and disposition. By birth a pagan, and by conversion a Christian, he understood the position of the two great parties in the world of religion. Born in Athens, personally acquainted with Italy, Syria, and Asia Minor, and finally settling in Alexandria, he combined in his own person the erudition and system of the West with the profundity and warmth of the East. In his boyhood he may have seen the keen eye and humorous play of feature in the face of Lucian, Pausanias investigating antiquities, and Diogenes Laertius collecting his anecdotes; in his manhood he must have seen Ammonius bending under his sacks of grain, and venting scraps of philosophy to his fellow-porters as he recovered his breath; and when he found that the two Philostrati and Sextus Empiricus were to be the leaders of his age, he may have thought that Diogenes Laertius had not lived too soon to write the lives of all the philosophers. In his boyhood he had heard the regrets of the old men who had seen the glory and prosperity of the golden age of the empire; during his travels he may have been one of the crowd which crushed into the Roman amphitheatre that day when Commodus, as the "Roman Hercules," slew with his own bow one hundred lions, and prostituted the imperial rank to a service which had been prohibited as scandalous to the senators and knights; and in his prime he felt the persecuting rage of Severus, and was forced to flee from his pupils to a safe obscurity in Cappadocia. He had the best opportunity, therefore, of judging what the real condition of the world was and was likely to be.

It is impossible to ascertain the exact date of his settlement in Alexandria. It was probably about the year 190;[1] and in a year or two afterwards he was ordained a presbyter of the church, and succeeded Pantaenus in the catechetical school. It was to Pantaenus that he owed the first satisfactory instruction he received; for all that he had acquired hitherto was a distaste for everything but the Stoic philosophy, which, as Brucker says, "ambabus amplexus est manibus," and the terminology of which he used to the last. Alexandria was at this time perhaps the greatest emporium in the world; allowed by the Romans to hold the second place. Every known race had

---

[1] Cave, who gives the opinions of the learned on this point, puts it somewhat later.

its representatives on the quays which Alexander had founded to be the exchange of the Eastern and Western worlds. Its climate was counted the most salubrious, and its natural beauty of position was equalled by the magnificence of its buildings. In the words of a traveller [1] who saw it two centuries after Clement, "I could neither satisfy myself with gazing, nor could I overtake all that was worthy of observation; whatever I looked at seemed to be unique and unrivalled, yet other sights pressed their claims, and could not be passed by. The extent of the city so strove with its beauty, and its size with the number of its inhabitants, that neither seemed to yield to the other. The size seemed greater than measure could include, and the population too great for number to overtake. As I continued to look around me, the city appeared too large to be filled by any number of inhabitants, and yet the number of men appeared so enormous that I was forced to doubt whether any city could be large enough to contain them." In this beautiful, busy, and dissipated city, every vice of heathenism, and the most sumptuous pomp of idolatry, were constantly before the eyes of Clement. He had

---

[1] Achilles Tatius, in the beginning of the fifth book of his romance.

witnessed the most impressive worship of nature in the gorgeous feast of the sun, when the city rivalled the sky in brilliance of illumination. Autumn after autumn, as the nights grew longer, and as the gay colours died away from the earth, he had seen the venerable priests of Isis lead out the sacred bull, with his horns gilt and his body veiled in black silk, to testify "their sadness and heavy cheer." And he had seen the same priests go forth by night to the seaside, clad in their sacred vestments, and carrying the consecrated ark and the vessels of gold, celebrating with shouts of triumph the finding of Osiris, and the restoration of life and fertility to the earth. Everything that paganism had to attract, to deceive, to bind, was matter of daily observation to the man who was destined to become not only the most voluminous, but in many respects the most sagacious of Christian apologists.

In Alexandria, Clement had also opportunity to acquire that learning which was essential to qualify him to meet the mental condition of religious inquirers in the second century. It was at least as important to gain the philosophers and scholars of the museum as the mechanics of the docks and building-yards, or the porters of the warehouses. It was not enough that he should be sufficiently acquainted with Homer and the other sources of Greek mythology to expose the infamy of the history of the gods; it was not enough that he should have sufficient acuteness and dialectic skill to divest the mysteries of their pretensions to bestow immortality on the initiated. His office as teacher of the Christian school exposed him to the interrogation of all who had difficulties about the new religion. The cavils which were concocted by the wits of the museum, the theories which were broached in the dining-hall of the professors, would naturally find their way to the ears of Clement. To gain a victory over the Christian teacher would be enough to make the reputation of an aspirant to the degree of the pagan doctors. And so Clement drew around the young plants which were under his charge the hedge, as he calls it, of a learning at least equal to, and probably very far superior to that of any who was likely to attack them. In the library of the Serapeion, doomed to be destroyed in another century by fanatics professing the same religion as himself, he found all that was needful to furnish him against the most erudite of his antagonists. That he made abundant use of the valuable stores here laid up, is sufficiently evident from the number and facility

of his quotations. Excepting Athenaeus, probably no ancient writer could be named who cites
400 authors; but if we are to reckon second-
hand quotations and sayings of the philosophers,
a much larger number than this must measure
the reading of Clement. Where so much time
has been spent upon reading, we do not expect to
find evidence of much time spent in reflection;
where the mass acquired is so great, we anticipate
that it has not all been assimilated, and that
much of it is carried as a burden, making the
movements of the mind heavy and uncertain.
Yet it is scarcely fair to say with Brucker,[1]—
"Suffocaverat vir eruditissimus immensae lectionis
copia judicium." He had, at least, a decided
aversion to foolish or useless learning, and would
have joined in the regret of our modern utili-
tarian—

---

[1] Every one who desires to understand the position, and to
estimate the teaching of the Alexandrine writers, will naturally turn to Brucker, and will be amply rewarded by the
dissertations in his third volume devoted to this subject. The
Dissertations of Le Nourry are long, but contain much useful
information. They are reprinted in Migne's edition of
Clement, which is very complete, and worthy of all praise.
An interesting, original, and satisfactory account of Clement is
given in Pressensé's *Histoire de l'Eglise Chrétienne.* To those
who merely desire a faithful rendering in English of large
portions of Clement's writings, Bishop Kaye's work will be
acceptable.

> "What numbers sheath'd in erudition lie,
>   Plung'd to the hilts in venerable tomes,
>   And rusted in; who might have borne an edge,
>   And play'd a sprightly beam, if born to speech."

Indeed, Clement expresses the same sentiment under what some may deem a prettier figure. "The wells," he says, "which are unused stagnate, but clear waters gush from those that are used. What profit is there in wisdom if it do not instruct the hearer?" There were many in his own day who told him that no good thing could by any alchemy be extracted out of pagan writings, but at the utmost he can only be accused of not being always judicious and logical in his use of pagan ideas. He might, perhaps, have been the better of the advice given afterwards by Gregory Nazianzen—

> "At ista, quaeso, cuncta fac cautus legas,
>   Prudenter ex his colligens quid utile,
>   Fugiensque quicquid noxium est et pestilens.
>   Apis aemulari cura sit sapientiam,
>   Quae flore in omni sessitans, ex singulis
>   Idonee carpit esse quod videt utile."

However, no one will deny that it was proper that a man in Clement's position at Alexandria should be a man of thorough culture, should understand his adversaries' position—

should be able to use against them suitable
weapons, and should strengthen the catechumens
with such instruction as would be of practical
value to them. The question which lies so close
to this,—How far the Christian teachers of Alexandria were justifiable in introducing Christian
ideas to the cultivated minds around them, under
philosophical garb and in philosophical forms—
how far they were right in Platonising—is a more
difficult question to answer. Much historical
investigation, much philosophical ability, and
much plausible argumentation have been ex-
pended by accusers and defenders. And probably the question will continue to be settled by
each investigator, in the same manner as it was
settled by the Fathers themselves: those who
had studied and admired the Platonic philosophy
making liberal use of it, and those who had not
done so condemning its use as profane. There is
no doubt, however, that even the fundamentals of
the Christian faith are obscured in the writings
of Clement, by the philosophic clothing in which
they are presented. It would be easy to select
passages from the *Stromata*, which would be
quite in their place in the *Phaedo* or the *Theaetetus*, not so easy to collect passages which would
fully exhibit the Scriptural doctrine of redemp-

tion. Yet, there is no mistaking the piety of Clement; his reverence for Scripture is equally unmistakable, and his anxiety to bring all men under its influence is patent on every page. And it cannot but occur to one who enters at all into the spirit of his writings, that there must have been some real efficacy in the mode of persuasion adopted by one who had himself been won from the same position as those to whom he appealed now occupied. He had been a highly educated pagan, he was now a sincere and devoted Christian; surely he must have had some knowledge of the path which led from the one position to the other. Is it likely, that when inducing others to the same transition as he had himself accomplished, he should have forgotten or omitted to use those inducements which had been effectual in his own case? Or is it likely that those inducements which had proved effectual with him, would be of no avail with others of the same cast of mind, and of the same habits of thought?

In estimating the service done by Clement, it has, perhaps, been too little considered that his position in Alexandria gave an apologetic cast to the whole of his teaching. We do not suspect Paley of Arianism because his *Evidences* contain no explicit teaching on the doctrine of the Trinity.

We do not consider the speech of Paul on Mars' Hill defective, because it does not enounce the doctrine of the Atonement. The writings of Clement are not all professedly apologetic, yet he has read them very carelessly who does not feel that this is the character of the whole, and that, if Clement is to be fairly estimated, he must be judged by an apologetic, and not by a systematic standard. What he would have done in those numerous works he promised to write, what he did in those nine which the old world saw and lost, we cannot tell; but his extant writings clearly show that if he was to teach in Alexandria at all, he must do so apologetically. Two of his three great works are professedly to the heathen; and the *Stromata* seem to be little more than a collection of such discourses as he held from time to time with his pupils, and with pagan inquirers. They bear all the characteristics of such a compilation. There is a great deal of repetition, and a want of order scarcely conceivable, except on the supposition that the work was written at intervals, as he had occasion to explain matters to his pupils. There is also a vivacity and animation which brings us into the presence of the author, and we seem rather to listen to one who speaks, than to read the words of a writer. Now, if this

K

be the origin of the *Stromata*, its excellence varies with its fitness to meet the questions and doubts of the most highly educated class in Alexandria at the close of the second century. These questions were of the same kind as had exercised the mind of Plato centuries before:—How are the finite and the infinite connected; or, what is the world, and how is it related to God? Has man any special connection with God, and how may this be realised and confirmed? What is the soul of man, and what may it become? And how is it to achieve its destiny; especially, is it by some kind, and what kind, of liberation from the body? If Clement did not answer these questions, he had no chance of being heard by the class among which his lot was cast. Christianity, by giving the real answers to these questions, and by putting the answers in the hearts of many whose ears were unused to philosophic diction, had excited an almost universal attention to the questions themselves. What had been interesting to the few, became important to the many. The appetite which had been dormant was excited as soon as the proper food was presented. Christianity no sooner put within men's reach communion with God, than men who had till now been content with the world thirsted after God. But at this juncture, paganism made a last stand. It saw now what the nature of man required; Christianity had developed the wants of the soul, as paganism had never done. But could paganism not satisfy these wants as plausibly as Christianity? Sagacious men began to see that there could be no going back now to the old state of things; but might not a pagan philosophy be framed which should satisfy these new demands? After all, had not Plato anticipated these very demands, and might not something yet be made of what he had done towards practically satisfying the craving of men after a higher life? It should at least be tried.

It was, therefore, with the beginnings of Neo-Platonism, which professed to be a saving religion as well as a philosophy, that Clement had in the first instance to do. He constantly endeavours to persuade men that Christ is the only teacher who has the truth to give. He does not deny that the ancient philosophers had some light, but maintains that they borrowed a great deal from the Jews, and that all that they had was given them only as a preparation for the fuller truth of Christianity. These are the ideas to which he devotes whole books of the *Stromata*, and which recur again and again throughout the whole. The attitude he maintains towards philosophers is that of an inquirer in the same path, but farther on. They are below, striving upwards; he stands above, where the dawn has struck. He continually assures philosophers that they are right so far—that there is a divine element in man—that men are capable of holding fellowship with God—that there is a life for the soul of man pure from sin. All this philosophy had taught, and all this, Clement insists, philosophy was right in teaching, and delights to recall the beautiful forms in which this teaching had often been embodied. But here, he says, is the difference between Christianity and philosophy, that Christianity has received the truth which philosophy was only groping after; that there is only One whose teaching can develop that divine element in man, only One who can bring man to God, only One who can heal, purify, and strengthen the soul. He comes even nearer to the philosophers still, by granting that this one teacher had been their teacher also, though he had not given to them the fulness of the truth. The Word, he says, who now enlightens Christians, has been in all antiquity the instructor of philosophers. All this is true, and may have induced men of philosophic leanings to look with a kindlier eye upon Christianity. Yet this uniform presentation of Christ in the one character of a teacher is not merely defective, but deceptive. Redemption comes to be nothing more than the reception of Christ's teaching, the soul being purified, and, in the Platonic sense, redeemed by the truth. Faith comes to be nothing more than the mental belief of the revelation of Christ, and this is placed as the foundation of all spiritual progress, in the same sense in which the older philosophers had postulated intuition as the basis of knowledge. Any other view of redemption will be found with difficulty in Clement's writings ; yet the occasional passages in which the correct view is found are satisfactory in regard to Clement's personal belief.

While, therefore, Clement can scarcely be said to have brought forward the characteristic differences of Christianity, he adopts the method which he judged most suitable for winning the attention of philosophers. And further, it is probably true that what Clement had both originally and habitually prized in Christianity was the solution which it afforded of the highest problems of philosophy, and the practical aid he received from it for leading a holy and godly life. He felt more keenly the distance to which sin had banished man from God, and the blindness and weakness it had begotten in the soul, than the guilt or danger of it. Having to do with men whose souls were aspiring, rather than with those whose consciences were condemning them, he took them as they were, and showed what there was in Christianity suitable for them. He was perfectly aware that his position was a doubtful one, and he maintained it, on the conviction that it was the most useful he could take up. That he had carefully considered the course he should adopt in dealing with incipient Neo-Platonists, is proved by the pregnancy of his sentences when he defends his position. He meets his assailants at three different levels, first maintaining that philosophy is a good thing ($\theta\epsilon\acute{\iota}\alpha\nu$ $\delta\omega\rho\epsilon\grave{\alpha}\nu$ $"E\lambda\lambda\eta\sigma\iota$ $\delta\epsilon\delta o\mu\acute{\epsilon}\nu\eta\nu$), meaning, however, by philosophy, "not the Stoic, nor the Platonic, nor the Epicurean, nor the Aristotelian, but an eclectic philosophy, compounded of all the good and wise things that have been found in any of these." Again, descending from the highest position, he maintains that "though philosophy were useless, yet if it be useful to establish its uselessness, it is useful." This is something more than a sophism, and would probably give pause to his assailants. But his favourite argument is drawn from necessity. He must become a Greek to the Greeks ($\tau\hat{\omega}$ $\gamma\grave{\alpha}\rho$ $\acute{o}\mu o\acute{\iota}\omega$ $\tau\grave{o}$ $\acute{o}\mu o\iota o\nu$ $\acute{\epsilon}\delta\iota\delta\alpha\sigma\kappa\acute{o}\mu\epsilon\theta\alpha$), he must fully appreciate their difficulties before he can remove them, recognise the truth they hold before he can add to it, and see their error from their own point of view (πιστὸς ὁ μετ᾽ ἐμπειρίας ἔλεγχος).[1] But in every defence which Clement makes of philosophy, it is implied that there is a better thing than philosophy, the ἀλήθεια καθ᾽ ἡμᾶς. With all that he grants to the philosopher there comes the appeal, Submit yourself to Him from whom all truth in every age has proceeded. Perhaps Clement had reason to be persuaded that the men to whom he was sent would not think of Christ at all, unless He were presented in this light. Perhaps the terminology, which to us appears defective and deceptive, may have admitted of a wider interpretation than we can now discover. While it touched philosophy on the one side, it may have comprehended more of the Christian idea than appears to us. If we take Clement's writings as we have and understand them; if we say, "This, and nothing more than this, is what Clement taught as Christianity, and would have men to live by"; if we form Clement's creed out of his extant works, and give to each article a higher or a lower place, according

---

[1] See the *Paedagogue*, throughout; and the *Stromata*, lib. i. c. 2-7, and lib. v. c. 3.

as it has a larger or a smaller place allotted to it in his discussions: then we must conclude that his views of Christianity were too much coloured by his philosophic upbringing and habit of thought, and that his hearers must have received a false impression of his religion. But if we conceive that what we have of Clement's teaching is only preliminary, if we look upon him simply as a guide to, and not as an expositor of, the truth; if we believe that he expected that those whom he won to Christ as his pupils, if not yet as his disciples, would go on to learn much more than he had led them to anticipate: our conclusions must be somewhat modified. "Cum enim hanc eclecticam philosophandi rationem non Alexandriam modo, sed et omnem fere orbem literatum atque philosophicum, occupasse cerneret, multaque passim adduci videret, quibus commendari posse gentilibus philosophis Christianam religionem credebat, eandem viam sibi ingrediendam statuit, ut rem Christianam juvaret" (Brucker, iii. 422). The redemption of which he generally speaks is certainly, in its mode, little more than the Platonic enlightenment and purification of the soul, yet without this there is no Christian redemption. The faith he argues for is short of the Westminster idea of saving faith; yet without the belief of the revelation of Christ, and the surrender of the mind to His teaching, there is no reliance of the soul upon Him. To have spoken of redemption and faith as we speak of them might have been unintelligible to those men out of whose speculations Neo - Platonism was rapidly taking shape; to speak of them as Clement spoke might introduce the Scriptural idea.[1]

The apologetic of Clement has, of course, a destructive as well as a conciliatory side. He is unsparing in his exposure of the folly and wickedness of the pagan worship and practices. As might be expected, his *Logos Protreptikos*, or hortatory address to the Greeks, differs considerably from the *Apologies* of Minucius, Justin, or Tertullian. He has not the advantage of Justin's hazardous position, nor does his fearlessness, though unsurpassed by any of the apologists, appear in so interesting a light as if he had been pleading at the tribunal of Caesar. His address does not possess the picturesque and dramatic

[1] Pressensé thus describes Clement's position : "Il est l'apologiste des gentils, l'apôtre de la Grèce cultivée, et il plaide la cause du Christ devant un aréopage idéal où siègent comme juges tous les grands philosophes de l'antiquité. Il parle leur langue, il les prend au point de développement moral et religieux où il les trouve pour les amener à la vérité complète."

attractions of the *Octavius*, but his impassioned earnestness, which throughout breaks through his reasoning in loving and pointed appeal, raises him above all his predecessors and contemporaries. His assault upon the heathen position is conducted with all the vigour of Tertullian, but with far more than his love, care, and skill. Whatever he says of idolatry is sensible and convincing, is based upon an unusually extensive acquaintance with the mythology and literature of the Greeks, and reminds us, by its animated and cogent reasoning, of the Epistle to Diognetus. "The Parian stone," he says (pp. 50 and 78),[1] "is beautiful, but it is not Neptune; the ivory is pleasant to the eye, but it is not Olympian Jove. Let your Phidias and Polycletus, your Praxiteles and Apelles come, and let them say which of them has made a breathing image, or out of earth moulded the soft flesh. Who liquefies the marrow? Who set and jointed the bones? Who strung the sinews? Who inflated the veins, and poured blood into them? Who stretched the skin around? Where is he who made the eye to see? Who breathed into the body the breath of life? Who endowed man with righteousness,

---

[1] The references are to the pages of Potter's edition, which are given in the other editions.

and promised him immortality? The Creator of all things, the supreme Artificer and Father. He alone made such a living image when he made us. But your Olympian Jove, the image of an image, widely differing from the reality, is the dumb work of Attic hands. Why, then, ye foolish and vain, have ye forsaken heaven to pay honour to earth? For is not this image of earth, and does it not receive the form which ye worship from the idea and hand of an earthly workman? I have learned to tread earth, and not to worship it." The characters of the gods are elaborately exposed, and their shameful histories brought forward from the most received authorities, poets, historians, and philosophers. "These gods," says Clement (p. 28), "let your wives worship, and bid them pray that their own husbands become like their gods in temperance. Let your boys be brought up to reverence these characters, that they may themselves become such men, and show in their own persons the image of the divine impurity." He dwells also upon the folly and immorality of many superstitions to which the heathen clung, for no better reason than that their fathers had sanctioned them by their practice. He rebukes (p. 82) "the pitiable and paltry superstition of the men who think that

God speaks through crows and jackdaws, but is silent through man; who honour the crow as God's messenger, but persecute the man of God, though he comes not croaking and cawing, but speaking articulately, and communicating reasonable and profitable instruction; him, alas! they seek to slay when he calls to righteousness, for they neither accept heaven's grace nor evade its punishment. For they believe not God, nor understand his might. But his hatred of wickedness is incomprehensible, whose love of man is ineffable. His wrath cherishes punishment for sin, while his love blesses the penitent."

Clement has also much to say regarding the narrowness of any philosophical religion. He presses the arguments that have since become common. "The teaching of our Master has not been confined to Judea, as philosophy to Greece. It has poured itself through the whole world, persuading Greeks and barbarians of every race, in all cities and villages, instructing whole families together, and enlightening individual believers wherever one was found hearkening to the truth; and having already won to the truth not a few even of the philosophers themselves." And not only has the truth thus an inherent property which secures its spread, it is also indestructible.

It is available for all kinds of men, and if crushed out of one region springs up in another. "Greek philosophy, if the ruler happens to prohibit it, there and then perishes; our doctrine has, from its first enouncement, been opposed and denounced by kings and princes, by governors and rulers, using against it armies of satellites and countless hosts of assailants, exerting their whole force to cut us off from the earth. Yet our doctrine flourishes but the more; for it does not perish like human teaching, nor fade like a powerless gift—for no gift of God is powerless, but remains unrebuked and undestroyed, since it is written that to the end it will be persecuted" (p. 828). He brings forward as a further distinction of Christianity, its applicability to women as well as to men. This distinguishes it from philosophy, and asserts its claim to universal reception. "If men and women have the same God, then one 'Paedagogue' belongs to both, and both have the same virtue. There is one church, one temperance, one modesty, common food, conjugal marriage, breathing, seeing, hearing, knowing, hoping, obedience, love,—all are alike to both. They whose life is thus common have also a common salvation" (p. 103). These words are sufficient evidence that Clement was thoroughly aware of the mission of Christianity, and confident in its power as the revelation of the true God. It is interesting, too, to find this early and distinct appreciation of the dignity of woman followed up in the *Paedagogue* by such precepts and counsels as would enable the gay and luxurious women of Alexandria to forsake the vicious and dissolute habits in which they had been reared, and become patterns in all modest, matronly, and Christian conversation.

From these passages it will already be conjectured what is the positive evidence on which Clement mainly depends for the proof of Christianity. From these it will already be seen that Clement trusts mainly to the truth being its own evidence. He views the heathen as "feeling after, if haply they might find God." His work is done when he has presented Christ to them. He starts from the truth received in common by himself and the heathen, that man is made to know, worship, and imitate God; he goes on to show that the gods whom they and their fathers have been worshipping deserve neither worship nor imitation; and this apology is complete when he has shown the true God revealed in the Word. Not that he follows this or any other order, but that these are the elements of his task. He believes that if Christ be set fairly before the soul of man, the soul will recognise Him and acknowledge Him. His aim is to persuade the φιλόσοφος to become φιλόλογος; and believing that man was made by the Word and for the Word, he believes also that there is that in man which will know and cleave to the Word. In the very first sentences of the *Logos Protreptikos*, in opposition to oracles, poets, and philosophers who had led men astray, Clement sets forth the Word of God (τὸ ᾆσμα τὸ καινὸν) in His office of teacher, and tells how He has come to open the blind eyes and lead the wanderers to righteousness, to declare God to men, to conquer death and bring corruption to an end, to exhort (προτρέπειν), instruct, and reconcile men to God. So that while he is careful to maintain that the love of God to man is not a new thing, nor his pity now for the first time active (ἀλλ' ἄνωθεν ἀρχῆθεν), the whole power of his address consists in his presentation of Christ as the one Teacher of truth and the sole Provider of life. These words may be taken as the motto of the piece,—παλαιὰ ἡ πλάνη, καινὸν δὲ ἡ ἀλήθεια φαίνεται.

It is impossible to reproduce in a translation the rapidity and rhythm of Clement's eloquence, and the surprising happiness of his phraseology, or to convey any idea of his inexhaustible vocabulary. It is difficult even to preserve the warmth and energy of his appeal; nor can a few detached passages produce an impression such as is felt on the perusal of the connected and cumulative whole.[1] Yet such is the wealth of the original, that, though much be spilt in the translation, enough may remain to show the nature of his argument, and that he is worthy of the title, "le fondateur de la grande apologie."

"Man is born to have connection with God. As, then, we do not force the horse to plough nor the steer to hunt, but apply each animal to its natural employment, so, of course, man, being made for the contemplation of heaven, a heavenly plant,[2] we exhort to the knowledge of God. We counsel him to prepare godliness as his proper, special, and peculiar maintenance (viaticum) for eternity. Till the ground, we say, if you are a tiller of the soil; but with your tilling, know God. Sail, whoever loves the sea ; but call upon the heavenly Pilot. Has the love of a military life possessed you ? then hearken to the Captain whose

---

[1] Yet what Pressensé says, with something of plaintive simplicity, is quite true : "Nos lecteurs ne sauraient se faire une idée de tout ce que ses écrits ont de confus, parce que nous n'avons cité que les passages les plus beaux sans le suivre dans les détours infinis de son style." The quotations in Pressensé must give every reader a high idea of Clement's power of expression.

[2] φιλόθεον ζῶον is a title of man in the *Paedagogue*.

signals are in righteousness. . . . Let us not, let us not be enslaved nor grovel in the mire like swine; but as the true children of the light, let us look up and use our eyes to the light, lest the Lord prove us bastards, as the sun the eaglets. Let us repent and pass from ignorance to knowledge, from foolishness to wisdom, from licentiousness to temperance, from unrighteousness to righteousness, from godlessness to God. It is a worthy venture to desert to God. 'The earth is the Lord's, and the fulness thereof.' How then do you dare to luxuriate in his possessions, and be ignorant of their Lord? Quit my earth, the Lord will say to you; touch not the water which I cause to spring, neither gather the fruits which I ripen; pay the price of your sustenance; O man, recognise your Lord; thou art the peculiar workmanship of God; how then can his property become another's? . . . Believe, O man, in man and God;[1] believe, O man, in him who suffered and is adored—the living God. Ye servants, believe in him who was dead. All men, believe ye in him who is the only God of all men. Believe, and receive salvation as your reward. 'Seek ye the Lord, and your soul shall live.' He that seeks God is taking steps towards his own salvation. Hast thou found God? Thou hast life. Let us then seek that we may also live.[2] For the reward of finding God is life in his presence" (p. 84).

---

[1] A title given to Christ in an early part of this address is ὁ μόνος ἄμφω θεός τε καὶ ἄνθρωπος.

[2] ζητήσωμεν ἵνα καὶ ζήσωμεν. For analogy of alliteration, cf. λήθη ἀληθείας. For the sense, cf. p. 89, where he says θάνατος γὰρ ἀΐδιος ἁμαρτία.

"The word which enlightens us is more to be desired than gold. Let us receive the light, that we may receive God. Let us receive the light, and we shall become the disciples of God, and it will instruct us how we have wandered in our search after God. Since thou, Lord, leadest me by thy light, through thee I find God, and from thee I receive the Father. I become thy co-heir, since thou art not ashamed to call me brother. Let us, then, cast off, let us cast off our oblivion of the truth, our ignorance, and the darkness which dims our vision like a mist ; and looking upon him who lives, the true God, let us greet him, Hail, Light ! for upon us who were plunged in darkness and buried in the shadow of death hath light from heaven shone, purer than the sun, sweeter than this life below. That light is life everlasting ; and whatsoever partakes of it lives. And the night does homage to the light, and setting through fear, gives place to the day of the Lord. All things are become sleepless light ; and the setting has believed in the rising. This is the new creation. For the Sun of Righteousness rides prosperously, and visits all mankind alike, imitating the Father, who ' maketh his sun to rise on the evil and on the good,' and sprinkles upon all the dew of truth. He it is who has brought the setting to the rising, and has raised death to life through the cross [literally, crucified death to life] ; and having snatched man from destruction, he has translated him to the skies, transplanting corruption into incorruption, and transforming earth into heaven, as the husbandman of God " (p. 88).

Throughout the *Paedagogue,* as well as the other treatises of Clement, there abound the fullest and most distinct assertions of the pre-existence and absolute divinity of Christ, often very happily worded and always delivered with a hearty and reverential warmth. Such passages as the following frequently occur, "The Lord, despised by the eye, was worshipped in act, the Expiator (ὁ καθάρσιος), and Saviour, and Propitiator, the divine Word, the most manifest and true God, equalled to the Lord of all (because He was his Son and 'the Word was in God'); neither disbelieved when first announced, nor unrecognised when, taking the person of man and formed in the flesh, he acted out the drama of man's salvation.[1] For he was a genuine combatant, and fought along with the creature; and, being very quickly made known to and distributed among all men, caused God to shine on us more swiftly than the rising sun diffuses his beams in obedience to the same fatherly will. He revealed God, and showed from whom and who he was, by the things which he taught and did—the Peace-bringer, the Reconciler, the Word, our Saviour; a fountain, giving

---

[1] These expressions, προσωπεῖον and ὑποκρίνεσθαι, borrowed from the theatre, might, in some writers, be susceptible of a Docetic interpretation, but are certainly free from suspicion in Clement.

life and peace, poured over the face of the whole earth ; through whom, so to speak, the universe has now become a sea of good." Shortly after, he again breaks into a laudatory description. " This is the word of incorruption who regenerates man, restoring him to truth ; the goad of salvation, who drives out corruption and chases death away; the builder of a temple among men, that he might make God to dwell among men. Sanctify this temple ; let pleasures and luxuries, like the flower of yesterday, be abandoned to the wind and the fire, and wisely cultivate the fruits of temperance, and dedicate thyself as the first-fruits to God, that not the work only, but the grace also, may be of God."

The address closes with an eloquent appeal put into the mouth of the Word, and opening with language familiar to Greek ears (p. 93) :

" Hear, ye myriad tribes, yea, all men who are endowed with reason, Barbarians as well as Greeks : I call upon the whole human race, whose Creator I am by the will of the Father, come to me that ye may be arrayed under the one God and the one Word of God. Be not satisfied with excelling all irrational animals in reason, since to you only of all mortal beings do I grant immortality. For I wish, I wish, to share with you this grace. I confer upon you a benefit perfect and entire, incorruption. I freely give you the Word, the knowledge of God ; myself I wholly give to you. This I am, this God wills, this is the harmony, this the whole good pleasure of the Father, this is the Son, this Christ, this the Word of God, the arm of the Lord, the power of all things, the will of the Father. Of these there have been from of old many images, but images without resemblance. I am come to direct you to the archetype, that to me ye also may become like. I will anoint you with the unction of faith, through which ye put off corruption, and I will show to you the naked form of righteousness, through which ye ascend to God. Come unto me, all ye that labour, etc. Let us hasten, let us run, O God-beloved and God-like images of the Word. Let us hasten, let us run, let us take his yoke, let us be urged forward to immortality by this noble charioteer of men. Let us form part of his triumph entering the presence of the Father. The noblest spectacle to the Father is the Son Eternal triumphing. Let us, then, be ambitious of sharing in such honours, let us be the favoured of God, and obtain the greatest of enduring possessions, God and life. Christ is our helper. Let us take courage in him. . . . But enough of words, yea, too much has been already said, drawn on as I have been by this opportunity which God has given me, of inviting you to salvation. For the words which tell of a life that has no end nor cessation are ready themselves to run on endlessly. To you, now, this remains, that you make choice of the most profitable, judgment or grace ; since, for my own part, I do not think it worth while deliberating which of the two is better ; nor indeed is it justifiable to weigh destruction with life."

In such passages as these Clement sets the Word in presence of the Greeks, declares His nature, His properties and His work. He makes abundant use of Scripture for the purpose both of defining more accurately the person of Christ, and of persuading men of the sincerity of His desire to guide them to God and immortality. He thus answers the questions which were being asked on all sides, and to which philosophy had professed to give the only satisfying answer. Clement tells men of Christ, and says to them, This is He who can bring you to all you seek. Is not this He whom you seek? Will not your destiny be achieved in coming to Him? Clement thus rose above the position of the earlier Apologists, and anticipated much of the modern Apologetic. If this religion, says Clement, be not what you need, reject it; if it be, acknowledge and use it. "We who are sick have need of a Saviour; straying, we need a guide; and blind, we need one who can lead us to the light; thirsty, we need the living fountain, from which, if we drink, we shall no more thirst; the dead need life; the sheep a shepherd; the children a paedagogue; yea, all humanity needs Jesus; lest, wandering and sinning to the end, we fall into condemnation, but rather, being separated from the chaff, be gathered into the

Father's garner" (p. 147). He knew that there was an absolute harmony between the necessities of man's nature and God's religion. To use his own language, there was an eternal religion subsisting between the Paedagogue, or the Word, and the men whom He had made. In all men there existed that which made them capable of recognising and following Christ, and this was to him final proof that Christ was to be followed. If any other teacher can teach more or better, if any other can penetrate the human spirit to a greater depth, or draw with a stronger attraction, let him be followed.

The detailed enunciation of Christian precepts, and the elaborate display of Christian life, which form so large a part of the writings of Clement, were necessary to the fulfilment of the task which his position demanded. The problem of philosophy, the great difficulty to all thinking men, had always been, and continued to be, How is the perfect man to be formed, and what, in the first place, is he? Man is, undoubtedly, a very superior creation; how is it that he so continually exposes himself to his own contempt, and falls short still of all the glories he seems with such justice to arrogate? Is there no possibility that he should actually achieve his high destiny, and become all he is capable of? To these questions philosophy had her answers; and Clement, in pursuance of his plan of meeting the philosophers as much as possible on their own ground, shows how the soul is purified in this life, and what conduct is proper to those who have entered the Christian school. After explaining, as was particularly needful to his audience, that the proper expression of our knowledge of God is in the life, he enters with much detail upon the inculcation of Christian duty. He has been much censured for his performance of this part of his task. It has been urged against him that, instead of laying down principles of action, he has busied himself with trifling and ludicrous minutiae, and that " he sets before us little or nothing that is at all fitted to promote the cause of genuine Christian holiness of heart and life." It would be nearer the truth to say, that while he does lay down (and with admirable terseness) principles of conduct, and sets before us (and with admirable power) much that is fitted to improve the spirit, all this is overlaid and partially obscured by a detail that would be wearisome were it not ludicrous. We expect a system of morality; we find a code of table etiquette. We expect to sit at the feet of a Johnson; we are introduced to a Chesterfield.

We lend our ear to the counsels of a spiritual adviser; and we hear the prescriptions of a valetudinarian. We are instructed how to lie at table, how to laugh without violating decorum, and how to sneeze or cough without distressing our neighbours. We are told that it resembles the lower animals to sniff the steam of a savoury dish, that it is unseemly to speak with the mouth full, and precarious to drink in the same condition. We are cautioned against lying in carved bed-steads, because such harbour reptiles; against using any perfumes which neither relieve the head nor strengthen the stomach; against wearing the hair on the head too thick, because that injures the brain, and against wearing it on the chin too thin, because that is effeminate, for the beard is older than Eve, and the sign of a superior nature. If our hair is gray, we must not dye it; and if we have no hair at all, we must not wear another person's. If we wear rings, they must bear no unseemly devices on them, but a dove, or a fish, or an anchor. A lady, however wealthy, ought not to wear dresses which attract the eyes and the calculations of men, though she may dress so as to please her husband. She must not wear sandals covered with gold and precious stones, nor so trim her hair that she is afraid to move her head. All this is curious, but not very edifying to a modern reader. But along with this, and interwoven with it, are found such manly and sensible injunctions, such devout though allegorising allusions, and all so well said, that one is carried on with not a little interest. And we believe that an age which was given up to such senseless customs, and which wallowed in such abominable practices as are here denounced, required as definite and detailed admonition as we find in the *Paedagogue* of Clement. As Bishop Kaye very well observes, " His intention was to deliver rules for the guidance of his fellow-Christians in the common intercourse of life. Many of his rules are puerile, many grounded on false principles ; but there is mingled with them much that may even now be read with profit, much that is fitted to give a religious tone to the mind, and to inspire it with the love of purity and virtue. When, too, we censure the minutiae into which Clement descends, we should bear in mind that, situated as Christians then were, it was desirable to draw as marked a line of distinction as possible between their manner of life and that of the heathens by whom they were surrounded."

As might have been expected, the Christian use of wealth was a favourite theme with the

Alexandrian censor. Not only is it handled at large in the excellent discourse entitled, "Quis dives salvetur," he also recurs to it in various parts of his writings. His view of it will be understood from the following:

"Wealth, indeed, seems to me to be much like a serpent; unless you know how to catch it without risk, and can lift it up by the tip of the tail, it will double back and fold round your hand and bite you: just so wealth, whether in the hand of the prudent or unwary, is a desperate thing to wriggle and catch and bite, but there is a possibility of a man using it so magnanimously and wisely as to charm the brute by the incantation of the Word and himself remain un-hurt."

Again, in the fine chapter on "Simplicity the best viaticum for the Christian," he says:

"Why are such dainties prepared? Is it to fill one belly? Why such an array of drinking vessels? Why such heaps of ornaments and such crowded wardrobes and cabinets? For thieves that slip into other men's clothes and for lickerish eyes. It becomes us rather to set out for the truth girt and light; as our Lord says, 'Carry neither purse, nor scrip, nor shoes,' *i.e.* do not burden yourselves with that wealth which can only be stored in purses; do not cram your treasuries as those who stuff a wallet with food, but share with them that need; neither trouble . yourselves with beasts of burden and a train of servants, who (because they bear the burdens of the wealthy) are figuratively called 'shoes.' Let us then dispense with a multitude of utensils, with cups of silver and vessels of gold, and a crowd of domestics, and let us receive industry and simplicity as the honourable and seemly companions of our journey. Let us walk in harmony with the Word, and even if we have wife and children, a household will prove no burden which has learnt to follow a wise guide, and the wife who loves her husband will walk as he walks.

"A good support on the heavenward journey is the double strength of simplicity and wise gravity. As the foot is the measure of the shoe, so is the body of each one's requirements. What is over and above, all ornate furnishings and movables, are merely a burden. One who is pressing to heaven, and has his way to force, should take bounty as his staff, and sharing with the afflicted and hard pressed, become himself partaker of the true rest. For as wells which are fed by a perennial spring rise always to their old level, however abundantly you draw ; and as the milk flows to the breasts which give suck, so bounty, the good fountain of benevolence, shares and distributes itself to the thirsting, and is yet again increased and filled. For he who has the Word, the Almighty God, is independent, and never runs out of anything he needs. For the Word is a sufficient possession, and the source of all welfare."

After these quotations, our readers will scarcely be prepared for the assertion that Clement " exhibits plain traces of the operation at once of what have been called the ascetic and the mystic systems of morality." There are, indeed, statements in Clement which might be set side by side with the sentiments of Fénelon's *Dissertation on Pure Love*, or Madame Guyon's *Torrents*; but there is throughout the writings of the Alexandrian a broad and wholesome practicalness, a modern common sense, which sets him at a distance from the French Pietists of the seventeenth century. The charge of mysticism may, however, be established, but the charge of asceticism cannot be allowed. The position of Clement as the orthodox champion against Valentinus and Basilides, if nothing else, forbade him to lean to asceticism. His attitude towards philosophy laid him under a like necessity to vindicate the rights of the body. "The soul," he says (p. 639), "is the better part of man, the body the inferior; but neither is the soul essentially good, nor the body essentially bad." The author quoted above as making these charges has been unfortunate in the instances he has chosen to confirm them. He says, "On the one hand, he prohibits indulgences which the Scriptures do not condemn (as second marriages); and, on the other hand, he releases men from obligations which the Scriptures impose,—as, for example, when he denies the necessity for regular times and seasons for prayer and religious exercises, upon the ground that men ought *always* to cultivate a devotional spirit." Upon the first charge we ask the reader's attention to the following words of Clement which represent his whole teaching on the point (p. 511): "A single marriage (μονογαμία), and the seemly dignity attached to it, we admire; saying, however, that we ought to be sympathising, and to bear one another's burdens, lest some one, thinking he stands, himself also fall. And respecting second marriage, the apostle says, If you burn, marry." The same opinion is expressed in the 12th cap. of the third book of the *Stromata*; and how any one can have read that book (wholly occupied as it is with the subject of marriage), and have failed to see that Clement is professedly and effectively opposing ascetic tendencies, we are at a loss to understand. The instance cited in support of the second charge is not more happy. Clement's own words concerning prayer, which he nowhere contradicts, but everywhere confirms, are these (p. 851; they occur in one of the most beautiful and instructive chapters of the *Stromata*): "The whole life of the Gnostic is a holy festival. His sacrifices are prayers and praises, and the reading of the Scriptures before meals; psalms and hymns during meals, and before retiring for the night: and during the night, prayers again." It is quite true that Clement declares that the Gnostic, or more advanced Christian, is not dependent on the seasons and places to which others confine their worship; at the same time, he distinctly commends both stated hours and special occasions of prayer He does maintain that the perfect man is always in the enjoyment of communion with God; in language of great beauty and force he represents the joyful and constant fellowship of the trusting soul with God, and tells how God hears not only the voice, but the thought; but he nowhere denies the necessity of stated and special prayer.

This latter point is, however, of less importance, as Clement is undoubtedly the forerunner of Dionysius in mysticism. The Gnostic of Clement is in all the leading features of his character the mystic of La Combe and the Archbishop of Cambray. Almost all that is found in the *Maxims of the Saints*, or the *Orationis Mentalis Analysis*, may be found in the sixth and seventh books of the *Stromata*. In these books it is Clement's object to describe the spiritual condition and outward deportment of the true Gnostic; and, in the judgment of one whose voice in such matters has much authority, "Clement's portraiture of the perfect Christian is one of the noblest things of the kind that the world ever saw ; yet the assertions cannot always be defended." It would have been marvellous indeed, if, in a communion swarming with heresies of every name, Clement had seen the simple truth and been able to declare it with power, and yet without over-statement. The errors of the French Quietists must be laid partly at the door of the Church of Rome, for, though they had no thought of abandoning her communion, the recoil from some of her doctrines drove them farther from the truth than they might otherwise have departed. Any one who takes an interest in mysticism will find it interesting to pursue the analogy between the ancient and modern forms of it, and to trace something of its history. The superiority of the Gnostic to the common believer, everywhere assumed in the *Stromata*, this is the very point which Bossuet saw to be the foundation of all Madame Guyon's error, and which he first assailed. "The doctrines which you advance, Madame, involve the fact of an inward experience above the common experience of Christians." That this is attained by contemplation of pure divinity, that this contemplation unites the soul with God in a manner that passes the experience of ordinary faith, and that this is the perfect bliss and final state of the soul, these are the assertions which are as unhesitatingly delivered by Clement as by any professed and full-blown mystic. The ἀπάθεια of Clement's Gnostic, *i.e.* the exemption from, and not the controlling of, natural desires and passions, his superiority to pleasure and pain, his effortless self-command, and his pure love of God, these are the well-known features of the later mystic, who has attained to the state of pure love, who has entered the blessed haven of abandonment and consecration, and has now no will but the will of God; who has ceased to form definite desires and expectations, but passes a life of silent prayer in mute dependence on the purpose of God

If Clement is guilty of all that is laid to the charge of the Pietists, it would be difficult to prove him quite innocent of helping out the philosophical mysticism of Plotinus. That Plotinus listened to as many teachers as were within his reach, until he found in the doctrines of Ammonius Saccas all that his soul sought, we know on the authority of his biographer, Porphyry. That he was very well acquainted with the teaching of Clement, we have therefore every reason to believe. That his system had much in it by which he might be convicted of purloining from Christianity, is recognised on the most superficial examination ; and it is scarcely credible that he should not have been most powerfully influenced by that Christian teacher who most nearly approximates to the tone of Plato, and who anticipates his own doctrine of the absorption in the divine essence of the soul that is exalted and purified by contemplation. Yet he who concluded that because Clement was philosophical and mystical he was therefore the father of Plotinus, and solely accountable for his birth, would show his ignorance of Neoplatonism, as much as he who argued that because Clement was a mystic he was also an ascetic, would show his ignorance of modern pietism. In this very article of asceticism there is a striking difference between the teaching of Clement, who recognised in the body the well-furnished palace of the soul, and that of Plotinus, who " refused to permit his picture to be taken, because it would unduly perpetuate the image of a body he deplored, and avoided all mention of the date and locality of his birth, as too dark and miserable an epoch to be remembered." [1]

We may be induced to be somewhat more lenient to the early philosophical theologians, when we compare their firm grasp of the doctrine of the

---

[1] Archer Butler's *Ancient Philosophy*, ii. 362.

Trinity with the shambling discourse of Tertullian regarding this fundamental of our Creed. And a little attention to the position of the Alexandrians convinces us that their Trinitarian teaching was in some degree dictated by their philosophical leanings. If the Word had been the teacher of philosophers from the first, then the pre-existence and divinity of Jesus are almost of necessity maintained. The necessary foundation of all Clement's apologetic is, "Our teacher is Jesus, the Holy God, the guiding Word of all humanity" (p. 131). Without the divinity of Christ the argument of Clement can make no way whatever; the doctrine of the Trinity is involved in each step of it. No doubt his position led him into error, as well as prompted him with much that was true. His defective view of the wrath of God was due partly to his philosophising tendency, and partly to his commendable but extreme opposition to those who believed in a Demiurge. His whole teaching on the articles of faith and free will bear evidence that it was directed against the false Gnostics. And in the chapters in which he most distinctly delivers himself on these points, he expressly combats the errors of Valentinus and Basilides. Had they not maintained that a man's spiritual destiny had nothing to do with his own will,

Clement might not have been tempted to pronounce that a man's own will had everything to do with his faith. But we cannot enter now upon the wide subject of Clement's dogmatic. Suffice it to say, that all his writings are very worthy of an attentive perusal, that they are not only historically interesting, both as reflecting his own times and as exhibiting the ages that were then past, but are also so fresh and vigorous, so erudite and yet so hearty and devout, as to command, if not our uninterrupted admiration, at least our constant love. And if his style has those faults which were mentioned above, it is also possessed of a characteristic beauty, purity of expression, and force of phrase, and is relieved by an occasional brilliance and rapidity of logical discussion which might vindicate for him, more than for any who has claimed the title, the epithet of the Christian Plato.

M. D.

July 1863.

V

FREDERICK DENISON MAURICE

During the last two or three years the Church of England has sustained losses which are lamented by multitudes beyond her own pale. With startling rapidity Dean Milman, Dean Alford, Dean Mansel, and Professor Maurice have followed one another to the grave. Intellectually the least of the four, Dean Alford, by his English common-sense, sagacity, and indomitable industry, as well as by his business-like concentration on one object, has produced a work, which, whatever may be the opinion as to its permanent value, must be admitted to have materially contributed to the advancement of exegetical study, and to stand as yet unrivalled as a first step in that study. Still greater diversity of opinion exists regarding the *magnum opus* of Dean Mansel, a diversity only equalled by the unanimity with which all who are capable of judging ascribe to him a learning and a mastery of it second only to that of one of his great teachers, Sir William Hamilton, together with a strength and closeness of reasoning and un-flagging vigour in speculation little short of his other great master, Bishop Butler. The writings of Dean Milman have the graceful massiveness of style and artistic completeness which belong to classical works; thoroughly equipped, laborious, and impartial, he is always accurate, and his narrative, never coloured by the prejudice or heat of the writer, presents undimmed the colour of his theme; dealing with the most perplexed and indefinite states of opinion, with Gnosticism, Neoplatonism, Manichaeism, he is always lucid and never shallow; universally informed, and able to condense into one paragraph more material than some historians furnish in a volume, and suggesting by a single word a new direction for thought or a revolution of opinion, he has the consummate historical tact which selects only what is requisite, and so felicitously groups it as to fascinate and substantially inform his reader. But our business now is not with any of these three serviceable and lamented Deans, but with one whose marked individuality caused him to miss preferment, but won for him a quite unusual esteem and affection.

Frederick Denison Maurice was born in the year 1805. He was the son of a Unitarian minister, esteemed for his intelligence and kindliness. At an early age he was sent to Trinity College, Cambridge, where he was fortunate enough to have Julius Charles Hare for his tutor and John Sterling for his friend. More congenial society could nowhere have been found for a disposition like Mr. Maurice's, nor society more likely to develop his undergraduate mind on its richest side and in its most promising direction. Had his lot been cast in Oxford his theological opinions might have been forced into more definite and stable forms; but from his Cambridge contemporaries, and especially from his philosophical, all-accomplished, and vigorous tutor, and from his truth-loving and courageous friend, there passed into his character and intellect, and even into his style, some of the elements most valuable in his subsequent career.

"Their life seems to have been an ardently speculating and talking one; by no means excessively restrained within limits; and, in the more adventurous heads like Sterling's, decidedly tending towards the latitudinarian in most things. They had among them a Debating Society called the Union, where, on stated evenings, was much logic and other spiritual fencing and ingenuous collision,—probably of a really

superior quality in that kind; for not a few of the
then disputants have since proved themselves men of
parts, and attained distinction in the intellectual
walks of life: Frederick Maurice, Richard Trench,
John Kemble, Spedding, Venables, Charles Butler,
Richard Milnes, and others." [1]

But paramount as the influence of such contemporaries must have been, it will not be
doubted by those who understand college life,
that the majesty of its intellectual ancestry had
much to do with loosening the student from the
narrowness of Unitarianism.   It is probable that
he could endorse the words of his distinguished
predecessor at Cambridge :

> "I could not print
> Ground where the grass had yielded to the steps
> Of generations of illustrious men,
> Unmoved.   I could not always lightly pass
> Through the same gateways, sleep where they had
> slept,
> Wake where they waked, range that enclosure old,
> That garden of great intellects, undisturbed."

But at no period of his career, and least of all
in the free and formative intercourse of college
days, could Mr. Maurice be merely acted upon
without powerfully reacting on those around
him.   Before leaving Cambridge, his marked

____
[1] Carlyle's *Life of Sterling*, p. 42.

individuality, strong will, and high character, had won for him a sway which was owned by many of his fellow-students. The peculiarity, too, of his religious position must have both reduced him to the happy necessity of thinking for himself, and been the occasion of some inquiry and revision of opinion among those with whom he familiarly conversed. Indeed, had he graduated and accepted academical position and work, we fancy that the fascination of Pusey's learning and devotedness to doctrine, and of Newman's combination of subtle intellectuality with practical knowledge of men and things, would have been more than rivalled in the sister university by Mr. Maurice's broad humanity and genuine love of truth. But his theological opinions prevented him from subscribing the Articles, and consequently from graduating. Such, however, was his reputation in his college, that on his declining thus to qualify for an academic appointment, it was proposed to keep his name on the College books for a year or two, in order that, if his views should undergo any modification, he might still avail himself of those emoluments and distinctions to which his under-graduate career had confessedly entitled him. Such an offer was highly honourable to him: his

rejection of it was still more so.   And it is interesting to find in the youth of two-and-twenty not
merely the courageous integrity which characterised him throughout life, but, what is rarer in
youth, an insight into the springs of human conduct which at once showed him that to keep open
the possibility of getting a fellowship was to offer
a bribe to himself, and thus to put an undue, however unconscious, pressure on the formation of his
opinions.   The temptations of young men are
commonly appropriate to their character and
future career, and it is not without significance
that Mr. Maurice should at so early an age have
been strongly tempted to sacrifice truth to custom, expediency, friendship, and advantage.

Taking leave of Cambridge, therefore, without
a degree, he went to London, apparently intend-
ing to devote himself to literature, in some
departments of which his singularly pure style
fitted him to excel.   His friendship with Sterling
continued, and Mr. Silk Buckingham having
recently founded the *Athenaeum*, enlisted the two
young friends as contributors.   About this time
also Mr. Maurice published a novel entitled
Eustace Conway.   We have somewhere seen it
mentioned that one of the characters in this
work of fiction being named " Captain Marryat,"

the novelist of that name, dimly conceiving that somehow his honour was involved, sent a challenge to the author. We can fancy the mingled pain and humour with which Mr. Maurice would pen his reply, explaining that his limited reading had left him ignorant of the existence of the celebrated novelist, his correspondent, but apologising, with certainly the faintest flavour of his irrepressible irony, for the indignity he had unwittingly put upon him. That Mr. Maurice might have attained eminence as a novelist will scarcely be denied by those who appreciate his great skill in dealing with character, his fondness for a dramatic vehicle for his thought, and his power of sympathetically understanding positions not comprehended in his own experience. It is possible that some may even believe that his choice of this form of literary effort was a sound and healthy instinct, and that his influence would have been both wider and of a less mingled kind had he not carried into the province of theology qualities which fitted him for the cultivation of a very different field.

At this time, however, the change which had been passing on his opinions culminated in his formal rejection of Unitarianism. How this change was accomplished, the steps in it, and the grounds of it, we expect to learn when his biography and correspondence shall have been published; although the public has more than once had occasion to learn that a man's *apologia* is not so satisfactory to other minds as to his own. Meanwhile the extent to which his views were modified may be gathered from his published writings, and also from the fact that he now saw his way to subscribe the Articles and take orders in the Church of England.[1] It has been more than once insinuated or roundly stated that he retained many of the opinions which characterise the Unitarian Creed; but this he himself indignantly and even fiercely denied. Such an accusation he declares is "an immeasurably more horrible libel—more destructive of my moral

---

[1] His idea of subscription may be gathered from the following: "1. When accepted in matriculating, the Articles are guides in the academical course, pointing out a method of thought on theological subjects, and warning of certain confusions into which I may fall in the study of these questions. 2. When I accept them as M.A., I say that I look on them as maxims of thought which I have found profitable, and mean to retain. 3. When I accept them at ordination, I signify that my teaching will not consciously contravene these maxims, but be in conformity with them."—Slightly abridged from his Letter on Subscription to a Resident Member of Convocation. Elsewhere (in one of his Letters to a Resident Member of Convocation) we find him declaring it "better to be brought up in a dame's school and become a dustman than subscribe the Articles dishonestly."

character—than if it had been said that on a certain day, I committed a forgery on the Bank of England, or that I had, in some court of justice, been guilty of a wilful and corrupt per-jury."[1]   It will afterwards appear that, notwithstanding this strong language, he did continue in substantial agreement with the Unitarians regarding some of the points on which the Church of England is supposed to differ from that sect; but the language he uses in speaking of the Trinity is certainly more Athanasian than that of the eminent, though scarcely Nicene, divine who believes in God in Nature, God in History, God in us.   Mr. Maurice laboured under the misfortune of a style so ambiguous that a habit of suspicion is bred in his reader, and his Neo-platonic proclivities were so notorious as to provoke unusual watchfulness when he speaks of the Trinity; but even such suspicion will find it difficult to fix upon any taint in passages such as the following:

"The names [Word and Son] are used interchangeably; but we should, I believe, lose more than we know, if either had been used exclusively. Experience has shown that those who determinately prefer the

---

[1] Dedicatory Letter prefixed to *The Doctrine of Sacrifice*, p. xxvii.

first soon fall into that notion of a mere emanation from some mysterious abyss of Divinity which haunted the Oriental mystics and early heretics, or else into the notion of a mere principle indwelling in man. The Word becomes impersonal; the Will becomes impersonal; very soon the man forgets that he is a person himself, and becomes a mere dreamer or speculator. The blessed name of Son, which connects itself with all human sympathies and relationships, is the deliverance from this phantom region. While we cleave to it, we can never forget that only a Person can express the will of the Absolute Being; that only in a Person He can see His own image." [1]

The manner in which he arrived at this faith he indicates in the interesting Letter to a Friend, published in his correspondence with Dr. Jelf, in which he says:

"The certainty of One absolute in goodness whom I could call Father, has more and more obliged me to believe in a Son, to believe Him, as the Church believes Him, to be consubstantial with the Father; the more have I recognised the impossibility of a perfect all-comprehending unity, or of any living fellowship between me and my fellowmen, or of any practical faith in myself, unless I confessed a Spirit proceeding from the Father and the Son, distinct from them, perfectly one with them."

Among the posts to which this adhesion to the

_____

[1] *Theological Essays,* p. 422.

Church of England gave him access and which he successively filled were the following: In 1834 he commenced his clerical duties in the curacy of a small parish in Warwickshire, from which he was removed in 1836 to the chaplaincy of Guy's Hospital, where he zealously ministered to its afflicted inmates for ten years. In 1840 he was appointed to the professorship of Modern History and English Literature in King's College, London, and subsequently held in the same institution the Chairs of Ecclesiastical History and Divinity, until in 1853 the Council decided that "his continuance as Professor would be seriously detrimental to the interests of the college." In 1845 he was chosen to deliver the Boyle Lectures, and in 1846 he was appointed Warburtonian Lecturer and Chaplain to Lincoln's Inn. In 1860 he became incumbent of St. Peter's, Vere Street, and in 1866 the University of Cambridge elected him Professor of Moral Philosophy.

It was shortly after his appointment to Guy's Hospital that he published *The Kingdom of Christ ; or, Hints on the Principles, Ordinances, and Constitution of the Catholic Church, in Letters to a Member of the Society of Friends.* It was scarcely to be expected that so comprehensive and intricate a subject could be satisfactorily handled by a man of three-and-thirty; and, as might have been anticipated, the author himself saw reason, a few years afterwards, in 1842, to issue a second edition, which was to a large extent a new work. Like too many of Mr. Maurice's writings, this bears evidence of undue rapidity of composition. There are many eloquent passages, many striking reflections, many thoughts so suggestive as to have deserved more patient and thorough examination and development, many remarks which evince extensive and intelligent reading; but through all there are manifest a determined refusal to run his thinking into the same moulds as other men had used and an evasion of the precise points at issue. These are blemishes which have already caused students to turn from this work, original as it is, to others which, though written by inferior men, yet more effectually solve their difficulties, and convey more available information. During this period Mr. Maurice had already earned distinction by his contribution on moral and metaphysical philosophy to the *Enyclopaedia Metropolitana*. This, as our readers are aware, has gradually grown under his hand, and now forms his largest, and possibly his most enduring work. He again and again disclaims the idea of producing a complete history of philosophy, or of furnishing the student with an adequate system ; but no work is more likely to quicken in the reader a love of truth, or to fill his mind with vivid, if not wholly adequate, representations of the profoundest thinkers of all time. In this book, as elsewhere, Mr. Maurice declines to deal with the mere external utterance and results of a man's opinions, but endeavours to get at the root of his thoughts by taking into consideration his personal character and circumstances. He has thus succeeded in producing what is certainly the most lifelike and readable *History of Philosophy*—a history which may be recommended, which will commend itself, to that large and increasing class of persons who are despairing of philosophy, and who are turning to physical science, politics, or history, in the hope of finding there something on which they can begin to build.

We have mentioned these two books together, not only because they began to occupy their author's mind about the same time ; but because, though the one is much, and the other little, read, —the one likely to live, the other likely to die,— they are yet generally spoken of as being of a les- "occasional" character than the remainder of his writings. These writings, for the most part, consist of lectures, sermons, addresses, which were called for by the passing events of the day, or by his position for the time being. We are told that five-and-thirty years ago Mr. Maurice expressed to a friend his opinion, "that a man who in that day was more desirous to serve God and his fellow-men than to win a name for himself, would give up the thought of producing any complete literary work, and employ himself in writing and teaching on the successive subjects on which the men of the day were thinking, and endeavouring to reduce thought to action; and his words implied that he had felt, but had rejected, the allurements of that last infirmity of noble minds, —the desire to win and leave a name for himself." The work, however, which, perhaps, may most justly be considered a manifesto of his opinions, is the *Theological Essays*, in regard to which he himself says: "The book expresses thoughts which have been working in my mind for years; the method of it has not been adopted carelessly; even the composition has undergone frequent revision. No labour I have been engaged in has occupied me so much, or interested me more deeply."

In the change of opinion to which we have referred, there are several points of much significance. First of all, it is obvious from his own statement that he was led to believe in the Son of

God, not by coming to a clearer understanding of Scripture, but by the necessities of his own nature or reason. We call attention to this, because it was not accidental nor exceptional, but was an instance of his ordinary theological method. In the *Theological Essays* (p. 416), there occurs a passage which every one who thinks it worth while to ascertain what Mr. Maurice's method was, will carefully read :

" I should," he says, " be abandoning the method to which I have endeavoured strictly to adhere, if I admitted that now at last I have come upon a mere dogma, which had no support but tradition or inferences from texts of Scripture ; or, on the other hand, upon a great philosophical tenet, which wise men may deduce from reason or find latent in nature, but with which the poor wayfarer has nothing to do. We may owe much to tradition for giving expression to the faith in a Trinity ; texts of Scripture may confirm it ; the context of Scripture may bring it out in beautiful harmony with all the divine discoveries to man. Philosophy may have seen indications of a Trinity in the forms and principles of the universe, in the constitution of man himself. But unless we are utterly inconsistent with all that has been said hitherto, these can be but indexes and guides to a Name which is implied in our thoughts, acts, words, in our fellowship with each other ; without which we cannot explain the utterances of the poorest peasant, or of the greatest sage ; which makes thoughts real, prayers possible ;

which brings distinctness out of vagueness, unity out of division ; which shows us how in fact, and not merely in imagination, the charity of God may find its reflex and expression in the charity of man, and the charity of man its substance as well as its fruition in the charity of God. What I have to do in this essay, then, is certainly not to bring forward arguments against those who impugn this doctrine, but only to show how each portion of that Name into which we are baptized answers to some apprehension and anticipation of human beings."

This passage enounces, as distinctly as Mr. Maurice ever enounces anything, that he had adopted as his theological *rôle* the task of exhibiting the harmony between human nature and truth, or between the unuttered longings and unformed thoughts of men and the Catholic creed. As a controversialist, he was weak ;[1] his mind was not objective and scientific, but reflective ; he shrank from systematic theology instinctively and in obedience to the same law of his nature which forbade that he should ever become an accomplished mathematician or physicist. He had found his own way into truth not by argument, but by feeling and conscience, and he wrote and taught on the understanding that men would

[1] Whatever view is taken of his controversy with Mansel, every one must regret the tone, form, and substance of the prolix *Letters to a Student of Theology.*

believe and accept what they found to strengthen their moral convictions, and satisfy their instinctive desires. He is always careful to guard his disciples against adopting what is merely supported by external authority. For example, in the *Essay on the Incarnation* (p. 104), he says :

"You are not to believe—you cannot believe—either fisherman or doctor, if the assertion itself is contrary to truth, to the laws of your being, to the order and constitution of the universe in which you are living. They may repeat it till doomsday. It may come, as it did, with no authority, against the weight of all opinion, breaking through the customs and prescriptions of centuries, defying the rulers of the world ; or it may come clad with authority, with the prescriptions of centuries, with the help of rulers and public opinion ; it is all the same ; you cannot believe the words, however habitual and familiar they may be to you, if there is that in them which contradicts the spirit of a man that is in you, which does not address that with demonstration and power. What we say is, that these words (John i. 14) have not contradicted that spirit, but have entered it with the demonstration of the Spirit and of power."

This is undoubtedly both true and important ; many who profess to accept the Bible as an infallible authority and rule of faith, do receive only what they find convenient, and no one can receive into, and hold in his mind what is contradicted and rejected by something which already has possession. It is admitted that we cannot believe a thing solely because we are told to do so, or accept as true what our own experience denies or our conscience condemns. An authoritative promulgation of truth cannot compel our assent, nor beget immediate faith in us; but it has nevertheless its proper function, and this function is discharged by its disclosing to us the truth, and turning our attention to it, and by constraining us to be dissatisfied with our belief until we are able to accept what the authoritative revelation enounces. When we speak of an authority in matters of belief, we mean a higher wisdom; and though we may not always be able at once to accept what this higher wisdom utters, we are able to put away from our minds whatever is clogging their action or dulling their perception, and so fit ourselves for apprehending what we indirectly know to be true. Such authority Mr. Maurice certainly ascribed in theory to the Bible. In his careful sermon on Balaam,[1] he says:

"We who acknowledge the Bible as the high and ultimate authority, must desire that our decisions should be revised, corrected, even reversed, by it, if we have adopted them from tradition, or fashioned

---

[1] *Patriarchs and Lawgivers,* p. 222.

them by our own weak, hasty inductions without con-
sulting it."

In his *Essay on the Atonement*, he rejects certain
notions on the ground that they "are not parts
of God's revelation or of the old creeds, but
belong to that Theology of Consciousness which
modern enlightenment would substitute for the
Theology of the Bible and of the Church."[1]   In
the face of these passages, we cannot identify Mr.
Maurice's views with "that system whose final
test of truth is placed in the direct assent of the
human consciousness, whether in the form of
logical deduction, or moral judgment, or religious
intuition."[2]   He did not consciously and theoretically assign a higher place to his own reason
than to the written Word of God; he believed
that the notions and feelings of each particular
mind must be brought into harmony with the
utterances and decisions of that Book which God
has provided for the enlightenment of mankind.
In arguing against the Friends, while he admits
the truth of what they have to say positively
regarding the indwelling Word and the Light
which enlightens every man, he shows the un-
reasonableness of their disparagement of the

---

[1] *Patriarchs and Lawgivers*, p. 132.
[2] Mansel's *Bampton Lectures*, p. 3.

written Word, and maintains that it alone can impart purity, clearness, and strength to the inward convictions and decisions of the individual mind.

But while Mr. Maurice would seem at times to set Scripture in its right position, and does always show the utmost reverence for it, every one who reads his writings must be struck by the extreme rarity of his appeal to Scripture. From the conclusions at which he arrived, one might suppose he was not scrupulous in submitting his own ideas to the modifying, not to say formative, influence of its statements ; and his writings abound almost equally in denunciations of those who put their own meanings into the language of the Bible, and in instances of interpretation which, we make bold to say, would receive the sanction of no other student of the sacred writings. No doubt, some of those doctrines which to us seem wild perversions of Scripture were arrived at through Mr. Maurice's strong tendency to measure truth by its practical results. So strongly biassed was he in favour of what immediately told on men's lives, so resolute was he in rejecting whatever did not find real application to his own inward experience, so careful to receive nothing which was responded to only by the intellect, that he was continually tempted to neglect certain aspects of truth, and to read the Bible in a narrow though truth-loving spirit.   But even this does not explain his neglect of difficult doctrinal passages of Scripture.   We have been at some pains to discover the precise attitude of his mind towards Scripture, and have been unable to escape the conclusion that he did not look to it as an infallible authority.   That he considered it the highest authority we have, that he placed it above the individual reason, we have shown; but though he had frequent opportunity for ascribing infallibility to it, he nowhere does so. The passage in which he most nearly approaches to a definite declaration of the amount of confidence he placed in Scripture occurs in a note to his *Essay on Inspiration.*[1]   Its importance justifies us in quoting it in full :

" A distinction is often hinted at, sometimes formally taken, between facts and doctrines. 'You may,' it is said, 'believe that the Spirit guides a man into a knowledge of principles.   But do you accept the facts of the Bible ?   Do you look upon them as divinely communicated to the seer ?'   Any one who considers doctrines as I have considered them in these Essays, finds it exceedingly hard to separate them from facts ; doctrines and principles he supposes to

---

[1] *Theological Essays,* p. 344.

be the meaning of facts. If, then, I am asked whether I receive the *transcendent* facts of Scripture, those which offer most occasion to disbelief, I appeal to what I have written here. If I am asked whether I believe the ordinary facts of Scripture, *e.g.* that such a city was taken at such a time? I answer, that when I find a man so free from biblical prepossessions as Niebuhr assuming Isaiah and Jeremiah to be better authorities about such facts than any he knew of, I am surprised that *our* divines and religious people should be so very eager to get confirmation of the testimonies in sacred books from profane authorities, as if they felt insecure of them till then,—a sentiment I cannot the least understand or share in ; that, believing the writers of the Bible to have been possessed by the Spirit of Truth, I am sure they will have more shrunk from fictions, and have been more careful to avoid mixing them with facts, than other men ; that it seems to me far safer, more Scriptural, more godly, to suppose they did *take pains*, and that the Spirit taught them to take pains, in sifting facts, than to suppose that they were merely told the facts ; that I most assuredly should *not* give up the faith in God which they have cherished in me, if I found they had made mistakes ; and that I have too much respect and honour for those who use the strongest expressions about the certainty of every word in the Scriptures, to suppose that *they* would. I will not believe any Christian man, even upon his own testimony, who tells me that he should cease to trust in the Son of God, because he found chronological or historical misstatements in the Scriptures as great as ever have been charged against them by their bitterest opponents. If I did suspect him of such hollowness, I should pray for him that he might never meet with any travellers or philologers who confirmed the statements of Scripture ; none but such as denied them or mocked at them ; because the sooner such a foundation as this is shaken the better it will be for him."

We cordially agree with Mr. Maurice in affirming that our faith does not depend on the accuracy of Scripture regarding "ordinary facts." Our faith remains intact though the histories of the Old Testament and the Gospel narratives be reduced to the level of the classical historians. We believe in the incarnation and death and resurrection of the Son of God on grounds which are not affected by such charges as are commonly brought against the strict accuracy of the evangelists. What Mr. Maurice calls the *transcendent facts* come down to us through a complex tradition of testimony which nothing now can destroy. The severest historical criticism has only exhibited that they are facts permanently unassailable. We go further, and maintain that though the doctrinal writings of the apostles were devoid of any authority beyond that which is implied in their truth, our faith, while it might be less full-bodied and complete, would, for all purposes of spiritual

life, remain very much as it was. Controversy
would be more difficult, but the formation of individual opinion would still necessarily proceed.
We find no fault whatever with Mr. Maurice for
declining to identify his faith with a faith in the
infallibility of Scripture; we think he was wise,
or, at least, ordinarily intelligent, in doing so.
We find no fault with him for supposing it possible that Scripture might misstate some things
but be most trustworthy in others; for this,
though not an easily defensible, is certainly an
intelligible position. But we are decidedly of
opinion that a writer who so freely criticises the
theories of others regarding Scripture should not
have left his readers in doubt regarding his own.
It is not to be denied that the current views of the
origin, formation, and authority of Scripture are
not perfectly satisfactory. We cannot shut our
eyes to the fact that some of the men who
are most strenuously and effectively defending
Christianity against Positivism or the false inferences of science, or other forms of error, do not
consider the Scriptures infallible even in points of
doctrine. It is wrong to neglect the difficulties of
such men; it is useless to fall back on arguments
which they know and have found unconvincing.
We had hoped that Mr. Maurice would mature his

views on this important subject, and would at least prepare the way for a fair, full, and friendly revisal of the whole subject. But we have found the *Essay on Inspiration* thoroughly unsatisfactory. It is directed against "those who, taking the Bible as their only religion and only rule of life, prevent it from being either, by saying that its inspiration has no relation to that of the writers whose dark sayings it illuminates, or that of the human beings it is intended to educate and console."[1] The only persons whom he sees it worth his while to contend with are those (whoever they may be) who hold that the inspiration of the Bible is "generically unlike that which God bestows on His children at this day." If by "generically unlike" he means proceeding from a different source, we think his time might have been better employed than in exploding such an opinion. If he means that the one was an inspiration effecting different results from the other, he himself believes it to have been generically unlike. If he means that the operation of the Spirit on the mind of the heathen poet is wrongly considered to be widely different from that whereby the apostles were fitted for their work, we imagine that this difference is asserted in

____

[1] *Theological Essays*, p. 337.

many passages of his own writings. From the
general scope of the *Essay* it would seem that he
considered that the chief point to be made out
was that it is the same Spirit who works all good
in the souls of all men, that inspired the apostles.[1]
This is not a very instructive discovery, neither
can one who has read the First Epistle to the
Corinthians be surprised to learn that the extraordinary influence of the Spirit is less precious to
the individual than the ordinary. We should
greatly have preferred that Mr. Maurice had let us
know by simple statement how much authority he
ascribed to Scripture, and on what grounds this
authority rests. As it is, we are left to gather
from his general treatment of Scripture the kind
of authority he attributed to it; and what we
gather is, that though he never explicitly dissents
from Apostolic teaching, as some of his most docile
followers are bold enough to do, he does leave
in the background such Scriptural statements as
directly contradict his teaching. Those who do
not acknowledge Scripture as the infallible rule

---

[1] We presume Mr. Maurice is alone in attributing to God
the manifestations of supernatural power among the heathen—
Dionysiac ecstasies, oracular rhapsodies, and so forth. In the
Essay on Inspiration he does not scruple to represent Paul as
"vindicating for the Father of Spirits," the "hideous hum"
and "words deceiving" of the oracles.

of faith, do yet appeal to it for sanction of such of their views as find confirmation in it. This Mr. Maurice does, but so frequently does he refuse to take any notice of passages which he must have known did contradict, or would by many be supposed to contradict, his statements, that it seems to us sufficiently plain that for him Scripture was not an infallible authority. In reading him, we are always reminded of that old heretic Faustus, who boasted that he could use the wholesome fish without being compelled to drink the brine he found it in.

Before passing from this subject we may endeavour to lay before our readers Mr. Maurice's theory of Scripture. The broad distinction between Scripture and all other books is that it reveals God. All questions of infallibility, inspiration, and so forth are subordinate and secondary; the one grand truth about Scripture is that, be its origin what it may, it does actually make God known to men. To a man who desired proof of this, Mr. Maurice would probably have replied, "Read the book; if a man who stands in the sunlight does not see that the sun is shining, you do not endeavour to convince him by astronomical diagrams and problems. This divine revelation also is self-evidencing; study it

and you will know God, and be convinced that
the light is shed from Himself." Mr. Maurice is
always explicit and instructive in maintaining the
possibility of such a revelation, and that it has
actually been made. He constantly affirms that
it is *à priori* a probable and likely thing that
God should make Himself known and declare His
mind to His intelligent creatures. Such a revelation being possible and likely, there is certainly
nothing impossible or unlikely in its being effected
by means similar to the ordinary means of communication between man and man, by the ordinary
forms of human discourse. In order to accomplish this communication, we should feel that
some selection of instruments was necessary, and
though we might not be able to conceive before-
hand how a number of men could be brought into
circumstances which should fit them to be more
efficient instruments than any others, yet if we
heard of a certain people being selected and sub-
mitted to a peculiar discipline that they might
be the universal teachers, we should admire and
acquiesce in the arrangement. We may not be
able to say what degree of inspiration may be
needful to effect this purpose, but we can have
no manner of doubt that if it is God's purpose to
reveal Himself, He will effectually do so. And

when this revelation, which is of necessity gradual and in accordance with the consequent progress of men in the knowledge of God, has been accomplished, when an adequate, though not a perfect revelation has been made, when there has been communicated all that men can in this life receive, the canon closes, and the book remains complete and separate from all others.[1] There must come such a time, a time when to add would be to dilute or to repeat, a time when it is fit that there should be henceforth silence. Obviously such a theory of the formation of Scripture may be held either with or without the idea of its infallibility. It might be argued, on the one hand, that if God meant to reveal Himself, He might be expected to secure that the revelation should be so made as to be an infallible guide. There are few stronger cravings in human nature than the desire for an infallible guide who shall save us from the responsibility, perplexity, and constant unrest which accompany the individual search after truth. Proselytising Romanists have no stronger argument by which to appeal to men than that which they found upon the likelihood that God would relieve men of this

---

[1] The above is chiefly derived from Letter V. of the *Kingdom of Christ*.

responsibility and provide for them an access to truth which should be free from toil and secure against the invasion of doubt. Men have persuaded themselves that it is useless to provide an infallible statute-book unless there be also provided an infallible interpreter and judge. And in the same plausible and persuasive manner it might be argued that it were useless to provide for men a declaration of God's nature and mind unless this were free from all mixture of error, and were in such a form that no man could be at a loss to discover the very truth. On the other hand, and more in accordance with Mr. Maurice's system of thought, it might be argued, that though this revelation is confessedly an exceptional thing, and therefore not to be judged by ordinary rules, yet, if one is to consider what is likely, the likelihood seems much rather to be that God will present this revelation in a form which shall disclose its treasures only to the man who is at personal pains to discover them. In everything else men are left to judge for themselves, to sift truth from error, to find what they bring the means of finding. In everything there are left stones of stumbling on which the dishonest and cavilling may break themselves, and there is no antecedent probability that this most important knowledge should be so given as to be equally available to the double-minded and to the pure in heart. Or Mr. Maurice might argue that this book is not given that we may frame a set of opinions, but that we may learn to live. This book is given us to enable us to fulfil the end of our being alive, and that is not to furnish out a complete system of doctrine, but to be righteous and loving. This position, which is certainly involved in every part of Mr. Maurice's teaching, has not been sufficiently weighed by his disciples. We are as cordial admirers of his character as they; we are very far indeed from grudging him the influence which could not but be exerted by one who so attractively embodied in his own person and life the principles of Christianity. There have been many better theologians, but few who have surpassed him in understanding human duty, few who have more courageously and consistently obeyed a highly sensitive and thoroughly enlightened conscience, few who have by purity, by strength of character, by patient labour, by self-abnegation, by belief in goodness and truth, caused men to acknowledge a Divine presence in their midst, and the substantial communication of grace from God to man. But our complaint is that Mr. Maurice at once professed to despise doctrine and meddled with it, denied the validity of system in theology and himself attempted to construct a system. His followers tell us that so genuine and truth-loving a man could not be deceived, could not be permitted to hold that as truth which is really error. This is a very convenient and summary mode of disposing of all objections to Mr. Maurice's teaching. We should have counted it unworthy of attention were we not convinced that the impressiveness of his character has done much more for the circulation of his opinions than their intrinsic value. His purity of character and openness to what is good made it likely—made it, we may say, certain—that he would be led to such knowledge as should suffice for the regulation of his own life and for his own salvation; and this was all that he encouraged men to expect from the Bible. But in the ascertainment of theological truth, no purity of intention or soundness of character can compensate for the lack of a sufficient theological education and of an exact study of Scripture.

Though Mr. Maurice was dangerous as a leader of thought, not so much from any results he arrived at as from the general principles and style of his theological procedure, his name has become associated with the special heresy on account of which he was expelled from King's College. At an early period he rebelled against the orthodox doctrine of eternal punishment, because it seemed to him a doctrine "full of the strangest complexities and incoherences; one which cannot be set before simple people without the most extraordinary devices to make it intelligible —devices which utterly fail, by the admission of those who resort to them."[1] The devices and their failure to which he refers are described in a previous letter to Dr. Jelf as "the continual experiments to heap hundreds of thousands of years upon hundreds of thousands of years, and then the confession, 'after all we are no nearer to eternity.'" Yet he admits that his own notion of eternity is incomprehensible. "I agree with you," he says in writing to Mr. Williams of Lincoln's Inn, "that it is impossible for any man whatsoever to have a conception of eternity." At the same time he maintains that simple people arrive, through the use of the Prayers of the Church of England, at a practical apprehension of that meaning of eternity which he deduced from the New Testament. If this be so, it is

[1] *Correspondence with Jelf*, p. 14.

somewhat strange that his most ardent admirers and pupils are at present differing among themselves as to what he really did teach on this point; and that they have so effectually imbibed the hazy unintelligible manner of their master, that their explanations have been declared to be more difficult than the teaching they endeavour to explain. It is pathetic to see men assuring themselves that certainly the enlightened world shall never again be terrified by the bugbear of eternal punishment, while yet they cannot quite understand how they have exploded the doctrine, and are perhaps even visited occasionally with the suspicion that after all their great doctor may have misled them by a metaphysical quibble. It will, in these circumstances, be safe to adhere pretty closely to Mr. Maurice's own statements.

The whole structure of his thought on this subject is professedly based on the meaning of the word *eternal* as determined by its use in the New Testament, and specially by its use as applied to God. It is this application of it which, he says, must determine every other. We must first ascertain what *eternal* means when it is used with reference to God, and then apply the meaning thus ascertained to every connection in which the word occurs.[1] With a loud and somewhat bombastic inculcation of exegetical integrity, he insists upon the extraordinary canon that the meaning of an adjective is not modified by the substantive with which it is connected. *Eternal*, when applied to God, does not mean "without beginning or end," and therefore when applied to punishment it does not mean "without beginning or end." Eternity, in relation to God, has nothing to do with time or duration; therefore, in reference to punishment or life, it has nothing to do with time or duration. Eternal life means life in Him who is eternal; eternal death means the loss of that life. "I am bound to believe that the eternal life into which the righteous go is that knowledge of God which *is* eternal life; I am bound to suppose that the eternal punishment into which those on the left hand go is the loss of that eternal life—what is elsewhere called 'eternal death.'"[2]

Now, no one will dispute that there is here much that is true. We may even say that Mr.

---

[1] We should have formed a higher opinion both of Mr. Maurice's candour and of his competence as an interpreter of Scripture, had he thought it worth his while to institute an inquiry into the use of the word among the Jews. Any one who takes the trouble to consult his memory or his Greek Concordance, will see passages which he cannot by any ingenuity interpret on this principle.

[2] *Correspondence with Jelf*, p. 6.

Maurice has done good service in showing what is the essence of eternal life and eternal death. The familiar idea that the possession of God is heaven, and the loss of Him hell, has been strikingly put again and again in his writings. We find no fault with his interpretation of his *locus classicus* on this subject: "This is eternal life, that they may know Thee, the only true God." These words may mean that, during this present life, men may enjoy a life which is above the conditions of time, life in God. But we are decidedly of opinion that this idea of eternity was quite unfamiliar to the persons with whom our Lord associated, however familiar it became to the Alexandrian school and to Augustine. Nay, we think it can be shown that as the ordinary conception men have of eternity is time indefinitely prolonged, so the words expressive of eternity and of indefinitely prolonged time were one and the same. Certainly the idea of an indefinitely long future was and is a common one; but if, as Mr. Maurice insists, αἰώνιος is to mean eternal in his sense, and nothing but that, what word have we left for the idea of everlastingness or endlessness? Mere assertion will not suffice in a case of this kind; and it became Mr. Maurice, as it would become any man of candour, to examine a little more carefully the meaning of common words before he ventured to alter our interpretation of some sixty passages of the New Testament.

But supposing that the meaning he seeks to attach to the word *eternal* be correct, it is to be observed that this alteration of meaning throws no new light on the duration of the punishment threatened or of the life promised. Eternity is not prolonged time, is not time at all; but is that state in which time is not. Eternity is not made by adding age to age, or century to century. If you take a bucket of water out of the sea, you diminish it by so much, and by so much approach to exhausting it. But no amount of time diminishes eternity, because the two conditions belong to different categories. Eternity is not made by time, however extended, but by its absence. Whatever is eternal is removed out of the conditions of time, and is no more subject to these conditions. It ceases to be affected by succession, by change, and becomes immutable and fixed. If therefore punishment be eternal, as Mr. Maurice of course concedes and maintains, punishment must be immutable and permanent. If any were to be delivered from what he will not call endless, but insists on calling eternal death, it is obvious that this deliverance from one state and entrance on another condition implies change and succession, that is to say, implies time. By Mr. Maurice's definition of eternal, he certainly precludes us from attaching the idea of duration to the phrase " eternal punishment," but he seems unaccountably to have overlooked the fact that, by that definition, he compels us to attach to it the idea of unchangeableness. Some of Mr. Maurice's disciples argue as if by showing that *eternal* does not mean " without beginning or end," he thereby showed that it meant " with beginning or end." But his definition of the word, when applied to the passages which speak of punishment, certainly consigns the lost to as irrevocable a perdition as is implied in the ordinary interpretations of these passages.

Dr. Candlish's criticism of the *Theological Essays* is in general too fragmentary and rapid to be very effective ; but in reference to Mr. Maurice's use of the word " eternal," his remarks are not merely ingenious, but true and unanswerable. To enforce his view of the meaning of the word, Mr. Maurice had referred to the use which had been made of it in the Arian controversy, maintaining that the error of Arius arose from his mixing time with relations which had nothing to do with time ; and that Athanasius, by asserting the *eternal* generation of the Son, declared that the relation implied in it was lifted above all notions derived from time. The heresy was that the Son had a beginning, and it was met by the assertion that He was eternal, and therefore by implication without beginning. Dr. Candlish challenges the same principle of interpretation for the expressions in question. When eternal punishment is spoken of, it is punishment to which the limits and laws of time do not apply; but on this very account the idea of change or end is excluded. The phrase to which Mr. Maurice appeals—the eternal generation of the Son—implies that this act had no beginning; the phrase eternal punishment implies that this state has no end.

This criticism, however, though it may be very serviceable in showing the fallacy of some of Mr. Maurice's arguments, does not shed much light upon the subject under discussion. The critique of Mr. Mansel,[1] besides being interesting as the germ of the Bampton Lectures, delivered four years afterwards, is a thorough exposure of the fallacy on which Mr. Maurice's views were founded. Mr. Mansel briefly, but conclusively, establishes

[1] This was published under the title, *Man's Conception of Eternity. An examination of Mr. Maurice's theory of a fixed state out of time, in a Letter to the Rev. J. L. Bernays, M.A.,* Oxford, 1854.

the distinction between regulative and speculative truths, and explicitly recognises the need of "a preliminary criticism of the laws and limits of religious thought, a work which, even had I the abilities or the leisure to attempt it, would be out of place here." He justly conceives that the whole controversy raised by Mr. Maurice's use of the word "eternal," depends on the distinction between positive and negative ideas, and the legitimate use of each in theology. Of absolute truth our conception is negative only ; we know it only as the condition of an intelligence which is not ours. Thus the idea of eternity as of a consciousness out of duration is negative, absolutely and totally inconceivable by us. Such a truth furnishes no basis for dogmatic teaching, but is yet necessarily included or implied in a revelation which comes from the infinite God. But in order to become practical, this and all other revealed truths must take a form adapted to the understanding of the recipient, and the form under which eternity is presented to the human mind is that of everlastingness. Mr. Maurice's mistake, therefore, however disastrous in its results, and however dangerous in the hands of less intelligent men, was in itself not of a very grave character. It was an attempt

to introduce into theology a metaphysical idea.
It was an attempt to supplant the familiar idea
of endless time which, if not absolutely true, is
yet conceivable and practical, and to put in its
place an idea which it is impossible to comprehend, and which would therefore become unin-
fluential in men's minds.   There are few readers
of theology who did not feel the thrill of important discovery when first they perceived that
eternity was something different from extended
time.   There are few who do not sympathise
with the late Dr. Duncan in his "hatred" of Dr.
Campbell for scoffing at the idea of eternity as a
nunc stans.   We see that probably truth lies that
way; but we also see that it is such truth as the
human mind can never comprehend, and that we
must be content to accept as our practical guide
the regulative truth which has been revealed as
a substitute for this possible speculative truth.
The conception of endless time is the nearest
approach our minds can make to the idea of
eternity: this is the fairest and most serviceable
working equivalent for an idea which only some
minds have any glimmering of, and which even
they can neither prove to be true, nor turn to
any better or different account than the familiar
and popular notion.

Other objections may be brought against Mr. Maurice's teaching. Especially it is reprehensible as having so slender an exegetical basis. Dr. Jelf's careful and scholarly inquiry into the meaning of the word *eternal* in the New Testament is treated as so much waste paper. The impartial inquirer is also disappointed at the easy mode in which Mr. Maurice sails along, considering an assertion or insinuation sufficient to overthrow proved positions, and leaving unsolved difficulties which must inevitably occur to every one who is thinking through the subject for himself. It is, *e.g.*, essential to his argument, if such it can be called, that we should understand in what sense or in what way a creature can be connected with the eternity he speaks of, but no effort is made to explain this.[1] It required proof

---

[1] We should have welcomed some such acknowledgment at least of difficulty and attempt at solution as we find in Augustine's *De Natura Boni*, c. xxxix.: "Aeternus autem ignis, non sicut Deus aeternus quod etsi sine fine sit, non est tamen sine initio; Deus autem etiam sine initio est. Deinde quia licet perpetuus peccatorum suppliciis adhibeatur, mutabilis tamen natura est. Illa est autem vera aeternitas, quae vera immortalitas, hoc est, illa summa incommutabilitas, quam solus Deus habet, qui mutari omnino non potest. Aliud est enim non mutari, cum possit mutari; aliud autem prorsus non posse mutari. Sicut ergo dicitur homo bonus, non tamen sicut Deus, de quo dictum est, Nemo bonus nisi unus Deus; et sicut dicitur anima immortalis, non tamen sicut Deus, de quo dictum est, Qui solus habet immortalitatem . . . sic dicitur ignis

that the Divine consciousness has no relation to time, still further proof that this idea of eternity being applicable to God, is also applicable when the future eternity of man is spoken of; but we look in vain for anything more than Mr. Maurice's assertion. Mr. Mansel's objections are, so far as we can judge, conclusive :

"It seems to be inconsistent with the whole design of Revelation, viewed on its human side—at variance with the whole object of regulative truths; it seems to be incompatible with the conception of the next life as a continuation and development of the present, or of the present life as a discipline and preparation for the next, to believe that our future consciousness will be exempt from the law of succession. It seems, moreover, though of this we cannot adequately judge, to be incompatible with the conception of a finite intellect at all, even of one perfect after its kind, or of a state of progress and increasing knowledge. It seems to substitute a negative notion for a positive one ; to exchange the vivid anticipation and foretaste of a real living futurity for the vague and meaningless intimation of some possible state of existence under no conditions which we can figure to ourselves of human consciousness or human personality."

It will be observed, then, that the proper difference between the teaching of Mr. Maurice

aeternus, non tamen sicut Deus, cujus solius immortalitas ipsa vera aeternitas."

and the current orthodoxy on the subject of eternal punishment consists in his introduction of this metaphysical meaning of the word eternal. This is the head and front of his offending. Had he only been consistent with himself, and represented the eternal state as a fixed and permanent state, no practical difference would have been introduced by this speculative distinction. Termination is quite as incompatible with the one idea of eternity as with the other. But this Mr. Maurice declined to insist upon or even to admit. He refuses to speak definitely of the duration of punishment, and labours only to show its nature. The word eternal teaches him much as to the nature of life and death, punishment and reward, but nothing as to their duration. But from other parts of his teaching we gather that he did not consider this life a final test of character, did not, in the straightforward sense, believe that "it is appointed unto men *once* to die, and *after this* the judgment." It is difficult to discover what views he entertained of the growth and fixity of human character, but it is certain that he believed that character might undergo a total change after death, and that men might pass from eternal punishment to eternal reward, and presumably from eternal reward to eternal punishment. We

are taught in Scripture that there are those whom
it is impossible to renew again to repentance; we
are taught that there are those for whom, even in
this life, nothing can be done which has not
already been done; but of such difficulties, verified
though they are by common experience and
observation, Mr. Maurice takes absolutely no
notice. Inevitably, therefore, we are driven to
conclude that Mr. Maurice, like many other men
and women, allowed impression and wish to stand
for reason and fact. There are many persons
who will not allow themselves to think that there
can be any real tragedy in human life, still less
any final perdition. The idea of permanent and
unrelieved, not to say endless, suffering, is intoler-
ably oppressive, and every one longs to see some
escape from it. Yet there is in the popular mind
a fundamental honesty and instinct for truth
which have hitherto prevented men from throwing off the belief in eternal punishment, though
few discoveries would be hailed with more
universal joy than that which enabled us to
believe that one day, however distant, all men
should be delivered from suffering. If we could
even take advantage of the cloud which undoubtedly does rest on the future of the wicked,
and believe that death eternal might amount to

an extinction of consciousness or of being, that would be a welcome alleviation. But certainly we can find little comfort and see little promise of alleviation in any theory of universal restitution that we have yet heard.

When he speaks directly on the subject of universal restitution, Mr. Maurice seems to be inconsistent or wavering. At p. 7 of his *Correspondence with Dr. Jelf*, he says, that though the human will can fix itself in misery, and defy that which seeks to subdue it, yet love does overcome this rebellion, its power being greater than every other. But in close connection with this we find that the ninth of his fifteen articles of belief or rules for his own assertions on this subject stands as follows: "Not to say that all will necessarily be raised out of eternal death, because I do not know." Now, alongside of this admission by Mr. Maurice, that it is possible there may not be an universal restitution, but that evil may, for all he knows, continue to exist for ever, how are we to account for his ungoverned indignation against Dean Mansel for expressing the very same idea? He quotes from the Bampton Lectures what he is pleased to term "nearly the most tremendous paragraph I ever read in a Christian writer." The paragraph is the one which contains the words, "Against this it is urged that sin cannot for ever be triumphant against God. As if the whole mystery of iniquity were contained in the words *for ever*." On this Mr. Maurice remarks:

"I was beginning to comment on these words. I was trying to tell you what impression they made on me. I cannot. I can only say, 'If they are true, let us burn our Bibles, let us tell our countrymen, that the agony and bloody sweat of Christ, His cross and passion, His death and burial, His resurrection and ascension, mean nothing.' . . . I believe, if we lose that hope [of the restitution of all things] altogether, we shall not stop at Mr. Mansel's point; we shall be certain that evil *must* reign for ever and ever, *must* drive out all that is opposed to it. We shall praise thee, O Devil, we shall acknowledge thee to be the Lord. And those who still retain the conviction that Christ has come into the world, will realise Jean Paul's tremendous dream. They will suppose that His message to men was, 'Children, you have *no* Father.'"[1]

It is no wonder that Dr. Jelf should have found it difficult to ascertain what Mr. Maurice's teaching on this subject was. He received a letter from him in which occur these words:

"I know from the express words of Scripture that God 'will have all men to be saved.' I know also

---

[1] *Letters to a Student*, p. 435-8.

that the will of man has an awful power of resisting
this will of God. How far that power may go, I dare
not ask myself. It is an abyss into which I cannot
look. I must believe that in some way the will of
God will triumph ; how, I know not."

These last words certainly seem to justify Dr.
Jelf in stating in his reply, that to him they conveyed the impression that Mr. Maurice meant to
say, "The *mode* I do not pretend to discover, but
the *fact* I am sure of, that God's will that all men
shall be saved will somehow finally triumph."
We venture to say that not one man in a hundred
would deny that this was a fair representation of
Mr. Maurice's meaning as disclosed in the words
quoted, and yet Dr. Jelf is assured by their writer
that this representation is "curiously wide of the
truth, as nearly as possible the reverse of it."
We may probably, then, lay ourselves open to the
charge of rashness if we presume to say either
that he did or did not believe in universal restitution. And, indeed, we think that his habitual
attitude of mind towards this doctrine was a
negative one. He would not dogmatise either on
the one side or the other. He would not say
that there was a place or time in which the
resistance of man to God should be effectual, and
when the resources of His converting grace should

be exhausted. Neither would he say that the
ultimate triumph of God's will could only be
accomplished by the restoration of universal good
and of every individual soul to the love of God.
He pled ignorance. "I am sure," he says, "that
restored order will be carried out by the full
triumph of God's loving will. How that should
take place while any rebellious will remains in
the universe, I cannot tell, though it is not for me
to say that it is impossible." So that, after all,
his universal restitution means no more, or little
more, than those hard Calvinistic theories he so
hates and repudiates. He dare not say that all
rebellious wills shall be softened and subdued, but
only, that somehow the will of God shall triumph,
even though some inferior wills be still out of
accord with it. His followers have judged this
part of his teaching rather by his well-known
leanings, and by certain of his loose and un-
qualified expressions; but it is significant, and
they should note it, that when he is called upon
to declare his opinion in terms as explicit as it is
possible for him to use, he declines to say that all
men shall yield to the love of God.

The doctrine of eternal punishment, however
essential to a complete creed, is not so central as

to modify all else that a man believes. In some cases, notably in that of John Foster, the denial of the ordinary teaching results from the vividness with which the state of the lost is conceived by the imagination. Men of feeble imagination, to whom the doctrine is little more than a form of words, and who are seldom distressed by the obvious consequences of it, have little temptation to rebel against it. But there certainly are men of, it may be, a morbidly sensitive nature, who cannot muffle their imagination, and prevent it from bringing them into sensible contact with what actually exists, and to whom life is rendered an intolerable misery, both by the consciousness they have of the present suffering in this world, and by the prospect that lies before so many of their fellow-men. Rather than resign mental comfort and happiness, men will resign their belief in eternal punishment, and attain thus a life free from visions so discomposing and grievous. There are other doctrines, however, which a man cannot thus discard without modifying his whole creed. The doctrine of sacrifice is notably of this kind. Knowing what a man believes on this head, we can deduce what he will believe on all other important points. Mr. Maurice's theory of sacrifice is well known, and his work on this subject bears evidence of care and matured thought. It is less profound and less complete than Bushnell's work, but it is equally eloquent, and as attractive in its ceaseless appeal to right feeling. Its fundamental defect, as has frequently been pointed out, is its neglect of the relation of sin to law. The moral law is assimilated to physical law. Consequence takes the place of penalty.[1] The scriptural idea of God as a Law-giver and Judge, inflicting judicial punishments, is set aside, and in its place we have an order of things which sin disturbs, and a Father from whom sin alienates the sinner. That which is required for the recovery of the sinner is not the expiation of guilt nor satisfaction to an offended government, but the renewal in the sinner's heart of right feeling towards God.

[1] The incompleteness of most of Mr. Maurice's statements here tells very seriously against him. He rarely anticipates and removes the objections to his doctrine which must inevitably occur to an inquirer. He furnishes no material for establishing his views, but is, for the most part, content to give them, and leave the reader the much more arduous task of proving, and defending, and developing them. In no case are we quite sure what a man believes, until we meet him face to face and cross-question him. And we cannot be quite sure we understand Mr. Maurice's position until we get his answer to the question : In what sense do you consider the whole order of things in this life penal ? And if you do not consider this order in any sense penal, do you consider that death itself

"The acts which express God's love to man; the acts by which the Son of God proves himself to be the Son of Man; these are the means of destroying the barrier between heaven and earth, between the Father and the children; the means of taking away the sin of the world. In each man the sin—the alienation and separation of heart—ceases when he believes that he has a Father who has loved him, and given His Son for him; when he confesses that this Son is stronger to unite him with his Father and his brethren, than sin is to separate him."[1]

This is a fair account of how sin in the heart is removed, and Mr. Maurice is angry with us when we presume to call past sins by the same name of sin, or to think of their guilt as well as of the sinfulness which still inhabits us. The Atonement is always represented by him as consisting of these two elements: there is in it, on the one hand, a proof of God's love, convincing the sinner that his fear and suspicion of God are groundless, and making him ashamed of his aversion or indifference to such a God; and there is in it, on the other hand, a persuasive example of sacrifice, a pattern of perfect living, an abnegation of self (the root of sin), and a dedication to God so

has nothing penal in it, but belongs wholly to the restored order of which you speak?

[1] *Doctrine of Sacrifice*, p. 196.

admirable and cogent that it constrains the sinner to a like sacrifice and return to God.

There is much else which is worthy of consideration in Mr. Maurice's theory, but it has so frequently and conclusively been dealt with elsewhere, that this brief statement must suffice.

So far as positive statements go, Mr. Maurice says little or nothing which is not embraced in the orthodox theory. We do not say that the side of truth to which he and others of similar views have called attention was made so prominent, or had even its due share of attention, before they taught and wrote. We think, indeed, that the one aspect of the Atonement as a deliverance from the guilt of sin, was by some teachers almost exclusively dwelt upon, and with very bad results. In many young persons the sense of guilt is extremely feeble, and becomes influential only after considerable conversance with divine things. Where the only point of attachment between the sinner and the Atonement, that is, between the sinner and Christ, was thought to be the hope it held forth of deliverance from guilt, this necessarily resulted either in the inoperativeness of the Atonement to attract the sinner, or in the production of forced and false feelings of guilt. If the Atonement be set before men as a deliverance from the bondage of evil habit as well as from the claims of a broken law, those will be attracted—and they are a very large number—who feel bitterly their helplessness and depravity, but who have no deep longing for pardon. But if orthodoxy has been practically one-sided, and we are far from denying that it commonly has been, Broad-churchism is theoretically as well as practically one-sided. It is a theology of reaction, and has its spring in contradictoriness. It has done eminent service in bringing to the front aspects of truth and ways of thinking which had been lost sight of; but, by refusing to see anything but these neglected truths, it has become narrower than the orthodoxy it condemns. The freshness and vitality with which some leaders of the school have handled doctrine have communicated a new and healthier tone to theological thought; but as this vitality has accompanied, if not resulted from, personal discovery of neglected truth, so this discovery of truth which personal experience had verified has tended to a depreciation of other truths which did not form an element in their own personal experience. It is very well to vivify doctrine by an infusion of experimental truth, but any one who tests doctrine by experience must be careful to include the experience of others. Certainly there are many who can find little comfort in an atonement in which there was no penal satisfaction for sin;[1] and there are none who understand the orthodox doctrine of the Atonement who do not find in it both this and everything which is promulgated by Mr. Maurice. There may be a difficulty in combining in one statement both the judicial and the ethical aspect of the Atonement, but we consider it an indelible blot on the Broad School theology, that they should suppose the two irreconcilable.[2]

The same incapacity to take account of both sides of a matter is discernible in Mr. Maurice's account of the mode in which men are practically restored to a righteous life. He denounces the

---

[1] It must not be supposed that Mr. Maurice's theology takes absolutely no account of guilt in any sense. He feels the guilt of having broken God's law, but thinks with Terence, "pro peccato magno paulum supplicii satis est *Patri*," or with Socinus, that nothing but repentance is required by God. Deliverance from guilt is necessary and longed for, and that deliverance is attained through the blood of Christ; but not because that blood is the satisfaction of the penalty of the law, but because it is an evidence of the love of God, a proof that He is waiting to receive the sinner.

[2] It will occur to most readers, as an objection to Mr. Maurice's theory, that if Christ's death were merely to exhibit the love of God, and so encourage us to trust Him, this was unnecessary, for all the believing Jews trusted God without knowing anything of Christ's death.

evangelical and ordinary style of preaching as incompetent, because it appeals to what is cowardly and evil in men. "We suppose men are to be shown by arguments that they have sinned, and that God has a right to punish them. We do not say to them, 'You are under a law of love; you know you are, and you are fighting with it.'"[1] Mr. Maurice and his allies persist in contrasting the power of love and the power of fear, as if a man must either be wholly governed by the one or wholly by the other. In point of fact, few men are uninfluenced by both. No one questions that love is the nobler and also the stronger motive:

> " Errat longe
> Qui imperium credat gravius esse aut stabilius
> Vi quod fit, quam illud quod amicitiâ adjungitur."

Or, as the same poet elsewhere puts it:

> " Pudore et liberalitate liberos
> Retinere, satius esse credo quam metu."

We all believe that ultimately love will be the only motive; but it is only when love has been perfected that fear is cast out as now useless. The two motives must together be brought to bear upon the uneducated, the child, and the depraved.

[1] *Theological Essays*, p. 27.

Every one who has had much to do either with
the education of the young, or the reclaiming of
the abandoned, is aware that there is a perfect
practical harmony between the persuasive " terrors
of the Lord " and the constraining love of the
Lord.   Certainly, Mr. Maurice's explanation of
the conversion of the Kingswood collier must
seem thoroughly incompetent to any one who has
either been in personal contact with similar cases,
or has carefully read the experience of Wesley,
Whitfield, and their followers.   We fancy that
Dr. Watts is on such a point as this quite as safe
an authority as Mr. Maurice, and we read that he,
" all mild and amiable as he was, and delighted to
dwell on the congenial topics, says deliberately,
that of all the persons to whom his ministry had
been efficacious, *only one* had received the first
effectual impressions from the gentle and attractive
aspects of religion; all the rest from the awful
and alarming ones—the appeals to fear.   And
this is all but universally the manner of the
Divine process of conversion." [1]

A theory of atonement such as Mr. Maurice
held implies a system of theology essentially
different from that which is currently accepted.
This system, in so far as he indicates it, we shall

[1] Foster's *Life and Correspondence*, ii. 260.

endeavour briefly to sketch. Mr. Maurice himself recognised that the real issue upon which the dispute between evangelical theologians and himself turned, was the question whether the Fall or the Redemption is the ground on which humanity rests.[1] This is true, but we think a more adequate statement of the fundamental difference of the two theologies would be brought out by their respective answers to the question, Is Adam or Christ the root of humanity? Mr. Maurice's whole system of thought springs out of his belief that the Son of God does not *become* the Head of humanity by His incarnation or by His designation to the mediatorial office and work, but that He is originally the Head or Root of the race.[2] In his own words, baptism "imports the belief that this Son of God, and not Adam, was the true Root of humanity; that from Him, and not from any ancestor, each man derived his life."[3] The Son of God is, in his theology, not merely

---

[1] *Doctrine of Sacrifice*, preface, p. xxxv.

[2] Thus Mr. Davies, one of the most moderate exponents of Mr. Maurice's doctrine, says: "The primordial creation of mankind in Christ underlies and explains our redemption by Him." He even ventures to make the surprising statement that "whenever St. Paul is setting forth broadly the message of Atonement through the Cross, he states as the ground of it the mystery of our creation or constitution in Christ.'

[3] *Theological Essays*, p. 202.

the Agent in creation; not only supplies life to men, but is in them. Whether he ever distinctly asked himself the question, Can God create life? we do not know; but throughout his writings it seems to be taken for granted that God can only enable His creatures to live by Himself living in them; extending, as it were, His own existence into new forms, so that still all His creatures may be called Himself. There is, according to this Pantheistic supposition, no more life in the universe than there was before creation; it only exists in new forms. Certainly no language can be plainer and stronger than that in which Mr. Maurice asserts "an actual relationship between the Son of God and human creatures of the most intimate kind which language can express—a relationship implying the closest communion of inward life, of inward love." He says he felt increasingly "the necessity of standing upon this principle, that *Christ is in every man.*'[1] Men are thus by nature and original constitution, in the most real sense, sons of God. Such an incident as the Fall could make no alteration in this relationship. He sets himself to "combat the great denial of our time—the one which is most at variance with the express letter of the Bible,

---

[1] *Doctrine of Sacrifice*, preface, p. xxiv.

and with its whole object and history—that man continued to be in the image of God after the Fall, with the denials which correspond to this and grow out of it; that man was originally created in the Divine Word; and that, apart from Him, neither Adam nor any of his descendants either had, or ever could have, any righteousness or any life."[1]   Christ thus dwelling in all men by their very nature, all that is needful for their restoration to the enjoyment of God and to a godlike character, is their recognition of this their true condition as God's children.   No obstacles exist preventing God's love from freely expressing itself to the sinner; the only change needful lies in the recognition by man of his true relationship to God.   This is effected by the manifestation of Christ in the flesh, which reveals God's love for men and their union or unity with the Son, and so inclines them to live no longer to themselves.   This revelation of the Son in them, and this knowledge of God as their Father, is eternal life, while the lack or rejection of this knowledge is death eternal.

Such a system manifestly evacuates the Catholic Christian creed of much that is peculiar, if not essential, to it.   Whether, and in what sense, our

[1] *Patriarchs and Lawgivers*, pref. to 2d ed. p. ix.

religion would have been Christian had we remained unfallen, we cannot tell. Whether in that case the Son of God would have become incarnate, we do not know. As things are, the incarnation is certainly presented to us in Scripture as a remedial arrangement, and the connection of men with Christ is spoken of as corrective of, and supplementary to, their connection with Adam. So far from it being the case that men are primarily in Christ, we are directly assured that we are originally connected with Adam, and only attain, by a change so complete as to be worthy of the name of a new birth, to a vital connection with Christ. We are distinctly and expressly warned against looking at things in this reversed order, and are taught that "that was *not* first which is spiritual, but that which is natural; and afterwards that which is spiritual." This is said with special reference to the two heads of humanity, Adam and Christ. And as the incarnation of Christ is, in the actual constitution of things, subsequent to the creation of Adam, and introduced as a remedial expedient, so in the life of the individual there exists first the natural connection with Adam, and only subsequent to that the spiritual connection with Christ—a connection which, being spiritual, is formed by the will of the individual. It is on this scheme very intelligible that this change should be called a new birth, and that by the establishment of a spiritual connection with the Son of God, men should become adopted sons of God ; but if men are by their natural birth sons of God, is "regeneration" not a misnomer for a change in which there is no real alteration of our relation to God? and is it not misleading to speak of a second birth? That there is some truth in the assertion that we are by nature God's children, we do not deny. We are far from maintaining that the description of God as our Governor or Judge is exhaustive, just as we should be slow to admit that the natural relationship between God and His human creatures is adequately represented by that of Fatherhood. We conceive that no single aspect of God's relationship to man is adequate, and that if we would understand the nature of His dealings with us, we must combine the love and longing of the Father with the Sovereign's regard for justice and indissoluble connection with law. If, therefore, men speak and think of God as their Father, understanding thereby that they may count upon a Father's tenderness in Him, and are receiving from Him a Father's care, no doctrine of Adoption or Regeneration would instigate us to rebuke them for so conceiving of God; but if they proceed to found upon this name of Father a scientific theology, if they argue that because they are in some sense children of God already, they need no connection with God's Son other than that which they naturally enjoy, we cannot but think that the entire scheme of salvation by Christ contradicts their position.

The influence which Mr. Maurice exerted was of that indefinable kind which proceeds from character, rather than that which is asserted by new and striking thought. His actual contributions to theology were small. He has not given us any substantial development of doctrine, he has not set any article of our creed on a more unassailable foundation. Some of his contemporaries have left behind them works full of well-digested thought and ascertained information, works of an impersonal kind, which communicate substantial knowledge, without giving us any hint of the character of their authors. In every line of Mr. Maurice's writings we are in contact with himself, and his books are useful mainly, if not solely, because they impart to the reader something of the earnest and living spirit of the writer. It is the tone in which he conducts all inquiries rather than the result of any special investigation which benefits his readers. As a preacher, this was the secret of his influence. From many pulpits there might have been heard much more lucid expositions of Scripture, and much more eloquent enforcements of truth, but it is not what a man says, but what he is, that influences. It is not the sermon so much as the man that preaches. A very commonplace truth heartily believed, and uttered because it is believed, is accepted by the hearer who is impregnable to the most skilful reasoning. Mr. Maurice, with his plain, hesitating manner of address, was an instance of this. His sermons were often crude, often dry, always obscure, but in them all the hearer was in contact with a soul seeking the light with holy and earnest purpose, hopeful of success, and resolute to seek till it found. Mr. Maurice became a leader among men because he followed none, but was always himself, true to his own convictions, open to more light, able to help others because himself immovably grounded, afraid of nothing, of no new discovery, of no outward changes; because he loved what was true and right, and had finally given himself to the truth, finding in it his blessedness. He had himself passed through the dark and difficult places into which intelligent, thoughtful, and God-fearing men are led, and he had that kind of imagination which enabled him to live through the experience of others. In dealing with the characters found under the Old Testament, his tendency was therefore rather to put too much of his own feeling into them than to handle them as fossil remains. Always successful in making these characters live before us, he sometimes falls into the Byronic error of putting himself into every character, and finding in others only what he has first found in himself. In spite, however, of this tendency, his writings on the Old Testament are not only full of interest, profound thought, and beauty of expression, but do present many views of persons and institutions which are of great value. Here he was in his element, and no hand is more successful than his in tracing obscure experiences, unravelling the mixture of motives and the subtle influences which express themselves in conduct, or in depicting the various attitudes which men assume towards God and one another. But we cannot persuade ourselves that he has been successful in handling theology proper. Indeed, to speak honestly, we have found few writers more disappointing. There are great difficulties in theology, and we, perhaps simply, betook ourselves to the writings of Mr. Maurice

with considerable expectations.   At first we were
encouraged by the earnest moral tone, but soon
his misrepresentations of evangelical truth convinced us that we had found only a one-sided
man still.   These misrepresentations, we are
bound to say, are so gross, so virulent, and so
ignorant, that they at once destroyed our confidence in Mr. Maurice as a theological guide.
We do not suppose that his theological reading
was extensive ; we have no evidence that he was
careful in ascertaining what Calvinism really is, as
held by its recognised champions, but it is difficult
to believe that he had no compunction in ascribing
to the Evangelicals such opinions as he represents
them as holding.   If we are to accept his representations of evangelical truth as a true account
of what he really supposed Evangelicals or
Calvinists to hold, then we must conclude that he
had never consulted any one leader of evangelical
thought, that he had never read Owen, or
Goodwin, or Edwards, or even Stillingfleet or
Charnock.   We are aware that Calvinism is the
red rag which renders a Broad-Churchman furious
and blind, but we are heartily disappointed that
Mr. Maurice should not have so far commanded
himself as to look steadily for a little at that
which he attacked.   In his *Theological Essays* his

uniform method is to describe the current opinion on the topic in question, and then gradually to disclose the view which he means shall supersede the old ideas, but in no case does he give us a reference to his source of information. No man is so free in ascribing hateful sentiments to large bodies of his fellow-Christians, and yet in almost no instance does he quote or refer to any authority. It is the merest caricature of the meagrest form of evangelical teaching which he gives; and we are persuaded that he could not substantiate his descriptions from the writings of any well-known teacher. This literary crime, like all other faults, has its own punishment; it renders his most systematic work utterly feeble and unsatisfactory. For who cares to hear magniloquent refutations of what no one believes? If Mr. Maurice chooses to call these creations of his own fancy orthodoxy, or if he chooses to identify the popular evangelical idea with some grotesque caricature of it, we are not bound to be so deceived. And if, having refuted this creation of his own, he erects his trophy and sings his triumphal ode over the fall of current theological opinion, we can but lament that a man who might have been usefully employed should so have wasted thought and language.

The obscurity, universally complained of as

attaching to Mr. Maurice's writings, arose mainly from his theological position and the attitude he assumed towards the orthodox creed. Accepting the dogmatic expressions of the Articles, the task of his life was to find the truth that underlies them. To him the Creed rather than the Bible was the source of theology. But he would accept no article which had not a meaning for his spiritual aspirations and experience; and his own intense hunger for what was real and nourishing to the spiritual life within him, caused him to reject with vehemence whatever savoured of merely notional or propositional theology. Terms and phrases, however venerable, were nothing to him. All formulas and creeds are dry bones, and he accepts it as his office " to create a soul under the ribs of death." In doing so he is guided solely by his own spiritual experience, and necessarily, therefore, by his own intellectual habits and forms of thought. He accepted the phraseology of orthodoxy, but filled it with a meaning peculiar to himself. He believed in an Atonement, a Resurrection, a Day of Judgment, but utterly repudiated what is commonly understood by these terms. He answers to his own definition of the " original man " as it is given in a characteristic passage in the Dedicatory Letter to his work on Sacrifice:

" I have affirmed continually—I have affirmed again
in this book—that I have discovered nothing; that
what I am saying is to be found in every creed of the
Catholic Church ; in the Prayers and Articles of the
Church to which I belong ; most emphatically in the
Bible, from which they derive their authority, and to
which they refer as their ultimate standard.   But
while I utterly disclaim *novelty*, which, I suppose, is
what Dr. Candlish means by *originality in matter*,
there is a sense in which I earnestly desire to be
original. . . . An original man is not one who in-
vents—not one who refuses to learn from others.[1]   I
say, boldly, no original man ever did that.   But he is
one who does not take words and phrases at second-
hand ; who asks what they signify ; who does not feel
that they are his, or that he has a right to use them
till he knows what they signify.   The original man is
fighting for his life ; he must know whether he has
any ground to stand upon ; he must ask God to tell
him, because man cannot."

It was this constant purpose and desire to hold
nothing for truth which he could not realise
within himself, and to give utterance to it precisely in that form in which it manifested itself

---

[1] Which will remind our readers of Carlyle's utterance in
his *Lectures on Heroes*. " A man can believe, and make his
own, in the most genuine way, what he has received from
another ;—and with boundless gratitude to that other.   The
merit of *originality* is not novelty ; it is sincerity.   The
believing man is the original man ; whatsoever he believes, he
believes it for himself, and not for another."

in his own spirit, which made him obscure. It is
his greatest excellence that to him no word is
merely a word; in all his thinking we feel that
he is not dealing mentally with propositions and
logical inferences, but spiritually with vital realities, with things and persons. This is his great
power and his great helpfulness, but out of this
arise his great defects, his narrowness and his
obscurity. It is to this doctrinal self-absorption
that the apparently egotistical character of his
utterances is due. We are never left alone with
the subject; the truth is never left to speak for
itself, it comes verified by Mr. Maurice's experience. This style of writing has its strength and
its weakness; it has the strength which belongs
to a personal statement, it has the weakness
which attaches to what appears as individual
opinion rather than the voice of the Church. A
man cannot always speak in the first person without leaving the impression that, however true to
his own experience, his words do not convey the
truth sanctioned by universal consent. It must
also be owned that there is in Mr. Maurice's
writings no large and liberal approbation of the
work of other theologians, but rather a frettingly
recurrent depreciation of those who have preceded him. Of course, every reader of his writ-

ings is aware that praise is occasionally distributed in the most unexpected directions, but accompanying the praise there is always found the modifying, detracting clause which leaves on the reader's mind the impression that truth lies with Mr. Maurice alone; and, in point of fact, the result of a belief in him is very frequently disbelief in all other writers. Indeed, it is scarcely too much to say, that in many instances there is no other visible result of belief in him than contempt for every other theologian.

We should be sorry, however, to seem to part from so rare a man in a spirit of hostility, or enmity, or detraction. We believe him to have been a man who has done much good as well as much harm. It may indeed be feared that he is one to whom the words are applicable, "The evil that men do lives after them, the good is oft interred with their bones." It may be feared that opinions which had no evil results in a character so pure and elevated as his, may in less genuine and reverential natures be productive of a thoroughgoing rationalism. Rejection of the traditional theology may have done little harm to Mr. Maurice himself, but may do much harm to the smaller spirits who take up the cry against all dogmatic teaching, and to those who merely wish countenance in renouncing what is commonly believed. It is very well known that a man's followers carry out his principles to conclusions little thought of by himself, and we think that already there are symptoms, among those who profess unbounded admiration for Mr. Maurice, of a loosening of faith in Scripture, which results from, though it far outsteps, his theory of its nature. There has got abroad a notion that this very excellent ·and able man showed little respect for the traditional theology, and some persons, omitting to consider that Mr. Maurice threw off the old habits of thought not that he might be "unclothed" but "clothed upon" with what he conscientiously believed to be more sufficient, imitate him in discarding what they have hitherto worn, but are in danger of being "found naked." But notwithstanding such disastrous results in pretentious, insincere, or feeble minds, we believe that the spectacle of a man who shrank from no test to which the Christian faith can be put, who advocated and displayed an absolute freedom of thought, and yet maintained to the end and increasingly his faith in God and in Christ, has saved many others from infidelity, and forced the acknowledgment that Christianity in some form or other is true.

This spectacle was all the more telling by reason of his departure from the orthodox faith; for few men can believe in an intellectual liberty which asserts itself only by agreeing with and corroborating existing beliefs. Though undoubtedly many adherents of orthodoxy are quite as unfettered and outspoken as Mr. Maurice, yet perhaps the time had come when the Church required to be reminded that theology, like every other science, has a tendency to convert living, life-giving truth into dead formulas and intellectual propositions. With immense industry, and with spiritual conflict which left its ineradicable traces on his resolute but tender countenance, Mr. Maurice verified the fundamentals of the Christian faith in his own soul, and in presence of every difficulty with which his wide knowledge and fearless inquiry acquainted him; and the result has been that men see that, even supposing the Westminster and every other Confession to be in many particulars wrong, there remains an indefeasible reality in religion. This result might perhaps have been gained without any counteracting detriment, but the Church must ever honour the man who has identified the name of Christian with the tenderest graces and the manliest virtues which adorn and enrich human nature, with the truest faith in God and an ardent devotion to the well-being of men. If we feel little sympathy with his theology, we do not the less love and admire the man : "omnes homines sumus ; non nos, sed errores et falsitates oderimus."

October 1872.

VI

CONFUCIUS

THE Chinese are supposed to form about one-third of the population of the world. And there is some ground for believing that for the last four thousand years they have held much the same numerical proportion to the entire human race. Yet it may be said that there is but one China-man who has earned a world-wide reputation, one individual who has been large enough to lift himself above the millions of unknown, unrecorded lives and force himself on the regard of the Western world. It is probably due to the absorption of the individual in the State that there is in China so remarkable a lack of great names. The individual exists for the State, not the State for the individual. Everything is crushed down to a dead level and monotony. No heroic spirits arise; no heroic deeds are done. Patriotism is enjoined by law, and the *spirit* of devotedness has never been evoked. Consequently, though no state has ever governed so many men, none has annals so poor and flat. Individual effort is frowned upon; improvement is branded as innovation.

By what singular qualities then did Confucius win for himself his unique reputation? He was not a conqueror stamping his name on the terror-struck imagination of surrounding tribes. He was not an inventor whose memory is kept green by the gratitude of those who daily enjoy the fruit of his genius. He was not a poet uttering men's best thoughts and deepest feelings for them in words more expressive than their own. He was not even a philosopher, or if a philosopher, his philosophy was on the level of that of Benjamin Franklin. In short, no ordinary avenue to fame seems to have been open to him; and yet, if numbers go for anything, what fame rivals that of the man who for twenty-three centuries has been worshipped as all but divine by nearly one half of the world, and whose words are regarded as canonical by a people compared to whose exclusive jealousy the Jewish exclusiveness is latitudinarian? The secret of his fame is mainly this, that he was the Chinaman of the Chinamen, the most conservative and ancestor-worshipping individual of the most conservative and ancestor-worshipping race. It was by his work that the national tendencies and popular instincts were recognised and definitely fixed. What had before been implicit was by Confucius made explicit. It was he who formulated the relations of ruler and subject which form so large a part of Chinese life. It was he who gave utterance to those maxims of personal conduct which the Chinese are justly proud of, though they do not scrupulously observe them. Especially it was he who gathered into a Chinese canon all the wisdom which had been tested by previous generations, and so set the seal of completeness on Chinese life and customs so far as this can be done by any man or by any books.

The facts of his life, which are at once well ascertained and significant, are few. Confucius, or Kung-foo-tsze, [*i.e.* Kung, the Master], like some of the heroes of Hebrew history, was the son of his father's old age — the long-coveted boy whom nine unwelcome daughters had preceded. He was born in the year 551 B.C., of parents who, though poor, were in good position. His father was a soldier of immense size, strength, and courage, and with the blood of emperors in his veins; so that even at the age of seventy he found it possible to contract a second marriage, from which sprang his famous son. The child was named Kew from a peculiar formation on the top of his head, which is still represented in some of the statues of Confucius. In his third year he lost his father, and of his childhood and schooldays only one characteristic trait is preserved. As it is recorded of Athanasius that he was observed when a child playing at church ceremonies, and himself enacting the part of a bishop, so of Confucius it is related that "as a boy he used to play at the arrangement of sacrificial vessels, and at postures of ceremony." At the age of nineteen he married, and entered the service of the State as a keeper of grain-stores and inspector of pastures and flocks. These duties were interrupted three or four years after by the death of his mother, an event which required that he should go into retirement for twenty-seven months. This period, however, was abundantly utilised for purposes of study and of inquiry into funeral and other religious observances and ancient customs. By slow degrees, and with some interruptions, he won his way at the age of fifty to a position in which he could practically carry out the social reforms he had long desired. As chief magistrate of the town of Chung-too he produced in a single year a marked improvement in trade-customs, in the private life of the citizens, and generally in the prosperity of the community. Rulers and people were alike sensible of the change. Neighbouring governors applied to him for draft-schemes for the government of their provinces; and when he was made Minister of Crime, so alive were the criminal classes to his integrity and thoroughness, that his mere appointment awed them into honesty.

His success, indeed, was his ruin. The province of Loo became the envy of surrounding provinces, and by an extraordinary appeal made to the sensual appetites of its prince, the neighbouring rulers succeeded in destroying the influence of the austere minister. When eighty dancing girls and one hundred and twenty of the finest horses arrived as a present to the prince, a discerning friend of Confucius said to him, "Master, it is time for you to be going." Reluctantly and regretfully Confucius withdrew, and the remainder of his life is a record of sorrow, disappointment, and unsettledness. Passing from place to place as the Apostle of Reform, he was everywhere rejected, though frequently treated with kindness and respect at the first. His wife, his son, his most intimate disciples, died during these melancholy years, till at last, broken with years and failure, he bowed to his fate. He died in his seventy-third year, a disappointed, saddened man, conscious of his own greatness, or at any rate of the importance of his teaching, and yet more than doubtful whether any lasting impression had been made by it. If we may judge from the pathetic significance of one of his brief sayings, he seems to have himself lost hope, and to have allowed his long-cherished ideal kingdom of Chow to pass altogether into cloudland out from among all practicable realities. "Extreme is my decay," he says; "for a long time I have not dreamed, as I was wont to do, that I saw the Duke of Chow." Dr. Legge gives the following touching account of his death: "Early one morning he got up, and with his hands behind his back, dragging his staff, he moved about by his door, crooning over—

> "'The great mountain must crumble;
> The strong beam must break;
> And the wise man wither away like a plant.'

After a little he entered the house and sat down opposite the door. Tsze-Kung had heard his words, and said to himself, 'If the great mountain crumble, to what shall I look up? If the strong beam break, and the wise man wither away, on whom shall I lean? The Master, I fear, is going to be ill.' With this he hastened into the house. Confucius said to him, 'Tsze, what makes you so late? . . . No intelligent monarch arises; there is not one in the empire that will make me his master. My time is come to die.' So it was. He went to his couch, and, after seven days, expired."

The acknowledgment so scantily given him in his lifetime was afterwards abundantly rendered by those to whom he was little more than a name. His reputation grew, until, in the year 57 of our era, it was enacted that sacrifices be offered to him in all the colleges of the principal divisions of the empire. A few centuries more, and temples were erected to him, and his worship became, as it remains to this day, the state religion. Twice a year the Emperor himself, the representative of the divine to all Chinamen, performs ceremonies in honour of Confucius with special solemnity; and this most exalted of potentates bows himself to the earth, and invokes the spirit of Confucius in the words, "Great art thou, O perfect sage! Thy virtue is full, thy doctrine is complete.

Among mortal men there has not been thine equal. All kings honour thee. Thy statutes and laws have come gloriously down. Thou art the pattern in this imperial school."

While, however, the career of Confucius as a practical statesman or reformer was almost wholly ineffective, his influence in private on the select circle that owned him as their Master and treasured his words was immense. He may best be understood as a kind of Chinese Socrates, quickening his disciples to think, rather than handing over to them a finished system, fearless and disinterested as the Greek sage, and with a like capacity of discriminating between the likely pupil and the unimprovable dullard. "Rotten wood," he said, "cannot be carved; a wall of dirty earth will not receive the trowel. This Yu, *who sleeps in the daytime*, what is the use of my reproving him?" Again: "I do not open up the truth to one who is not eager to get knowledge, nor help out any one who is not anxious to explain himself. When I have presented one corner of a subject to any one, and he cannot from it learn the other three, I do not repeat my lesson." As a teacher, he maintained throughout his whole career a perfect independence, for which we cannot but honour him. A provincial governor who had been captivated with his conversation offered him the revenues of one of his towns, but Confucius declined the gift, saying to his disciples, "A superior man will only receive reward for services which he has done. I have given advice to the Duke, but he has not yet obeyed it, and now he would endow me with this place. Very far is he from understanding me." Threats moved him as little as bribes or rewards. His vigorous reforms and reassertion of forgotten and inconvenient customs often made him obnoxious both to rulers and people. But he argued that if Heaven had wished to let the cause of truth perish, he would not have been impelled to proclaim it, and "if Heaven intends that the truth shall not perish, then what can the people of Kwang do to me." Always accessible to the earnest inquirer, he never declined to give instruction, though his pupil might, to use his own words, have nothing to give him but a bundle of dried flesh. He was himself profoundly interested in human duties and relationships, willing always to receive or to impart light. "There were four things," his disciples used to say, "from which the Master was entirely free. He had no foregone conclusions, no arbitrary predeterminations, no obstinacy, no egotism "—

important qualities, certainly, in any one who proposes to find the truth. Of his sincerity no one can entertain a doubt. "I detest," he says, "that which has appearance without reality; I detest clever men, for fear that they shall confound justice; I detest an eloquent mouth, fearing lest it confuse truth; I detest the colour of violet, because it mimics the colour of purple; I detest the most respectable people of a neighbourhood, because they mimic virtue."

The subject-matter of the teaching of Confucius was Ethics. In his day there was a remarkable stirring of the Chinese mind, and this mental movement naturally revolved round the popular religion. This religion was one which could satisfy neither the speculative nor the morally earnest men. It was a degenerate nature-worship, each natural agency being under the control of departmental spirits, who had to be consulted and propitiated on every occasion. No better soil could be found for charlatanry and superstition. Two reformative reactions appeared in the sixth century B.C., the one associated with the name of Lao-tsze, the other with that of Confucius. The work of the former was an attempt to elevate the popular religion by rationalising it, or finding a sufficient speculative basis for faith.

To Confucius fell the more congenial task of introducing a higher morality. Both were dissatisfied with the state of matters around them. The one said to himself, Let us see what basis in fact there is for religious worship; let us find out what existence is, and what this world is, and whence we are. The other said, Let us look at the things immediately before us, and speak only of what we know, and regarding which we can make positive affirmations. The one was the Hegel, the other the Comte of China. They had no sympathy with one another. Confucius had a dry, prosaic, practical mind, which could only gaze in wonder at the speculative flights of Lao-tsze. He was not ashamed to make the admission to his disciples, "I know how birds can fly, how fishes can swim, how animals can run. But there is the dragon: I cannot tell how he mounts on the wind through the clouds and rises to heaven. To-day I have seen Lao-tsze, and can only compare him to the dragon."

The position of Confucius may best be understood through the analogous position of the statesmen-philosophers of Rome, such as Cicero, Seneca, and Plutarch. Confucius could not break with the religion of his country, and he had no desire to do so. A reverence for antiquity was his chief characteristic. "I am a transmitter, not a maker," he was fond of saying. All his reforms were conducted in a conservative spirit, and on the principle that all wisdom had been given to the ancients. He would not meddle with the established worship which had satisfied his fathers. It was part of his duty as a good citizen to render that worship, and therefore he would unquestioningly give it. To him, as to every Chinaman, the State was the supreme entity. It was to it he owed his allegiance, and his aim was to discover how men could best live together and serve the State. Like Aristotle, he is devoted to ethics and politics, and has nothing to say about the Divine. The bent and constant attitude of his mind is given in his words, "To give oneself earnestly to the duties due to men, and while respecting spiritual beings, to keep aloof from them, this may be called wisdom."

We must not look to Confucius, then, for any light upon religious matters. He had evidently no convictions about the supernatural. He was an Agnostic pure and simple, declining to dogmatise where he had no grounds for affirmation. Even when questioned regarding the most universal custom and belief of the Chinese religion, he made evasive answers. Ke Loo, *e.g.*, asked him about serving the spirits of the dead, but Confucius replied, "While you are not able to serve living men, how can you serve their spirits?" Not daunted by this clever snub, the irrepressible disciple went on to ask about death; but the ready fencer met this assault also with an equally skilful parry: "While you do not know life, how can you know death?" These replies might indeed be supposed to lie in the same plane as the remark of the Apostle John, "He that loveth not his brother whom he hath seen, how can he love God whom he hath not seen?" They might, that is to say, be construed as merely intended to remind men that there is an order and gradation in human duties, and that no man can accomplish the higher by evading the lower; and to rebuke the tendency to exonerate ourselves from duties that lie under our nose by professing to be engaged in higher matters. But this construction cannot always be given, and will not account for the uniform indisposition which Confucius manifests to commit himself to any statement regarding things supernatural. He was, in fact, a high-minded secularist or positivist, who believed that care for present duty was the only preparation for the future, that men should concern themselves with what they know, and that the unseen and unknown will reveal itself in due time. "Have the dead knowledge," asked one of his disciples; "or have they not?" The Master replied, "If I were to say that they have knowledge, I am afraid that filial sons would injure their substance in paying the last offices to the departed; and if I were to say that they have not knowledge, I fear lest unfilial sons should leave their parents unburied. You need not wish to know whether they have knowledge or not. There is no present urgency about the point. Hereafter you will know it for yourself." Obviously Confucius was not possessed by that intense religious craving, nor by that keen speculative instinct, the one or the other of which drives many men past secularism, bidding them search above all else for God, bidding them renew the search, however baffled, however weary and perplexed, because they feel that till the question of God's existence is settled all other questions can receive but a partial and provisional solution.

Yet the moral intensity and practical earnestness of Confucius never relaxed. And if he ever questioned himself regarding the source of moral obligation and found that he could not satisfactorily answer the questions that pierced to the ultimate aim of human life and the fundamental ground of human duty, this seems only to have made him cling more tenaciously to whatever in conduct he felt to be good, and to trust more to the leaven of personal influence than to carefully elaborated systems of ethics for the regeneration of society. His consciousness of the inefficacy of reasoned systems of morals is remarkably expressed in the following: "The Master said, 'I would prefer not speaking.' Tsze-Kung said, 'If you, Master, do not speak, what shall we your disciples have to record?' The Master replied, 'Does Heaven speak? The four seasons pursue their courses, and all things are continually being produced, but does Heaven say anything?'" Increasingly he felt the insufficiency of teaching to make men moral,—and here again he resembles Aristotle,—increasingly indeed he felt how far off he himself was from living up to his own ideal. "The sage and the man of perfect virtue," he said, "how dare I rank myself with them? In letters I am perhaps equal to other men, but the character of the superior man, carrying out in his conduct what he professes, is what I have not yet attained to." "The leaving virtue without proper cultivation, the not thoroughly discussing what is learned, not being able to move towards righteousness of which a knowledge is gained, and not being able to change what is not good— these are the things which occasion me solicitude."

The work from which a knowledge of the teaching of Confucius may best be gained is entitled *The Confucian Analects*.   This work may, in respect of its *form*, be compared to the gospels ; not that it contains anything approaching to a biography of Confucius, but because it comprises a vast number of his sayings, which were set down in writing or committed to memory by those who heard them.   In the *Analects*, therefore, we must not expect to find such an exposition of his views as a philosopher would give who sat down, pen in hand, to do so ; neither have we the artistically finished and long-drawn discussions familiar to the reader of Plato, but only a collection of brief sayings evoked by some trivial circumstance or incidental question.   Some of these sayings are indeed full of shrewdness, and worthy of the universal introductory formula, "The Master said."   For example : "In ancient times men learned with a view to their own improvement : nowadays men learn with a view to the approbation of others."   Again : " He who requires much from himself and little from others will keep himself from being the object of resentment." Two other of his sayings are worthy of the attention of all students: "The Master said, Learning without thought is labour lost; thought without learning is perilous." And again: "In *all* things success depends upon previous preparation, and without such previous preparation there is sure to be failure. If what is to be spoken be previously determined, there will be no stumbling. If affairs be previously determined, there will be no difficulty with them. If one's actions have been previously determined, there will be no sorrow in connection with them. If principles of conduct have been previously determined, the practice of them will be inexhaustible." Of course it would be easy to quote pages of trivial, flat, commonplace observations; on the other hand, if any one wished to establish for Confucius the character of profundity, he might cite such a saying as this: "Is virtue a thing remote? I wish to be virtuous, and lo! virtue is at hand"; or as this: "What the superior man seeks is in himself; what the mean man seeks is in others."

But it is not by scattered sayings such as these that a teacher can exert a lasting influence. In the *Analects* we find traces of something more than the faculty of felicitous expression and acute observation. We find a moral earnestness that penetrates to some of the most important principles of human life and conduct. Perhaps the most remarkable instance of this ethical insight is found in the Chinese teacher's anticipation of the *golden rule* of the Gospel. One of his disciples, weary of maxims and rules, said to Confucius, " Is there one word which may serve as a rule of practice for all one's life ? " The Master replied, " Is not *Reciprocity* such a word ? What you do not want done to yourself, do not do to others." This was not a mere accidental hit or happy thought. In the little work entitled *The Doctrine of the Mean*, in which he elaborates his ethical ideas somewhat more fully, it is still this principle which pervades the whole. Indeed he formulates it in the ever-memorable expression, which is probably profounder than any ethical truth uttered by Greek philosophy, " Benevolence is Man." Again and again we find him unfolding this central truth in some such style as the following : " In the way of the superior man there are four things to not one of which have I as yet attained : to serve my father as I would require my son to serve me, to this I have not attained ; to serve my prince as I would require my minister to serve me ; . . . to serve my elder brother as I would require my younger brother to serve me; to set the example in behaving to a friend as I would require him to behave to me—to this I have not attained." But the prominence he gave to this ethical principle is perhaps most convincingly shown by the fact that this doctrine of his was taken up and developed by the philosopher Mih Teih, who *demonstrated*, in a work still extant and accessible to English readers, that universal mutual love is the root of all virtue and the cure of all social evil.

There are two uses to which this slight acquaintance with the great Chinese moralist may be put. The first is to guard ourselves against the common error of supposing that it is by inculcating a wholly new and previously unthought-of morality that the Christian religion proves its divine origin and establishes its transcendent importance. The Christian morality is more complete, more consistent, more penetrating than that inculcated elsewhere. The Christian morality is perfect, being the morality of the Incarnate God. But it is an extremely rash, not to say unfair, procedure on the part of those who have no personal acquaintance with other moral systems to institute comparisons upon special points, or to declaim at large against the defects of uninspired teachers. For what is the consequence? The consequence is this, that having heard the ardent but reckless Christian Apologist declare that this one Christian injunction, "Do to others as ye would be done by," is enough to prove the divinity of our religion, you turn to Confucius and find the very same sentiment, or you consult the Hindu sacred books and you read: "Hear the sum of all righteousness, and when thou hast heard, ponder it, Do not to others what would be repugnant to thyself." It may then be insinuated that these are only negative precepts informing you what you are not to do, but not directing you to positive duty; you look, therefore, a little further and you find it written: "That the wise man should in whatever manner he can promote the satisfaction of every embodied creature — this is the worship of Vishnu." "What makes the birth of embodied creatures fruitful is this, that they should with their life, with their means, with their understanding, and with their speech, seek to advance the welfare of other creatures in this world." "The good show compassion even to worthless creatures. The moon does not withdraw its light from the house of the Pariah." "Suitable hospitality should be shown even to an enemy when he comes to one's house. A tree does not withdraw its shade even from the forester who comes to cut it down."

Manifestly, if we have been taught that the chief distinction between Christianity and other systems lies in the contents of their moral teaching, our faith must receive a shock when we discover how much of what is true and high these systems contain. Hence the reluctance of many to admit the facts regarding pre - Christian teachers ; hence their jealous, unloving criticism of their teachings. Mr. Kinglake has admirably shown that the unusual bloodshed at the battle of Inkerman was in great measure due to the false issue on which for some part of the day that battle was fought. The Sand-bag Battery, for the acquisition of which hundreds of brave men fell, was utterly worthless when won, and was not by any means the key of the position ; and yet it was round it again and again that the tide of the fight was drawn. And similarly it is only through an entire, and in many cases disastrous, misapprehension that the contest between Christianity and opposing systems can be drawn to a position of second-rate importance. That men should be able by their unassisted mental powers, or under the influence of those sporadic and mysterious impulses which God seems to have communicated from time to time to the heathen, to analyse their own moral nature seems to me almost as likely as that they should be able to anatomise the human body and discover the ends and uses and legitimate treatment of its organs. At all events it is a mistake to treat Christianity as if it were chiefly a system of morals, and to lay the stress of the argument in its favour on its distinct superiority in moral teaching; because though this position be gained we do not thereby command the whole field, and the opponents of Christianity are well aware that there is no point at which they are more likely to succeed in making a serious breach in our defences.

A system of morals carries in itself no moral dynamic, no propelling force, no regenerating power. Neither is morality co-extensive with religion. However we answer the question, Was the teaching of Confucius and Mih Teih essentially different from the teaching of the Gospel? there remain the far more vital questions, Did these teachers enable men to attain the ideal they set before them? and, Did they bring them into a right relation not only to their fellow-men, but to their God? To both questions Confucius himself constantly and dolefully replies in the negative. Yet it is these two questions which are quietly evaded or kept in the background while our attention is called to the comparison of the contents of the Chinese ethical code with the contents of the law of Christ. Here, for example, is perhaps the most graceful and telling attempt to level up all religions to one standard that has been made :

" Children of men ! the unseen Power, whose eye
  For ever doth accompany mankind,
  Hath look'd on no religion scornfully
    That man did ever find.

  Which has not taught weak wills how much they
    can ?
  Which has not fall'n on the dry heart like rain ?
  Which has not cried to sunk, self-weary man,
    Thou must be born again ?

  Children of men ! not that your age excel
  In pride of life the ages of your sires,
  But that you think clear, feel deep, bear fruit
    well,
    The Friend of Man desires."

But if there be a Friend of Man there is one

thing He must more earnestly desire, and that is, the personal recognition and love of the children of men. And it is idle to measure any mere system of morality with the religion of Christ in this respect. It is in this religion we meet God as we meet Him nowhere else, and so receive that link to what is higher than ourselves without which knowledge of our duty to one another always becomes inoperative. To the question, Can morality exist without religion? the history of China gives a broad and unmistakable answer.

But if the grand feature of religion is that it brings a personal element into morality, if Christianity is what it is because of the Person it reveals, if it owes its power to the personal connection established between men and God, if it gives a motive and a strength to us by bringing all our life into fellowship with Him, then the help we derive from our religion will vary precisely with our success in introducing this personal element into our own life. A hearty Confucian is a more respectable man than a nominal Christian, or than a Christian who takes to do with his religion as a system of laws, observances, regulations, and counsels, and who fails to find in it the means of entering into fellowship with God and a love that is stronger and more enlightening than all law. Like many more of his words, these of the great Richard Hooker are worthy of letters of gold: "They that love the religion they profess may have failed in choice, but yet they are sure to reap what benefit the same is able to afford; whereas the best and soundest professed by them that bear it not the like affection yieldeth them retaining it in that sort no benefit."

The second use to be derived from a study of the Chinese moralists is of a kindred nature. I think we should be neglecting our advantage in living so late in the world if we refused to see in the history of China positivism on its trial. Evolution was not scientifically made out by the Chinese, but from a speculative point of view it was accepted. The existence of a personal Creator was not denied; it was merely relegated to the limbo of uncertainties. Man was accepted as the highest known manifestation of the world-soul or productive energies of nature. Worship of ancestors was the sole religion, and duty to men was the only duty. In fact, feature by feature the modern philosophy was represented by the school of Confucius. And so far as I can see the experiment of a morality without any higher religion than filial piety could never be made in more favourable circumstances. In Greece the moralists were not canonised; even the dramatists, influential and didactic as they were, cannot be called authoritative. But the teachings of Confucius have been for two thousand years accepted as canonical, and no boy has been educated without having his mind imbued with these teachings. Philosophy had a chance in China which it is never likely to have in any other country. No population can reasonably be expected to yield itself so passively and so steadily to this species of influence. Nor is it credible that a purer non-Christian system of ethics will ever be devised. Yet what has been the result? Ask any man who has lived in China, read the narratives of the most impartial travellers, and you find that with one voice they denounce the Chinese as among the most immoral of peoples. They do indeed possess virtues, and virtues of a substantial and efficacious kind. They set an example to the world by their filial piety, their industry, their contentment to live at peace with neighbouring nations. It has been urged that they have had virtue enough to preserve them as a prosperous people for four thousand years; and Chinamen who have visited England are as much astonished that we should compare our moral condition with theirs as we are astonished that they should fancy themselves on a level with us in the ordinary virtues. These are points which must be left to other inquirers, and meanwhile we would commend the study of the Chinese to all who desire a practical or experimental answer to some of the questions which are agitating our own society.

VII

CHRISTIANITY AND CIVILISATION

CIVILISATION has for its aim the perfecting of civil society; the discovery and establishment of the happiest possible conditions of social life in this world. All the movements and life of the social organism, all legislation, commerce, war, emigration, administration of justice, exist for the sake of securing further advantages to society and for making life in this world less difficult and oppressive. On all living forms there is impressed a law of growth and improvement; and in accordance with this law society continually strives after a perfect condition in which every man shall have all his rights, and enjoy every aid to self-development and success that society can give him. Now Christianity proposes to accomplish this very thing, to establish the kingdom of God upon earth, or, in other words, to bring all human affairs into the happiest possible condition.

And if Christianity is the great civilising power, it would seem to be the duty of every good citizen to uphold and promote it, as far as in him lies.

In order that we may clearly see the relation which subsists between civilisation and Christianity we must first of all apprehend what civilisation is, and what it is not. There is unfortunately no concrete instance of a perfect civilisation to which we might point. It need scarcely be said that we in this country are not in a perfectly civilised condition. In some respects the ancient Greeks were more civilised than we are. A holiday in Athens was celebrated by magnificent spectacles, by artistically devised choruses and processions, by the public recital of some new work of genius, history or drama; and it was disfigured by no rowdyism. So long as our amusements are so coarse and sensual that the quieter part of the population shrinks from a public holiday; so long as labour remains so much like slavery; so long as hundreds of thousands among us live by vice and crime; so long as there are countless social problems awaiting solution, we cannot suppose ourselves to be perfectly civilised. No doubt when we compare our condition with that of our progenitors five centuries ago, when men lived in mud hovels, when reading and writing were the accomplishments of a profession, when a few powerful nobles kept the entire population in subjection, and often in misery, we may claim to be comparatively civilised. In some outward and material respects, indeed, we may affirm that we are already perfect. In means of communicating, for example, with distant places, the telegraph cannot be surpassed. Improvements in the collection and distribution of intelligence may be introduced, but the maximum of rapidity in transmission has plainly been reached. In the enormous multiplication of power by means of steam, in the permanent acquisitions of knowledge made by science, and in the methods which certify us that these acquisitions are but the introduction to a measureless advance, we enjoy the outward equipment of a very advanced civilisation.

But civilisation itself consists not so much in these material advantages and achievements as in the underlying conditions which have made them possible, and in the refinement and intelligence and charity of which they may become the instruments. The civilisation of a country is to be measured, not by its wealth nor by its skilful adaptations of scientific discoveries to social convenience, but rather by the character of the uses to which these things are put, and the aims and purposes they fulfil.   Are men better educated? are law and order more generally maintained? are the relations we hold to one another and to other states better understood?—these, and such as these, are the questions we must ask if we would learn our stage in civilisation.   The vital refinements, as Emerson justly says, "are the moral and intellectual steps."   The appearance of great moralists and seers and legislators

"are causal facts, which carry forward races to new conditions, and elevate the rule of life.   In the presence of these agencies, it is frivolous to insist on the invention of printing or gunpowder, of steam-power or gaslight, percussion-caps and rubber shoes, which are toys thrown off from that security, freedom, and exhilaration which a healthy morality creates in society.   These arts add a comfort and smoothness to house and street life ; but a purer morality, which kindles genius, civilises civilisation, casts backward all that we held sacred into the profane, as the flame of oil throws a shadow when shined upon by the flame of the Budelight."[1]

And precisely to the same effect says an higher authority than Emerson, Dean Church :

[1] Macmillan's edition, V. 292.

" The degree of civilisation depends a great deal more on whether the citizens are manly, honest, just, public-spirited, generous, able to work together in life, than on whether they are rich, hard-working, or cunning of hand, or subtle of thought, or delicate of taste, or keen searchers into nature and discoverers of its secrets. All these things are sure to belong to civilisation as it advances ; and as it advances it needs them, and can turn them to account more and more. All I say is, that they are not civilisation itself as I understand it." [1]

Statesmen and moralists in modern times have frequently had occasion to point out that mere amelioration of the social condition does not in itself constitute civilisation. Life may be easy and safe, taxation light, labour abundant and remunerative, the sources of health and prosperity open to all ; but if this happy condition do not contribute to the development of what is best in man, there lacks an important element of civilisation. In fact, unless humanity itself be developed, unless human nature itself be helped towards perfection, there is not much to choose between a highly civilised and a barbarous social state. In a state of barbarism, as has often been pointed out, there is much from which we are debarred

<hr>

[1] *The Gifts of Civilisation*, p. 155.

by a highly organised external civilisation. There is

" the pleasure of individual independence ; the pleasure of enjoying oneself with vigour and liberty, amidst the chances of the world and of life ; the delights of activity without labour ; the relish of an adventurous career full of uncertainty and of exciting peril." [1]

But the freedom and ease and excitement of this barbaric condition are sacrificed for the sake of those more important functions which can be performed by the civilised. Men submit to the many limitations which a highly organised civilisation imposes, because they are conscious that a higher mental culture and a more extended influence belong to the members of a state than to the loosely-cohering individuals of a savage tribe. They perceive that the civilised man is a larger, more capable, finer product than the uncivilised. But if the outward material of civilisation do not secure this finer product, then it fails, and is the mere body of civilisation without the living spirit.

In a word, man himself is the important thing in history. We judge all the past movements of

<hr>

[1] Guizot, *Civilisation in Europe*, p. 40

history and of civilisation by the question, What have they done for man? Is the race as a whole distinctly in advance of its former position? Are there even here and there appearances of a promising kind? Do the forces now operating in the world produce a finer type of man than formerly? There is no doubt that in many respects great advances have been made. The rights of the individual are much more considered. The claims of weaker nations to just treatment are at least understood, if not always admitted. Social problems are freely and candidly discussed, and must eventually be wisely determined, even if after foolish and hurtful experiments. But even though every state in the world had the wisest internal organisation, giving to every individual the utmost of advantage, and though it had a perfectly adjusted relation to all other states, the question would still remain, What type of man is thus produced? It is with what is directly and distinctively human that civilisation has to do. And without attempting to determine whether the individual exists for the sake of society, or society for the sake of the individual, we may safely affirm that neither has attained its end until the best possible in human nature has been developed. Now, the best possible in human nature is certainly that which belongs to character. It is not by what is physical, nor by what is mental, but by what is moral, that men touch their highest.

Without morality, then, civilisation is inconceivable. We cannot imagine a high civilisation existing without law, without literature, without art, without scientific knowledge, without institutions; but least of all can we conceive any high civilisation which is not penetrated by moral principles. An absence of morality or the presence of a very imperfect moral ideal, marks with imperfection any state, however richly endowed and equipped it may otherwise be. High and noble as in many respects the civilisation of Athens in the age of Pericles was, it is yet branded as imperfect by the uncondemned immorality of even its most cultured men.

Herbert Spencer has shown that

"the character of the aggregate is determined by the character of the units";[1]

and as a corollary from this principle it may, I think, be affirmed that where the individuals composing a state are immoral, the state itself will be immoral. And if it be true—as without question

____
[1] *Sociology,* p. 48.

it is—that "morality is the nature of things," and therefore an essential element in all permanent success, then it follows that all civilisation must be moral, or is destined to decay. In short, as it is true of the individual that in order to his making the most of himself for this life, he must take into account the life to come; so is it true of society, that in order to a perfect civilisation or order of life for this world, it must be founded on a morality which civilisation itself has no power to create, if it has even the means of preserving and propagating it.

Now here we seem to touch solid ground. There can be no satisfactory or enduring civilisation without morality. And certainly whatever else Christianity may be, it is a religion whose object is to make men moral. True, it may not have been conspicuously successful in accomplishing this object. But this, as Rousseau had the shrewdness and candour to remark, does not prove that it is superfluous, but only that as yet few persons are Christians. And any one who affirms that Christianity did not introduce into the world new moral forces, merely convicts himself of ignorance of history. Granted that the Christian Church has made many mistakes and committed many crimes; granted that she has on particular occasions retarded science and obstructed healthy political movements; yet it is not to be denied that the Christian religion tends to make men moral, and does so with a persuasive and effective force which belongs to no other influence which has ever been brought to bear upon men. The individual is necessary to society; and the morality of the individual is essential to the well-being of society. In the interests of civilisation, therefore, Christianity is indispensable as the only hitherto discovered efficient and universally applicable conservator of the morality of the individual.

If we descend from the "high *priori* road" of argument from generally admitted premisses and follow the surer path of historical research, we shall be guided to the same conclusion—that Christianity is essential to civilisation. History affords us the crucible in which we can analyse our actual civilisation, and ascertain what ingredients have gone to its composition. History can with exactness answer the question: Are we in any measure indebted to Christianity for such civilisation as we have? Should we have made the same or even greater progress, supposing Christianity had never been heard of? Is Christianity a factor of any importance in our social well-being? A recent writer of unquestioned authority in his own field has charged Christianity with destroying two civilisations. Can this charge be sustained? These questions will be answered if we allow history to show us what had been accomplished in civilisation before Christianity appeared in the world, and what impulses Christianity has in point of fact imparted to modern civilisation. And I think this appeal to history will make it clear that in two respects Christianity has been a most important factor in the production of modern European civilisation. It has (1) supplied the fatal defect in ancient civilisation, the defect of morality; and (2) it has assimilated and adapted to the uses of modern society, all that was valuable in ancient civilisation. These two points I will endeavour briefly to establish.

I

When we turn our gaze upon that critical period when Christianity was introduced to the world, the eye is at once attracted by a civilisation, which, if not of the most refined type, yet possessed many qualities which seemed to promise a great future. In Rome there was amassed an immense accumulation of wealth, and of all the raw material of enjoyment, of culture, and of power. Everything which could gratify the taste or contribute to an easy and luxurious life was there in profusion. And yet life in Rome became increasingly hideous and repulsive. The bright cities of the Empire, splendid with buildings which are the envy and despair of modern architecture; their baths and gardens and amphitheatres, the mere ruins of which are the wonder of to-day; their streets crowded with tokens of the wealth and power of these masters of the world; their picturesque and peaceful country seats; their wonderful applications of art and mechanical contrivance to all household conveniences, and their power of saturating their whole life with the achievements and spirit of art; their facilities for rapid and safe communication with remote places, and the accessibility of justice—all this which lends to life under the Empire so much brilliance, and makes it live before us in colours so various and so unfading, was after all but the garnish of a sepulchre, only partially hiding away a loathsome corruption.

It is needless here to describe with any detail the licentiousness and degradation which characterised Rome in the first century. The main features of the picture are sufficiently known, and even those who know little else about that period have been made acquainted with its corruption by the powerful condemnation of it which occurs in St. Paul's Epistle to the Romans. The most decisive and ominous element in the general demoralisation was the shamelessness of the women. Adultery and divorce were so common as to excite no remark. A law had to be passed prohibiting the prostitution of women of rank, who bore the names that were identified with the history of their country. Never surely was a legislative assembly called upon to pass a measure more calculated to bring a blush to the cheek of every member. The dissolute sensuality of the leaders of society betrayed itself in banquets, on which the host would spend his whole patrimony, and which terminated in dances compared to which the most shameless of modern performances are decent and respectable. The natures thus glutted with sensual gratifications, and throwing off the guidance and restraint of natural feeling, craved the sharper stimulant of the spectacle of suffering and blood, and found an unnatural and deadening enjoyment in the mutual slaughter of thousands of captives, or the deadly combats of trained gladiators.

In point of fact the world has never been so ingeniously and exhaustively wicked as in Rome during the first century. A writer whose leanings are certainly not unduly Christian says :

"In no period had brute force more completely triumphed, in none was the thirst for material advantages more intense, in very few was vice more ostentatiously glorified." [1]

This judgment is confirmed by their own contemporary writers. Tacitus finds in the period a subject congenial to his tragic and scathing pen, and concentrates his indignation at the shameless degradation in the epigrammatic but strictly true remark that "Virtue was then a sentence of death."

Juvenal, who had an unrivalled genius for holding up the mirror to wickedness, whose every word was a blister, his every adjective a poisoned arrow transfixing character after character for the contemptuous gaze of all time, yet occasionally throws down his pen in despair and contents himself with general invective :

"Vice," he says, "has now attained its zenith ; nothing is left for future times to discover or to add ; the sons can but repeat the vices of their fathers."

The Emperors themselves were probably the most miserable series of men that were ever

<hr>

[1] Lecky, *History of European Morals*, i. 191.

mocked by the apparatus of happiness. The throne was fatal. One after another of its occupants died by poison or by the dagger. Julius married four times, Augustus thrice, Tiberius twice, Caius thrice, Claudius six times, Nero thrice; yet not one of these was succeeded by his own son. Domitian caused the ends of the corridor where he took exercise to be lined with highly-polished marble, that he might detect any would-be assassin approaching from behind. Claudius was a gourmand, but could not touch any dish that was set before him till a physician had tasted it, and pronounced it free from poison. Caius, with nerves strained by every caprice of self-indulgence, so that his naturally excitable temperament seemed to totter on the verge of delirium, would, night after night, spring from the wild and terrifying dreams that tormented him, and pace the galleries of his palace, shouting for the dawn. Such were the men who represented the highest point touched by the most powerful of ancient civilisations.

Now in this case it cannot be said that there were racial defects which precluded Rome from enjoying the highest type of civilisation. No race could have more promising natural qualities than those which distinguished the primitive citizens of Rome. They were sober, truthful, hardy, chaste, industrious, daring, enterprising, self-reliant, and eminently gifted for colonising and governing. Indeed, for the practical work of this world it would be difficult to imagine a race better equipped. Neither were their circumstances unpropitious: they inherited the civilisation of Greece, and their position as masters of the world gave them opportunity of observing and adopting whatever art or useful institution or custom had been in any place developed. But from each conquered province the intoxicated Roman brought back some novel vice, along with the additional wealth which put the gratification of every desire within his reach. The old Roman honour and virtue, the chastity of their women, the incorruptible manliness of their men were broken down by the rapid increase of wealth, and the absence of any worthy purpose, or high aims in conquest. The absence of any ennobling hope, and of any grand exhibition of the spiritual significance of life, left them a prey to greed and lust, to lowering ambitions and degrading appetites. And as the absence of a popular and high morality debased the character of the Roman civilisation, so it prevented it from becoming progressive and permanent. Among other lessons that may be read in the decline and fall of that great Empire, this is not the least important,—that a nation's continuance depends upon the morality of its citizens. It was not left to a Christian apologist to point this out. Horace was neither prude nor pharisee; he was not easily shocked, nor was it his interest as a courtier to become an alarmist, but in verse that no one could misunderstand or forget, he warned the people that the Empire they so strenuously defended against barbaric foes was being inevitably destroyed by their own licentiousness. And I suppose it will be generally agreed that the ultimate dissolution of the Roman Empire was the result, not of any grave political mistake, nor of any irreparable disaster, or only of such political mistakes and disasters as were occasioned by the tide of immorality, which sapped the manliness of the race and the other true foundations of empire.

It is true one historian ascribes the fall of Rome to the despotism of the emperors, another to the bad economic and moral results of the institution of slavery, a third to the disappearance of the landed or middle class of society; and to dogmatise in connection with so perplexing and complicated a problem would be presumptuous.

But it will scarcely be questioned that Juvenal laid his finger on one true cause of decay when he said that

"luxury, more ruthless than war, had fallen upon the city and avenged a conquered world";

although his words were not fulfilled for some centuries. As the territory of Rome increased, so did its dangers multiply; and the greed that incited to fresh conquests led also to the abuse of the power acquired, and to an incapacity to face the deeper responsibilities of conquest. Had there remained in the Roman the old public spirit that loved country better than sons, and counted it glory to die for Rome; the old reverence for purity that preferred a daughter's death to her dishonour; the old truth which kept faith with an enemy, even when to do so was certain death; the masculine contempt for wealth, in which the breed of conquerors had been nursed, it cannot be doubted that the Empire would have adapted itself to changing conditions, and survived the gravest emergencies.

But what we are here concerned to show is mainly this, that the absence of a high morality, fed by a true and popular religion, to a large extent blighted the civilisation of Rome, and deprived it of a chief refining influence. The manner in which Christianity supplied this lack can be clearly traced. And it may not be out of place to exhibit its work in one or two directions.

1. Perhaps the most striking general result of the introduction of Christianity is the renewal of hope among men. It was as if the race had become conscious of receiving a new lease of life. It was a dying world it entered : full of activity and apparent strength, but full also of despair ; ringing with shouts of victory and of amusement, but with a chilling melancholy cramping the heart. As Salvian said, the Empire "*moritur et ridet,*" it laughs with the death-rattle in its throat. Pessimism of the most despairing kind possessed many of the best and wisest men. Suddenly in the midst of this sated and despairing world appeared a people with the radiance of renewed youth and undoubting hope on its face ; its eye brilliant with new-found truth, its bearing erect from very gladness. The Christians were incomprehensible to the ordinary Roman. Their confidence was judged to be obstinacy ; their hope delusion. But as this same hopeful bearing was found to survive martyrdom and every kind

of ill-usage, it was examined, and the contagion of the Christian confidence in the future was caught by many.

This hopefulness about the race was partly the hereditary bequest of Judaism.   Renan says that

" what more than all else characterised the Jew was his confident belief in a brilliant and happy future for humanity."

But the Christian hopefulness was fed by the fuller knowledge of God communicated by Jesus Christ.   In the life and especially in the cross of Christ, God was revealed to men as a God of unimagined holiness and unquenchable love. When it came to be understood among men that when they looked for their God they were to see Him bearing their sins upon the cross, loving them and hating their sins with an equal intensity, a new hope flooded their minds.   They felt at once that this was a God whose purposes were worth fulfilling, and that they themselves were bound to fulfil them.   Once the idea of God as the Father of all men was grasped, the whole conception of history and of the future of the race was altered.   It was impossible that God's purpose should fail, impossible that His purpose should not include all men, impossible that it should not be beneficent in the highest degree. The mode in which this purpose was to be fulfilled and the date of its consummation were misunderstood. So elate was the Christian heart that at first it anticipated an immediate consummation. But the essential elements of its hope were abiding, and were not mistaken. Men were taught to look at humanity as a whole, and at history as a whole, so that even when the vast and great Roman Empire itself was broken up, and when men bewailed its fall as if the order of nature itself were coming to an end, the Christian knowledge of God as the Father of men and ruler of all events enabled them to believe that still His wise purpose was running on to fulfilment, though on lines that were new and as yet obscure. It was when the profoundest men were exclaiming that human affairs were the sport of the higher powers, and when all men felt as if

> " The pillared firmament were rottenness,
> And Earth's base built on stubble,"

that the calm voice of Christianity restored sane strength to men's hearts by proclaiming, " The Lord reigneth, let the earth rejoice." To any one who observes the Roman Empire as Christianity dawned upon it, it is obvious that men are conscious that a new life has entered the world, and that germinant ideas and principles of abiding influence have lodged in the human mind.

2. The manner in which Christian principle has permeated society and strengthened all civilising influences, counteracting the results of pagan ideas, is very well seen in the gradual extirpation of slavery.

In empires extended and maintained by conquest and force of arms, slaves were of necessity very numerous, and a very broad and marked distinction subsisted between the conquering race or governing class and the captive slaves. In the palmy days of Rome the number of slaves her citizens owned was enormous. Sometimes a wealthy person left at death as many as four thousand. Many citizens possessed a hundred; and he was a poor man who had not ten. On one occasion it was proposed in the Senate that the slave should wear a distinctive dress, but the proposal was at once quashed on the ground that it would be most impolitic to give the slaves so ready a clue to their own immense numbers. But the abundance of slave labour, which seemed so inexhaustible a source of wealth, really turned to the impoverishment of the Roman Empire.

All the ordinary handicrafts, being practised by slaves, were considered discreditable to the free-born. Even in the time of Cicero we find that labour was considered unworthy of a gentleman:

"The gains of all hired workmen whom we pay for manual labour, and not for artistic skill, are ignoble and sordid: for in their case the very wages they receive constitute a sort of obligation to serve as slaves. Also, all retail traders are to be considered mean; for they would never get on unless they lied enough. And all artisans are engaged in vulgar business, for in a workshop there is nothing that befits a gentleman."

The free-born citizen thus became an idler, for his legitimate pursuits of law and arms could not occupy his whole time; and as slaves were also employed in manufacture, it became impossible for free labour to enter into competition. Beyond the city of Rome the results of the employment of slave-labour were equally disastrous. The peasantry or yeomen were gradually exterminated, their lands being absorbed in the huge properties of successful courtiers or administrators, and farmed by gangs of slaves instead of the indigenous peasantry. These slaves were treated as we treat convicts, compelled to work in fetters, and lodged at night in huge and unhealthy prison-houses.

Christianity introduced new ideas, which have at last made themselves felt.   It inherited the Jewish ideas of the dignity of labour, and to this it added its own care for the slave.   The gradual amelioration of the condition of slaves, and their eventual emancipation under Christianity, form a history full of significance.

Had our Lord or His apostles commanded the emancipation of slaves we should have lost one of the most conspicuous and instructive instances of the *manner* in which Christian belief and sentiment do their work in civilisation.   No edicts of emancipation were issued by our Lord, nor even by His Church for many centuries after it had power to do so.   The earliest trace of a command of the Church to put an end to slavery occurs in the ninth century.   They are the words of St. Theodore of Stude :

" Thou shalt possess no slave, neither for domestic service, nor for the work of the fields ; for man is made in the image of God." [1]

At first there was no thought of emancipation in the Church.   Individuals here and there perceived the incongruity of retaining in a servile condition men who were their brothers in Christ,

[1] Brace, p. 59.

and often their superiors in character and Christian conduct. And sometimes where a slave belonged to a household in which he was subjected to cruel persecution, or in which it was well-nigh impossible he could live a Christian life, he might be ransomed by the Church. But in general the Christian master retained his slaves, and the Christian slave was exhorted to be content with his condition. Indeed, one canon of the Church (council of Gangra) explicitly enacts :

"If any one, under the pretence of piety, advises a slave to leave his master and run away from his service, and not to serve his master with goodwill and full respect, let him be anathema."

What the Christian teachers of the early centuries press upon their hearers is not the duty of emancipating, but of instructing and caring for their slaves. Says Augustine, in an address to slaves :

"Christ did not make slaves freemen and masters, but He made bad slaves good slaves."

Indeed, the Church herself continued to hold slaves as Church property until the middle ages. But from the first, although there was no thought of emancipation, which was too large and revolutionary an idea to be soon conceived, the condition of the slave was improved. The Christian master was positively forbidden to ill-use his slave: if a woman even accidentally caused the death of her slave by punishment she was excluded from communion for five years. The Gospel was preached as cordially to the slave as to the freeborn : the Church was as open to him. He sat down at the table of communion with his master, and instances are not wanting in which slaves became bishops in the Church. And as early as 321 A.D., the manumission of slaves from religious motives is recognised as common enough to require regulation, and accordingly Constantine encourages it in the enactment :

" He who under a religious feeling has given a just liberty to his slaves in the bosom of the Christian Church will be thought to have made a gift of a right similar to Roman citizenship." [1]

In accordance with the growing humanity and the erring piety of the times, the emancipation of slaves came to be looked upon as a good deed which could not fail to redound to a man's credit in this world, and to his advantage in the world

[1] Brace, p. 54.

to come. The monk in abjuring all his possessions necessarily parted with his slaves and frequently gave them their freedom. Those who to
a more limited extent abandoned the luxuries of
a merely worldly life often parted with some of
their numerous slaves, and these also were commonly emancipated.

Slowly indeed, very slowly, but surely, all
these influences worked in Christendom. Only
in our own day has the last blow been given to
an institution which has probably inflicted more
suffering than either pestilence or war—which
has indeed been a perennial fountain of degradation, despair, and vice, wherever it has existed.
As mercy is twice blessed, blessing him that
gives, as well as him that receives; so inhumanity
in the form of slavery has been as great a curse
to the slave-owner as to the slave. The horrors
of a slave-raid as now accomplished in Africa, the
physical miseries, the unparalleled cruelties, the
ruthless slaughter of the incapable, and the worse
fate of the surviving, all these horrors that make
the heart sink in helpless indignation, are outdone
by the extinction of human feeling, the excitement of the vilest passions, the slow demoralisation of the slave-owning class. This blackest of
stains Christendom has at length washed off her-

self, and there is the clearest evidence that the final extinction of slavery among Christian peoples was due, not to profounder economic views, nor to any natural instincts of humanity, but to the principles of Christianity. Garrison in the early stage of the final conflict in America said :

"Emancipation must be the work of Christianity and the Church. *They* must achieve the elevation of the blacks, and place them on the equality of the Gospels."

And Clarkson, when fighting the same battle in our own country, said :

"If we oppress the stranger as I have shown, and if by a knowledge of his heart we find he is a person of the same passions and feelings as ourselves, we are certainly breaking by the prosecution of the slave-trade that fundamental rule of Christianity which says we shall not do that unto another which we wish should not be done unto ourselves."

Here then is a fact in the history of civilisation of a large and easily appreciable kind. It was impossible that the world should be civilised while one half of it lay under disabilities so crushing, and in a degradation so frightful. Indeed it was impossible that those who were exempt from these disabilities should be civilised, so long as their inhumanity or ignorance of human rights suffered them to hold their fellow-men in such a bondage. Yet no institution seemed so firmly established as slavery. To many most discerning men it seemed an ordinance of nature. It was a universal custom. It appealed to the self-interest of men. But by the slow leavening of Christian sentiment, and by the vigorous assertion of Christian principle, society has at length thrown off this incubus, and in the very act of doing so has made a really measureless stride in civilisation.

II

But besides introducing into the ancient civilisation principles which have eventually eliminated some of its most glaring evils, Christianity has also preserved to the modern world, if not all that was valuable, certainly the best elements in ancient civilisation. I am far from meaning to claim for Christianity the credit of being the sole agent in producing all those beneficial results which are compendiously known as modern civilisation. Much, no doubt, is due to the experiments made in civilisation by races whose history was closed before Christianity appeared. Christ came "in the fulness of time" to a world prepared by the energies and fortunes of various nations. Much also is due to the natural tendency in the race to progress. Doubtless "the thoughts of men are widened by the process of the suns." The collision of mind with mind; the constant call made upon human invention to meet new emergencies, and to take advantage of accidental discoveries; the introduction of fresh races, with their characteristic ideas, upon the field of universal history; these and other natural causes tend to produce a progressive civilisation. But the claim I am now urging is, that whatever the ancient world produced of a worthy kind, has been handed down to us by the agency of Christianity.

When Shelley said,

"We are all Greeks, our laws, our literature, our religion, our art, have their roots in Greece,"

he spoke somewhat at random. But had he said that to Greece we are largely indebted in art and literature, and to Rome in law, he would have uttered unquestioned truth. But it is the Church of Christ which, though it did not create, has conserved these great heritages to us of modern times. Rough as the transition from the ancient to the modern world was, and apparently haphazard as was the partition of advantages between

the old Latin and young Northern races, it would
have been attended with far more disastrous results had not Christianity smoothed the transition, and moderated the disturbance. It was the
Church which alone maintained its historic con-
tinuity in those wild centuries, when every
nationality was altered, when immemorial bound-
aries were obliterated, and ancient tribes driven
from their ancestral homes, when all that was
most stable in civil society seemed tottering to
its fall, and when life and property were in such
hazard that men had no leisure to think of literature or of art. Only within the Church did men
find security and peace ; the Church alone retained the respect of men, and enabled them to
hope that something would survive the universal
shaking of everything that was old.

That the Church preserved to us the literature
of the ancient world is not disputed. And with
the literature the Church has preserved the knowledge of all that was worth celebrating in literature, the history, the thought, the life of antiquity,
and has thus kept the modern world in sympathy
with all that was most noble and most precious
in pre-Christian times. And this service it has
rendered, not by the mere accident that monastic
libraries were the only safe places in which ancient

MSS. could be preserved; but by the deliberate conclusion of the Church, that the writings of the heathen should be preserved. No doubt there was at all times a party in the Church which condemned pagan learning, and adopted the watchword of Tertullian:

"What is there in common between Athens and Jerusalem; between the Academy and the Church; between heretics and Christians?"

Even Jerome, who alleviated the rigour of his monkish fasts by reading Plautus or Ovid, had some twinges of conscience for this dalliance with pagan literature. Falling dangerously ill one Lent, he dreamt that he stood before Christ's throne. "Who art thou?" said the Judge. "I am a Christian," answered Jerome. "No," replied Christ, "not a Christian, but a Ciceronian." But notwithstanding his dream, and the flagellation he received from the angels, he continued to carry with him on his journeys Cicero or Plato, and to teach to the Christian children in his schools the lyric and comic poetry which charmed himself. His contemporary, Augustine, defended the Christian use of the genius of heathendom on the ground that the Israelites had been commanded to spoil the Egyptians. In fact the common attitude of the Church towards the literature of antiquity is best represented by the monk who burst into tears at the tomb of Virgil, or by the Christian poet Dante choosing the same great bard as his guide in the unseen world.

There would seem to be in some quarters an impression that the introduction of Christianity has not proved favourable to the development of Art, and that it cannot claim to have preserved to modern times this conspicuous element of ancient civilisation.   Closer scrutiny of the actual history of Art removes this impression.   It is true that the sense of sin which Christianity aroused, as well as the perception of the moral discord between the world and God which it quickened, made Hellenism for ever impossible.   No longer could it be believed that to be moral one need only be natural.   The taint in human nature as it actually appears on earth, its need of regeneration, could not be overlooked.   It was recognised that the sense of harmony or beauty, to which the Greek had trusted as his guide in morals as in Art, was, like everything else in man, dulled by carnal and selfish desires.   And no doubt the tendency for a time was to underrate the importance of physical culture, and to condemn whatever glorified the mere outward form and appearance. In point of fact, Art had become in the first century to a very large extent the minister of idolatry and of luxury ; and to any one who is familiar with the public and private life of the time, it can seem neither surprising nor deplorable that there should have been a reaction against it. There are certain manifestations of Art, as of human nature, to which Christianity, in common with every healthy human sentiment, must always be opposed. They are the worst freinds of Art who degrade it, by making it the pander to appetites of which healthy natures are ashamed. In order that Art might take its true place as the interpreter of beauty to men, it was necessary that it should not be suffered to allure men, through loveliness of form and colour, to what was morally hideous. As Canon Westcott truly remarks :

" A formal severance from the past was the prelude to the new birth of Christian art." [1]

This is recognised by those who have studied Art profoundly, and without any bias in favour of Christianity. Mr. Symonds says :

" Together with the separation of the flesh and spirit wrought by Christianity, came the abhorrence of

---

[1] *Epistles of St. John*, p. 325.

beauty as a snare, the sense that carnal affections were tainted with sin, the unwilling toleration of sexual love as a necessity, the idealisation of celibacy and solitude. At the same time humanity acquired new faculties and wider sensibilities. A profounder and more vital feeling of the mysteries of the universe arose. Our life on earth was seen to be a thing by no means rounded in itself and perfect, but only one term of an infinite and unknown series. It was henceforward impossible to translate the world into the language of purely æsthetic form. The striving of the spirit marks the transition of the ancient to the modern world."[1]

Any fanatical contempt for Art, or hostility to it, which may have been displayed by Christians in the first fervour of the new and exciting ideas, must be set down as mere reaction against what was vicious in the uses Art had served. The spirit in which Epiphanius tore the picture of Christ he found in a church, and ordered the veil on which it was wrought to be used for a pauper's shroud, was not the spirit of Christianity, nor was it the spirit which long prevailed among Christians. Christian ideas and the training to which Christian principles subject men, have immensely deepened human nature, and have imparted to human experience a variety and a

---

[1] *The Greek Poets.* First Series, p. 434.

colour unknown before.   The expansion of horizon which results from the hope of immortality, the quickening of new aspirations, the suggestion of endless possibilities, the awakening of slumbering desires, the revealing of unthought-of connections with our fellow-men and with the world, all that adds significance and abiding interest to life is brought with Christianity, and inspires Art with new conceptions.   It is the function of the artist to show us beauty we have overlooked, either because it has been hidden among unlovely things, or because it has been isolated.   The artist brings out its beauty by setting it in a new relation, which draws our attention to what before we have missed.

" For, don't you mark, we're made so that we love
    First when we see them painted, things we have
        passed
    Perhaps an hundred times, nor cared to see ;
    And so they are better, painted—better to us,
    Which is the same thing.   Art was given for that ;
    God uses us to help each other so,
    Lending our minds out."
                        BROWNING, *Fra Lippo Lippi.*

But the artist who merely sees a beauty in form or colour, where other men pass it by, the poet who merely recognises and can reproduce an interesting and dramatic situation in human life, has the eye and the brain of the artist, but may yet lack the only legitimate aim of all true art. Art may not amuse or delight at the expense of what is highest in man. Through its power to appeal to man's instinct for beauty, it must bring an elevating and purifying joy. Life as it actually is, it must show men,—yes, if it can maintain the moral proportions of things, and by its representations lead men to loathe what is loathsome, and admire only what is admirable. Otherwise it becomes a curse, and not a blessing to man; a demoralising, not a civilising influence. It is a chief agent in civilisation when it trains men to admire and love, to pity and to grieve, to pardon and to condemn, where these feelings are appropriate. And in this grand function it receives help of the most valuable kind from a religion which teaches that

"this world's no blot for us, nor blank; it means intensely, and means good";[1]

which tells us that between God and man there is a real affinity, and which shows us how far-reaching in result are all our words and actions. The immensely increased richness and variety of

[1] Browning's *Fra Lippo Lippi.*

music, painting, and poetry in modern times will be ascribed, at least in considerable measure, to the influence of the Christian religion, by those who patiently investigate the growth of the human mind.

Even more essential to civilisation than Literature or Art, is Law. Where there is no Law civilisation is impossible.   But

" where you have in a society a strong and lasting tendency to bring public and private affairs under the control of fixed general rules, to which individual wills are expected and are trained to submit ; where these rules are found to be grounded, instinctively perhaps at first, methodically afterwards, on definite principles of right, fitness, and sound reason ; where a people's habitual impulse and natural disposition is to believe in laws and to trust them, and it is accepted as the part of common sense, duty, and honour to obey them ; where these characteristics of respect for law as an authority, of resort to it as an expedient and remedy, are found to follow the progress of a great national history even from its beginnings, it cannot be denied that there you have an essential feature of high civilisation.   They of whom this may be said have seen truly, in one most important point, how to order human life. And law in that sense in which we know it, and are living under it, in its strength, in its majesty, in its stability, in its practical, business-like character, may., I suppose, be said to have been born at Rome." [1]

---

[1] Dean Church's *Gifts of Civilisation*, p. 163.

This the early Christians were forward to admit. They did not hesitate to ascribe the Roman legislation to a Divine source.

" *Leges Romanorum divinitus per ora principum emanarunt,*" said Augustine.[1]

But though born in Rome, Law certainly owes to Christianity a great part of its development. In its early days it reflected too plainly the stern and fierce features of the Roman character. The son was the property of the father, and had no rights of his own. The wife was the bought possession of her husband; and the slave was the living tool, to be thrown aside when worn out. The amelioration of this extreme harshness is due, not to Christianity alone, but in the first place to Stoicism. The Stoic philosophy has the distinction among philosophies of exercising a direct, and extensive, and beneficial influence upon society. Contemporaneously with Christianity this great and inspiring philosophy made itself felt in Rome, and through the saddest years of the Empire nursed many of the best and greatest of her citizens. But it was through the legislation of Rome that Stoicism exercised

---

[1] The laws of the Romans came from God through the lips of their rulers.

its most powerful influence. The leading Roman jurists of the early centuries were Stoics, and in becoming jurists they did not cease to be philosophers. There were, no doubt, tendencies in Stoicism which somewhat obstructed the free operation of its philanthropic principles; but if Stoicism did not make men pitiful, it made them sane and just. It elevated what was spiritual in man, and under its light the brutal cruelty of the Roman character was ashamed of itself, and even the Roman insolence which despised the slave and the foreigner was curbed.

"As far as natural law is concerned, all men are equal."

"By natural law, all men are born free."

Such maxims fell naturally from the lips of Stoic jurists, and a marked amelioration of oppressed conditions set in under this new regime. The son, the slave, the wife, all classes of society began to feel the breath of a new and happier era.

The improvement begun by Stoicism was carried on by Christianity. Even before Christian principles were allowed directly to influence legislation, the leaven of Christianity had found its way into many social relations. The Church

had from the first been recognised as a great
institution for teaching and enforcing a pure
morality. The ancient religions concerned themselves little with morals : the priesthood was
not a preaching institution, and took no over-
sight of conduct, save in matters ceremonial.
It was a new thing in the world to see a great
religion devoting itself to the task of elevating
the morals of its adherents. Christians were not
admitted to the Communion of the Church if
they were known to be guilty of certain sins, of
which the civil law took no cognisance. A new
system of law arose within the Church, as rigor-
ously administered as the law of the Empire, and
finding offences where the imperial law found
none. This system of law regulating the life of
the Christian population brought clearly before
the minds of men the intention of Christianity,
and furnished all men with an ideal of character
and conduct which was new to them. In this
code every transgression had its penalty attached;
and while the door of the Church was held open
to the penitent, some adequate representation was
at the same time given of the high requirements
of the Divine holiness. Ecclesiastical law thus
became the pioneer of civil law. It educated the
public sentiment, and indicated the direction in

which civil law should be revised and amended. It was the rising tide which lifted the whole body of Roman law to a higher level.

This brief sketch is sufficient to indicate the manner in which Christianity preserved the best elements of the old civilisation. It may fairly claim, not only to have directly contributed the most important element of civilisation, the highest moral ideal—the example of Christ; a sufficient motive—the sacrifice of the cross—to strive towards it; and a sufficient power to realise it—the power of the Holy Spirit; but also to have indirectly influenced for good everything for which society exists, and the whole of human life. It has stimulated thought, and opened new fields for its exercise; it has purified and deepened art, and by giving to love a new meaning and scope, has entirely altered literature, and given it a range of human interest it never before possessed. It has improved and extended education; it has dignified labour, and thus enormously stimulated mechanical invention. It has greatly lessened the misery of human life, introducing justice and charity on a large scale; and it is now labouring heartily and steadily at remaining grievances, endeavouring to bridge the chasm between rich and poor, to sort the balance between labour and capital, to adjust satisfactorily the relation of man to man, and of nation to nation; to minimise disease and all individual disabilities, and to supplant war by arbitration. In nothing that is essential to a perfect civilisation can a Christian be uninterested, and from none dare he withhold a helping hand, because he believes that Christ has come for this purpose, to establish His kingdom on earth.

Guizot, in his most instructive and lucid analysis of European civilisation, makes the pregnant remark that the great distinction between ancient and modern civilisations is that the ancient were simple, while the modern are complex: in other words, that while each ancient civilisation depended on one social power, the modern depend upon several. The Egyptian civilisation, *e.g.*, was theocratic, or religious, depending on the priesthood; the Assyrian was military, depending on the army; the Tyrian was commercial. There are in society these distinct sources of power and of well-being — religion, military strength, education, commerce. Each of these has something to contribute to the civilisation and well-being of the State. But if one of these powers usurps exclusive rule and becomes autocratic, the State will be rapidly developed in the direction nourished by that power, but it will be atrophied in other departments, and must either die or become stationary and barren. In China, for example, the State has been for two thousand years dominated by the educated class. Admission to offices of State and to all posts under government is regulated by competitive literary examinations. This system has its obvious advantages; but the result of its exclusive influence is that China has been comparatively stagnant for all these centuries. In Europe this bar to progress has not existed. Its civilisation is many-sided. It has derived much from Rome, much from the barbarians, much from Christianity.

It might also, I think, be shown that the solidarity of European civilisation is largely the result of Christianity. The gifts and discoveries and customs of one nation more readily become the property of all those in other parts of the world. What is the unifying element? It is not race. Races as antagonistic as Celt and Saxon are combined in this unity. It is not language. What languages could be more diverse than Spanish and Hungarian? But the Christian element and ideas in literature make the literature of Europe interesting to all Europeans, and tend to unify the culture of the various races. The same radical ideas influence their legislation, and prepare one nation to understand and to appreciate the political and social conceptions of the rest.

No doubt the student of history is often perplexed to find that Christianity has often done so much less than might have been expected. He will be grieved to read in the unalterable facts of history a grave indictment against the Church. He will see that while undoubtedly softening the barbaric ferocity of the northern races, she has herself been guilty of most unpardonable cruelties: that while resisting the tyrannical oppression of kings and nobles, she has often kept the people in a still more degrading bondage; that through fear of a rival authority she has retarded science and fostered superstition; and that in several respects, which her enemies have never been slow to proclaim, she has in great measure forfeited her claim to be for the healing of the nations. It is incontestable that the Church of Christ might have done much more and much better than she has done. But we contend that the candid reader of her history, if he find much to blame, will also own that she has done for civilisation what no other known power could have done, and certainly what no other power has done.

When the circumstances are considered in which Christianity had to maintain itself, the work it had to do, and the material it had to work with ; when it is considered that Christianity took possession of rude tribes, barbarous in their manners and ideas, living for plunder, war, and the chase, without settled abodes, without education, with barely the rudiments of social order ; when it is considered that Christianity had to engraft its own principles of justice and humanity on national usages and laws which in many particulars repudiated these principles ; when it is considered that out of the chaos and night of the centuries between the fifth and the twelfth, modern Europe has by the help of Christianity emerged, one is disposed to wonder not at the meagreness, but at the grandeur of the results accomplished.   And where the Church did fail, she failed not by being Christian over-much, but by failing to be Christian.   Even now the Church is only slowly apprehending what the religion of Christ really is, and we can hardly wonder that ten centuries ago it was not per-fectly understood.

One or two considerations may be urged which

may serve to mitigate our soreness that Christianity has not, as a healer of society, accomplished all that might be expected.   In the first place, it must always be borne in mind that Christianity is not like civil law which can be enforced by authority.   It could not work magically, irrespective of the laws which govern moral growth.   It could not produce its effects save through the intervention of human understanding and human concurrence.   It had no power to constrain the will of man; but it had to wait till men should learn the genius and spirit of it, and till they should willingly yield themselves to its influence.   Its supreme influence is seen only in those who are personally born again.   The full power of Christianity for the regeneration of society could only be seen if all individuals were regenerate.   Such results are not quickly obtained.   The world is only very slowly convinced of civil truths; how can we wonder it is slow to believe what is spiritual?   If you tell men of earthly things and they believe you not, how shall they believe if you tell them of heavenly things?

Besides, it is a commonplace of science and of history that great ends are slowly achieved. Geology demonstrates that with God a thousand years are as one day.   History reads us the same lesson. Slowly and patiently God advances towards His ends. And the more we understand God's ways, the less shall we resent that society is not regenerated in a day, nor all the world civilised in one generation.

In conclusion, we may appropriately ask, what is the significance of the fact that outside of Christendom there is no high or progressive civilisation? The old civilisations, magnificent as in some respects they certainly were, carried in themselves the seeds of decay. The very rapacity and lust of conquest and of splendour, which gave them brilliance, indicated the unchastened vigour of youth, and foretold premature, rapid, and irremediable decay. The sudden blaze of civilisation which accompanied the early successes of the Mohammedan arms was the result of an intense but one-sided conviction; and being one-sided it remains for ever restricted, it cannot educate the whole man, cannot fit him for the whole of life, cannot give him growth beyond a certain point. Mohammedanism can turn a naked African into an armed, drilled, and efficient soldier; it can educate and satisfy man's capacity for an ornate and luxurious life; it can hold men together in common enterprises and inspire them to endure great hardships, but it has yet to learn two at least of the radical elements of civilised life, respect for woman and for liberty. Only in Christian countries have men steadily aimed at giving their rights to the weak, to women and slaves. Only in Christian countries has the natural equality of all men been taken seriously, and been allowed practically to influence legislation and social arrangements. Only in Christian countries can you trace a ceaseless striving and steady advance towards that happy condition in which there shall be "neither male nor female, bond nor free," so far as the rights and possibilities of human life are concerned.[1]

This limitation of the highest forms of civilisation to Christian countries is sometimes explained by racial differences. Mohammedans keep women and slaves in bondage because they are Orientals. Freedom is in the blood of the Western races, and they cannot either be slaves or hold slaves. Now it is not to be denied that racial distinctions have most substantial results in civilisation. Nor is it to be denied that the Germanic races before they were brought into contact with Christianity had an exceptional reverence for women and an exceptional regard for independence and liberty. At the same time it must remain doubtful to any

[1] See Brace, p. 291.

one who compares the primitive German races with the primitive Romans, whether there was any appreciable difference between them. And all that I would claim for Christianity in this particular is that it cherished the natural gifts of these races, and saved them from being degraded and destroyed as those of the Romans were. And it is incontestable that the historian can lay his finger here and there upon legislation in favour of the slave expressly dictated by Christian feeling and upon ameliorations of the condition of woman which arose directly out of Christian sentiment. The facts are so: and it is idle to say that if Christianity had not emancipated oppressed classes, racial instincts would have done so. We must abide by history; and history tells us that neither racial instincts alone, nor Christianity alone, effected the great work of civilising Europe; but the two working together in that close combination which defies analysis and which was intended by God, the Author of both.

The conclusion, then, to which the mere historical inquirer is inevitably led, would seem to be that history discloses no power which has been so efficient in civilisation as Christianity. That no stimulus to moral growth and individual improvement is comparable to that which flows from the person and cross of Christ will be granted by all who have experienced it. But the inquiry now conducted shows in addition that the same vital forces which avail for the regeneration of the individual, avail also, though in methods less direct, for the regeneration of society ; and that no other forces do supply a permanent and sufficient elevating power. Other forces, no doubt, have their place and their results, but whether we consider the operation of these forces in ancient civilisations or in modern races outside of Christendom, we are equally compelled to recognise that they lack some essential factors, which only Christianity supplies. From Christianity we have received what we justly prize as the very flower of civilisation, and in Christianity have we the guarantee for all noble endeavour in the future, for all sympathetic consideration of actual human conditions, and for all the zeal, self-sacrifice, and labour that may be required for their improvement.

VIII

ON PREACHING [1]

I CANNOT enter upon my subject without most sincerely congratulating you upon your desire to learn something of that art which you are to spend your life in practising. In my college days the prevalent ambition was to be foremost in study; and a number of thoroughly good students were formed. But along with this laudable ambition there existed something verging on contempt of the popular preacher. We respected a man who had a great deal in him; but if he was able to bring it out, and had not only much that was worth saying, but could say it in a worthy manner, and so that people were compelled to listen and believe, we regarded him with some measure of suspicion. The consequence is too obvious to be overlooked by the

---

[1] An address delivered to the students of the Free Church College, Glasgow, 1880.

blindest adherent of our Church. We possess an unduly large proportion of small congregations. There is a greater waste of the raw material of good preaching among ourselves than, I suppose, among any other body of Christians. By dint of a curriculum whose chief fault is that it is too ambitious, and by the help of a staff of professors who would contrive to use the most opaque and unintelligent curriculum as a medium of light, we succeed in turning out a large proportion of educated theologians. But they are trained to be anything rather than public speakers. The training is only partly professional. Our licentiates are like graduates in medicine who have never seen a patient nor heard a clinical lecture ; or like licentiates in law who have never sat at an office desk nor drawn up a deed. We produce athletes instead of skilled mechanics. Our young ministers are full of unavailable resources, and are as helpless in presence of a congregation as a historian in presence of an invading army. Hence our small proportion of success. Partly, no doubt, this is due to the musical and liturgical attractions studiously provided by the Churches which are wise in their generation, while culpably neglected by ourselves ; but it is due even more to the fact that in other Churches a larger proportion of ministers have acquired the art of public speaking. If some of them have little to say, they can yet say it with a grace.

I congratulate you, then, on your wish to learn how to preach ; and I fancy you have asked *me* to come and give you some rough notes on the subject, on the principle that it is generally the man who cannot himself do the thing who can best say how it ought to be done—that is, on the converse of Matthew Arnold's fundamental rule that "the critic should abstain from practice." At all events, I am very glad to be here, and sincerely thank you for your invitation.

There are two preliminary observations which, although you have all made them for yourselves, it may be as well to repeat, that we may be sure we know exactly where we are. 1st. The first is, that it is the *man* who preaches. Certainly in the long run it is the man that tells rather than the sermon. The sermon is but the medium through which the personality of the preacher communicates itself to the audience. So that we ought not too readily to despise people for praising preaching they do not understand, nor for being moved by what is very little more than bodily exercise, because it is in the subtlest ways that communication of vital force is made. Faith is much more a matter of contagion than we are sometimes disposed to admit, and where there is strong religious vitality it will find its way through almost any medium. Hence the initial, grand difficulty of preaching. It is not an art that can be acquired, so that at last you can write sermons mechanically; on the contrary, the whole man must be in good order before you can effectively preach. What Milton says of the poet is still truer of the preacher: "I was confirmed in this opinion, that he who would not be frustrated of his hope to write well hereafter in laudable things ought himself to be a true poem . . . not presuming to sing high praises of heroic men or famous cities, unless he have in himself the experience and practice of all that is praise-worthy." And as he elsewhere says: "This is a work not to be raised from the heat of youth or the vapours of wine, like that which flows at waste from the pen of some vulgar amourist or the trencher fury of some rhyming parasite: nor to be obtained by the invocation of dame *Memory* and her siren daughters, but by devout prayer to that Eternal Spirit that can enrich with all utter-ance and knowledge, and sends out His seraphim with the hallowed fire of His altar to touch and purify the lips of whom He pleases. To this must

be added industrious and select reading, steady observation, and insight into all seemly and generous
acts and affairs." Do not suppose that in pressing
this point I am seeking to make you good men
under pretence of making you good preachers.
Not at all. It is solely in the interest of good
preaching I speak, and because I am deeply persuaded that the *initial* hindrance to effective
preaching is the lack of strong religious convictions and a personality penetrated with religious feeling. Let me add that the absence of
genial human nature is often as great a hindrance.
If you have no interest in men and women, if
you like books better than life, ancient history
better than what is going on to-day, you may
become extremely useful, but scarcely as preachers.
He is most likely to succeed as a preacher to whom
nothing is more interesting than human character,
and who has chosen his profession not because it
commits him to a life of quiet study among books,
but because it promises to him much contact with
men and influence upon them.

2d. It is obvious to remark that no rules will
avail to make men preach well; that every man
by practice, and reflection on his own practice of
the art, will arrive at the method which is best
for him. The sooner this practice begins the

better, so long as it does not interfere with your
study; and the more uneducated and in a state
of nature your audience is, the better. My first
experience of preaching was in a model lodging-
house, to an audience of labourers, with a thief
here and there by way of seasoning, all in their
shirt-sleeves, and seated round a deal table in a
room that opened off the kitchen of the establishment. The door between the rooms was always
open, and I believe I had a better chance there
of learning to preach than ever I have had since;
for I felt myself pitted against the alluring smell
of cookery and the frizzling of bacon, and whenever I became uninteresting I was made distinctly
aware of the fact by the increase of conversation
in the kitchen.

But though practice alone will teach you how
you can best utilise your own gifts, this knowledge is often obtained by a most humiliating
experience. The first years of a ministry are
often just a scramble from one mistake to
another; and if one who has been through the
bog can shout loud enough to be heard by those
who have yet to pass it, he may show them where
the softest bits of the ground are, and warn them
where *not* to go. And I understand this is very
much what you wish me to do—not to descant

on the higher qualities of the preacher, nor to give you a theory, but to lay before you one or two practical hints which experience has shown me to be serviceable.

What I have to say I will arrange under the three heads of Substance, Form, and Delivery.

1st. As regards Substance. Success in preaching very much depends upon a judicious choice of subjects. If you take up a volume of popular sermons you see that the titles indicate subjects about which people will naturally wish to hear. "The Moral Consequences of Single Sins," "Unreal Words," "Obedience without Love," "Religious Conversation"—these are subjects on which you would willingly listen for half an hour to the talk of a sensible man. There are subjects which have a never-failing interest to all classes and kinds of men, and these are the subjects which are closely connected with human character and human life. Unless you speak to men of the actual circumstances and objects with which they have to do, they at once perceive you are but vapouring, maundering unverifiable platitudes, and it does not concern them to listen. The Bible furnishes large material and suggestion for character-preaching, and our Scotch method of lecturing enables us to touch upon delicate matters of personal and home life which we could never have the audacity to select for treatment, however welcome they are when they come in ordinary course. Lecturing has this other unspeakable advantage for an uninventive and irresolute man, that it saves him spending many hours weekly in the endeavour to find a suitable subject—an endeavour sometimes vain, for I have known one of the wisest, fullest, and ripest of men to burn three almost finished sermons in one week.

It is chiefly in two directions that preachers are apt to go astray in choosing their subject. They choose what is too abstruse or what is of too limited application to their audience. A young preacher is under strong temptation to treat his audience to speculations on points they have never been in sight of. To him it is natural to take up a subject with which study has made him familiar, and to start with his investigation at the point where others have been brought to a stand, and so to launch his hearers into a wholly unintelligible and uninteresting region. Or he is tempted to avoid the commonplaces of preaching—the Atonement, the love of Christ, reasons for accepting God's offer of salvation, or such universally applicable themes, and to choose minute points or fine threads of Christian experience, which are off the beat of almost every mind in his audience. I have known and now know. preachers of admirable parts who have failed to get churches from one or other of these mistakes —from the choice of subjects either quite remote from the thought of common people and unintelligible to them, or so particular as to interest only a few. And to myself it has always seemed to be the most difficult part of the whole work of preaching to discover themes which are at once capable of carrying some considerable weight of Christian truth and likely to interest people.

The method I long ago adopted to secure, as far as possible, a constant supply of such subjects, is to keep a register of suitable and unworn texts. In reading the Bible, a few words will sometimes leap out from the context and take possession of your mind as the final representation of some truth. Whenever this occurs, follow the dictate of nature, and mark a large T on the margin of your working Bible, or transfer the words at once to a note-book kept for the purpose. Unless your memory is exceptionally strong, do not trust it. After twenty the memory of nine men in ten is almost worthless for many purposes. If the books in your college library had been simply thrown into the room one on the top of the other as they were bought, it would represent the state of that important faculty on which we have to depend for so much of the work of life. It is only those who have taken time, and been at pains to carry each acquisition to its right shelf, that can at a moment's notice lay their hand on what they require. And this is given to few. For the most part, knowledge is tumbled in upon us, and the labour of assorting it is too great to be undertaken, and so it lies in an utterly useless heap. Do not scorn, then, to keep a pen-and-ink memory, and set down at once the texts that occur to you and the subject they preach to you, in the words coined by the first impression. If you allot to each suggestive text the two pages of a note-book as it opens, and if you add from time to time what your reading or observation contributes to the elucidation or amplification or illustration of the subject, you will sometimes find, to your great joy, a sermon almost ready-made. I have kept such a book for years, and have found it one of the most tangible and appreciable helps to preaching. I find in it such notes as these : "Num. xii. 14, 'The Lord said unto Moses, If her father had but spit in her face should she not be ashamed seven days ?'"—obviously, *the* text for a sermon on the comparative shame we feel on receiving tokens of God's displeasure and expressions of men's displeasure. Again, as a text from which to preach on the influence which other men's judgment has on our conduct, or more generally "on the motives of human conduct," I find this text marked: "Exod. ii. 12, 'He looked this way and that way, and *when he saw that there was no man* he slew the Egyptian.'" Again, for a sermon on the hindrances which prevent prayer from being answered, I find that text in Daniel x. 12, marked: "Fear not, Daniel, for from the first day that thou didst set thine heart to understand and to chasten thyself before thy God, thy words were heard, and I am come for thy words." The very finding of such a text goes far to precipitate you into a sermon.

Sometimes the best sermons you are capable of making are, however, not suggested by a text, but by some defect in religious life that meets you wherever you go among your people, or by some deep-cut experience in your own history. These are the sermons that tell. There is always some similarly wounded soul that recognises that you are touching the critical point in its experience, and that eagerly hails your explication of its difficulty. Sometimes it is not easy to find a text for such sermons. You will occasionally

finish the writing of such a sermon before it
occurs to you that in order to satisfy popular
expectation a text is needed. If you know your
Bible as Newman knows his, you will always get
some suitable words, but not without careful
search. Even for prominent points in Christian
teaching, you will sometimes be at a loss to find
the suitable motto—and I do not know that it
matters much, so long as your subject is clearly
enounced and really runs on the lines of Christian
teaching or Christian experience.

For your selection of preaching material you
must be guided mainly by the needs of your own
spiritual life. You will always command attention when you speak of what is of vital moment
to your own spiritual well-being. There is no
subject so trite and commonplace that will not
acquire freshness when spoken of by one who is
dealing with it as matter of life and death to himself. It is almost useless handling Justification,
Sacrifice, the Divinity of Christ, His Intercession,
if you are merely wishing to fill up a Sunday-
service with an adequate treatment of such a
theme ; but these are the subjects which tell most
powerfully when you approach them, because you
find that for your own soul's peace you are driven
to take to pieces all that has been taught you

about them, and to reconstruct them for yourselves. "All language and literature," says John
Stuart Mill, "are full of general observations on
life, both as to what it is and how to conduct
oneself in it; observations which everybody
knows, which everybody repeats or hears with
acquiescence, which are received as truisms, yet
of which most people first truly learn the meaning
when experience, generally of a painful kind, has
made it a reality to them." This is especially
true of the truths of religion. Preach what you
have verified in your experience, and people will
be interested.

Even, however, when you are not deeply
exercised about any important topic, you must
preach upon subjects objectively important. It
.is the duty of every settled minister to be sure
that he is preaching with sufficient frequency on
the central facts and truths of the Gospel. In
some Churches the ecclesiastical year compels the
preacher to a regular cycle of the most important
Christian themes, and if we do not approve of the
method, we should be careful lest with the method
we throw away also the end it achieves.

Subject, then, to the limitations stated, it may
be laid down as a law that whatever is thoroughly
interesting to yourself, and has a religious bearing,

is fit material for preaching. But do not fancy that because a subject ought to interest you, it therefore does so. Nor yet conclude that because it has interested some one else, and he has made a good sermon out of it, that therefore it will interest you. Not at all. You have learned that you have just to wait your time until your interest spontaneously attaches to certain books the world admires. You have perhaps found that even in the Book of Job, or in Homer, or Dante, or Milton, you do not find all that the leaders of opinion find ; and that the book which four years ago you could see nothing in is to-day your meat and drink. So with preaching you will grow up to the best subjects. Be yourself. Preach what is of present interest to you, and other things will become interesting. But do not throw yourself off the line, or run off upon a false scent, by trying to be interested in some other man's subjects. The only legitimate method of creating or forcing an interest in a subject is by working hard at it.

But in finding such material for preaching, is no help to be derived from books? From books of sermons I think you cannot *directly* get much material. It seems to me that in sitting down to write a sermon you will come better speed if you refuse to look at any sermon on the same topic.

At the same time, I think it is every preacher's duty to make himself acquainted with the best work in his own department; to study and analyse and learn the secrets of the sermons which have approved themselves most decidedly to the hearers. But this analytic study of sermons pertains more to the acquiring of a suitable form for our own preaching. And probably the best way of using published sermons for the supply of material is to keep a volume of Newman, or Temple, or Beecher, or Spurgeon, by you for devotional reading. It is a good beginning to a day, and it contributes in a two-fold way to your work. The ideas you thus receive become assimilated to your own mental possessions and enter into your own spiritual life, so that your mind is gradually filled with material for your own thought to work upon in the preaching line. And, better still, it keeps you up to the right preaching level, and gives you the proper tone in which to begin your own work. It is the distinctive mark of genius, as John Foster said, that it lights its own fire. We who are not the gifted ones must often be content to catch light and kindling from another. Even the greatest writers have not despised such aid. Burke had always "a ragged Virgil" at his elbow; and the orator and statesman of our own day who most nearly rises to the level of Burke—I mean Mr. Gladstone—goes, as every one knows, to a still deeper and purer source of inspiration. Plutarch tells us that Caius Gracchus was frequently carried away by passion while speaking in public, and therefore kept a well-educated slave at his back, who, as often as the orator's voice became shrill and discordant, sounded a soft, sweet note on his flute, and so restored his master to the proper pitch. And it is by giving ear to the sweet, true, and manly tones of our best preachers that we are most likely to be recalled to our highest and best self, and to begin our day's work at the right level.

There are books, not volumes of sermons, from which much preaching material can be derived. Of course, as it is each man's own observation of life and of men that will best fill his mind with ideas for preaching, so each man has his own books that nourish and stimulate him; but I would recommend you to try the Puritan Goodwin, and the Romanist Faber. I cannot conceive of any one reading their volumes without receiving most substantial aid for preaching. But all good books are helpful. In the measure in which they are honestly studied, they widen the view, strengthen the judgment, and inform the mind. Only, nothing is more difficult than to *study* when you are not going to make immediate use of what you learn. It is one of the great snares of our profession to mistake reading for studying. There is many a minister who has been irretrievably ruined as a student by giving way to the fancy that when he got hold of a good book, and spent the day with his feet on the hob, he was studying. We all learn in time the truth of Bishop Butler's remark, that reading is the idlest of human occupations. And many of us learn that we read too much. As undigested food burdens the body, and impedes the free action of its organs, so undigested reading clogs the mind, and interferes with intellectual activity. It is when we are spending thought of our own on a subject that the appetite for mental nutriment is restored, and that we can actually assimilate what we receive. But there is almost no kind of literature that will not help the preacher, either by refreshing and enlivening the mind, or putting him on new lines of thought, or making him more familiar with the real motives of men and the actual issues of certain lines of conduct, or by supplying him with illustrative matter.

On the subject of illustration I have only two

remarks to make—1st. That every preacher should cultivate his faculty of illustration, because there can be no question that his success largely depends upon it. Of course I do not mean his popularity, but his power to impart and infix truth. And I would recommend, as perhaps one of the best ways of cultivating this faculty, that the young preacher should take up as his subject one or other of those laws of Christ's kingdom which are so frequently enounced in the gospel—I mean such laws as these: Except a corn of wheat fall into the ground and die, it abideth alone; or, To him that hath shall be given—for in order to enforce the working of a law you must of necessity cite *instances*, and it is easy to find suitable examples of the working of those great laws that rule both in the spiritual and physical sphere. 2d. The second remark I would make is this: Never introduce an illustration with the formula, "Suppose a man"; never, that is to say, illustrate by a hypothetical case—rather begin in the nursery style, "Once upon a time there lived a man." It is the direct affirmation of fact that commands attention. It occurred to me when Mr. Moody was preaching here that a great part of the secret of his success lay in this, whether he knew it himself or not, that he always drew his illustrations from actual life, from something his boy had said that morning, or that he had heard on the street. The reason of the different effect produced is obvious. If you begin your illustration with "Suppose," your dullest auditor instinctively feels that you may suppose whatever suits you, and that of course you will only suppose what makes for your own position. Masters of illustration, such as Aristotle and Homer, will always be found to draw from the actual.

Even where illustration is almost wholly wanting, vividness is always secured by writing in presence of your audience. As you sit at your desk gather your people before your mind's eye, and you will never treat your subject abstractly, and apart from their living necessities. To write sermons as a probationer is difficult in the extreme ; but as soon as you have a people of your own, and become friendly with them and interested in them, they haunt you as you write, and not only suggest the fit things to say, but put all the liveliness of personal intercourse into your sermon. Never allow your sermon to be a monologue, but make it an address from beginning to end. And no sooner do you get a real interest in the mental condition of any one of your people than it becomes so—nay, even though you have no special interest in them, yet if you set three or four of your people before your mind while you write, their shadowy presence will act as a test, making you at once feel where you are becoming dull and uninteresting and abstract. And be sure that in this small representative congregation that sit round your desk, your most obtuse and uneducated hearer has a place. You will thus, and thus only, take the sting out of that ill-natured but wholesome criticism uttered two hundred years ago, and no less needful now—" Preaching for the most part is the glory of the preacher, to show himself a fine man. Catechising would do much better."

2d. Let me now say a few words on the form of your preaching. And I would say—1st. Do not begin to write until your plan is mature. Have clearly in view what you wish to enforce, and let this rule all the parts of your composition. Your plan will probably take shape somewhat in this humble way: you will sit down, pencil in hand, and jot down various things that occur to you as requiring to be said on the subject. This is often terrible work. When the note-book fails me I have sat for hours at my desk, unable to think of one thing worth saying, and have had the mortification of seeing the whole forenoon slip by, leaving my paper as clean as it came from the mill. In such circumstances you will be tempted to wish you had devoted your life to smith or wood work, or rope-making, where you could measure your work by the yard, or to any occupation in which you could always uniformly go on and produce something. It is at such times you learn to sympathise with Lessing when he says, "Among all the wretched, I think him the most wretched who must work with his head, even if he is not conscious of having one." But in your happier moments various things will occur to you to be said, and as you jot them down you will gradually see how best to group them so as to form an effective treatment of the subject. Once your plan is vividly conceived, the heaviest part of your work is over. Many preachers, indeed, do no more. And men of a certain temperament will, perhaps, preach better with no further preparation than merely the conception of a well-balanced plan, and the accurate perception of the leading points by which it is to be worked out. If you see clearly what you mean to enforce, and know where you mean to begin and where you mean to end, and if you have also well in your head the arguments you mean to use and the illustrations by which you wish to enliven them, and the points you mean to make, you are well furnished for effective preaching, supposing always you have nerve.

Divisions are not always necessary; and some of the greatest modern preachers, such as Canon Mozley, never use them. Others again are strong in division. Frederick Robertson, *e.g.*, shows remarkable skill in so dividing his sermon that great scope is given for fully handling the subject. It is noticeable that almost invariably his division is twofold.

It is, I think, as essential to success to break up your discourse into brief paragraphs, each of them clearly enouncing and completing a single idea. A sermon thus broken up is as much more effective than a continuous, prolonged dribble of ideas as a succession of blows of a hammer is more effective than a prolonged and continuous pressure. You see a number of writers nowadays adopting the practice of numbering their paragraphs—this is the mechanical expression of the idea that thought becomes easier and more profitable when it is conveyed in compact pellets following one another consecutively. You will also find that it greatly relieves and enlightens a sermon if you can vary the tone of each paragraph. If one is explanatory, let the next be hortatory; if one is dogmatic, let the next be illustrative or emotional, and so on.

And when each paragraph is written, and stands before you in black and white, ask yourself these questions: Is there anything here that will do the people good, or that they ought to know, and do not already know; and have I put it so that it is impossible for them to miss understanding and being impressed by it?

3d. You may nullify by bad *delivery* what is admirable both in matter and in form. Indeed, it is pitiable to think how much waste goes on weekly in Scotland in this respect. You must, in the first place, bear in mind that a large part of your hearers when they say that they like your preaching better than that of some one else, simply and solely mean that they hear you better. You will be astonished to learn how many people find comfort in having a voice come clear and pleasantly on the ear. Cicero had some little experience as a public speaker, and he advises regarding the voice "*ut clara sit, ut suavis.*" For a large number of our hearers, the first requisite of preaching is that it be heard with perfect ease and satisfaction. You cannot help listening from the first to Mr. ——'s preaching, because he begins in a clear, resonant, masculine voice—a voice which somehow comes home to the mind with the intimation that it has something to say. Whenever you find yourself beginning your sermon in a tone of friendliness and lively interest, you may feel sure of holding the people's attention. When you can put yourself, in your own mind, on thoroughly good terms with your audience, without being patronising or childishly coaxing, you are ·sure to catch their attention. On the other hand, when you get annoyed with the coughing of a miscellaneous audience or sulky at their inattention, you become conscious that this betrays itself in your voice, and you may as well be done. The pulpit voice assumed by some preachers is not to be commended, nor the lugubrious or preternaturally solemn tones in which you sometimes hear a man begin the service, as if his wife were lying dead in the vestry. Yet this solemnity has a great effect in quieting an audience, and possibly acts as the tones of the organ do in quickening religious sensibility. Still, I would say, above all things be natural. Do not speak as you speak across a table to a friend, for it is not natural to address a thousand people as you address one; but do not assume a voice.

But, above all, cultivate the art of preaching without notes. I do not know any art that is so much worth acquiring as that of public speaking. Miseries unspeakable must be endured by some in acquiring it; agonies of nervousness before each attempt, and agonies of shame afterwards; but the price is not too heavy. The man who has acquired the faculty of addressing a body of his fellow-men wields the most effective instrument that man can wield. Of all technical faults of which I this day repent there is none which I more constantly and deeply regret than that I did not thoroughly acquire this faculty. A read sermon, and, still more, a read lecture, may be instructive and impressive, but undoubtedly the highest form of address is that in which a man speaks face to face with his audience, without even the slight intervention of his own manuscript. I have no faith in committed sermons, in which the man stands like an automaton that has been wound up to say certain words, the eye fixed on emptiness, and empty as that which it is fixed upon—a more painful, depressing spectacle rarely appears in the pulpit than this. This is the deadest form of all public speaking, in which a man reads off his memory, and is so anxiously absorbed that he has not a tithe of the freedom the reader of the manuscript has. But where a man can be at pains to master his subject, and get thoroughly interested in it; where he has broken it up into natural consecutive divisions; where he has spent time in revising and selecting his material, and so holds it in his mind freely; and where he is so sure of his grasp of the whole that the presence of his audience only animates and gives him his opportunity,—there you are sure to have the utmost success the man is capable of achieving.

And not only does carefully-prepared speech tell on every one, and with tenfold more force than written discourse tells on the few, but the practice of such careful preparation reacts powerfully and advantageously on your written style. You acquire the habit of holding a complete subject in your mind : you are compelled to find a plan which is distinct and memorable—else you become entangled as you speak—and so you learn to frame such plans, even for your written efforts ; and in speaking to your audience you instinctively choose modes of presentation, words and illustrations, which are suitable. On the other hand, to speak without writing is perilous, for written discourse tells as powerfully on spoken, as spoken on written. You have the highest authority for the assertion that the habit of careful, slow, exact writing, is the only school for ready and effective speaking. "*Stilus,*" says Cicero, "*optimus et prae-stantissimus dicendi effector ac magister.*" And in addressing your predecessors in study in this city one of the greatest of modern orators, Lord Brougham, used these words: "I should lay it down as a rule, admitting of no exception, that a man will speak well in proportion as he has written much."

I opened these scattered remarks by congratulating you on your desire to know something of the work on which you are to spend your life. I close them by congratulating you on your having chosen preaching as the work of your life. There is no work in which the opportunities are greater; nor any in which the stimulus is so constant and sufficient. It will never cease to fill you with astonishment and with delight, tempered by a sense of responsibility, to see people, Sunday after Sunday, returning for the express purpose of being influenced by what you have to say. No doubt that is not the universal attitude of mind, but it is the general attitude. Undeterred by past experience, forgiving you all your past poverty, hoping always the best, the people return and put themselves under your influence. They wish to be impressed; they come open-mouthed for whatever will truly feed the spirit; they watch and wait for the merest crumbs of instruction or edification. They hunger for the fruit of your study.

And this opportunity, grand as it is, is one which every honest man who will faithfully stick to his work can adequately use. I fear you may have asked me to speak to you this evening under some vague impression and hope that there is some royal road to preaching,—that you have only to learn the trick of the thing and it will come easy. If so, I trust you are disappointed. There is no royal road, and he that is not prepared to live for his work, and to be at it from week's end to week's end, will certainly fail. I know one or two men who have every natural qualification for good preaching; they are sound-hearted, intelligent, kindly men, with large knowledge of life and great accuracy of general information, and, moreover, gifted with much natural eloquence, and yet they fail as preachers. Why? Simply because they do not work at their preaching resolved that in that they shall excel. Instead of beginning their work early in the week, and being at it as their main business always, they make a rush at it on Saturday or

Friday, and are carried through respectably, by dint of their exceptional natural ability; but they fail regularly and throughout to make that impression which they might make did they give themselves to their preaching as their main work.

When I began preaching I greatly underrated its importance, and consequently had far too little ambition about it; and I see nothing more clearly than that I might have been helped to much more effective work could I have seen from the first what I now see of the very great importance of the function. I would therefore say to each of you, with all the earnestness that a conviction wrought by experience can give: Resolve that you shall be a good preacher. Do not be content with getting and keeping a church, but be resolute to excel; and, for this end, live for your preaching; make it your centre, round which all your reading and observation revolve; have stated hours of work with which nothing is allowed to interfere; keep a severely true record of the hours you have spent on work each day, of what you have read and what you have written, and do not think you are likely to preach well unless you spend six hours of each day at your desk in real hard work for your pulpit. Men will tell you they cannot work save under pressure, and must put off till Saturday, that the steam, I suppose, may be sufficiently compressed to become fully energetic. Why is this? Simply because they are lazy, and can do no work till compelled; and because they have trained themselves to neglect their work till Saturday, until an unconquerable habit is formed. Another class of men will tell you that they find they can perfectly well prepare on Saturday for their one service on Sunday. To spend more time would be waste, as much as if they spent an hour on lacing their boots or brushing their hair. But if a minister finds that this is so, he ought to be all the more apprehensive of forming what I fear is the great blot on our profession—lazy habits. Unless a man is working hard all the week it will become most irksome to work on Saturdays—just as the first sermon after one's midsummer holidays is the most difficult to write in all the year. And nothing will persuade me that a minister's life is healthy, if he is not working hard for a certain number of hours each day in his study. I know how plausible the excuses are, and I know what relaxation of study results in—laziness in the morning, increasing excesses in the daily papers, increased interest in gardening, several more pipes a day, and so forth.

Breakfast comes finally to its long-deferred end about ten, then there is a consultation with the gardener—which is, of course, *business*, and makes the idler feel that really his active habits are returning; then two letters have to be answered; then, just as he means to go to his study, he sees Mr. Fritterday passing, and before he has finished his colloquy over the hedge with him it is past mid-day. When he does get to his study, *Macmillan* or *Blackwood* is lying on his table, and he feels he cannot settle till he knows what is the fate of the heroine of the current story; or his window overlooks the busy hayfield of his neighbour, and he becomes ten times more interested in that work than in his own; and so his whole forenoon is gone, and he is summoned to dinner before he has earned his salt by one decent hand's turn. And so his whole life goes; and when he is put under the sod by his people, they regret the loss of a good-hearted, kindly friend, but they inwardly resolve that whatever their next minister is, he shall at all events be a student.

If you wish to maintain the respect of your people, and what is much more, if you wish to maintain self-respect, make a point of spending a fixed number of hours in your study each day— not merely reading, but studying, working resolutely at something profitable, if not directly bearing on the coming Sunday's sermon. You may be perfectly sure that if you thoroughly prepare yourself for a place of influence in the Church, the place will one day be given you. Good preachers are not so common among us that one may easily be overlooked in the multitude. And every hour of honest work you spend, and especially every written thought you have fabricated with care and effort, will stand you in good stead before you are done with your ministry. In a word, magnify your office, and recognise it as rightfully claiming the whole effort of your manhood, the most skilfully trained intellect, and the utmost grace that pure and healthful living, constant prayer, and hopeful self-control can secure to you. No work makes so constant a demand on all our best energies, and none, therefore, yields so constant a return of keen and healthful happiness.

IX

MARCUS AURELIUS

It is much to say, yet I think it is true, that it
would be impossible to find among men a character more stainless than that of Marcus Aurelius.
When he died, his bereaved subjects felt that
Heaven had reclaimed its own: they thought of
him as still their patron above, and the young
men called upon "Marcus, my father"; the men
of middle age on "Marcus, my brother"; the old
men on "Marcus, my son." A century after his
death his bust was to be found in the house
of every Roman whose means could afford the
slightest decoration. Disturbed as the empire
was, there was no party in it that did not
acknowledge the integrity and unselfishness of
his character. Set in that "fierce light that
beats upon a throne and blackens every blot,"
judged by the lofty standard his own philosophy
erected, no fault was found in him that the

bitterest enemy could have dared to point at, and no enemy was found who would have used such opportunity had it been given. The one solitary rebellion which a mistaken officer of his own strove to raise against him only stood as the occasion for one of the most signal acts of magnanimity that history records. The consenting judgment of his contemporaries is ratified by the impartial and unsparing criticism of modern times. It is the most authoritative critic of our own day who says that Marcus Aurelius "is perhaps the most beautiful figure in history. He is one of those consoling and hope-inspiring marks, which stand for ever to remind our weak and easily discouraged race how high human goodness and perseverance have once been carried, and may be carried again." Born with the disposition of a Christian saint, his destiny made him a pagan emperor: born amidst the dregs of pagan vice, he lived to put to shame the effeminacy and insincerity and selfishness of Christians.

From the year 96 to the year 180 the Roman Empire was governed by that succession of rulers commonly known as the five good emperors: Nerva, Trajan, Hadrian, Antoninus Pius, and Marcus Aurelius Antoninus. These princes followed one another in the occupation of the imperial throne not by hereditary succession, but by nomination or adoption. Marcus Aurelius was the nephew and son-in-law of his predecessor, and aided him in the government until his death in the year 161. After this Marcus reigned as emperor for nineteen years, dying on the 17th of March 180, in his fifty-ninth year. While quite a child, and known by his family name of Verus, he had caught the fancy of Hadrian, who in playful admiration of his bold candour and integrity used to call him Verissimus.

He was educated with the greatest care, and was singularly fortunate in the society of wise and faithful men. As he himself afterwards said, " To the gods I am indebted for having good grandfathers, good parents, a good sister, good teachers, good associates, good kinsmen and friends, nearly everything good." From the hand of Aurelius himself we have a characteristic record which enables us to form a tolerably accurate picture of his youth. This record takes the form of an analysis of the influences which entered into the formation of his character, together with a grateful reference to the various persons from whom those influences were derived. "From my mother I learned to abstain not only from doing evil, but even from thinking it," and so forth. He records his thankfulness that he had been brought up, not at a public school, but at home, and amidst influences which, while they compelled him to be hardy and laborious, requiring the barest food, and content with a plank bed and a skin, yet kept him out of the vitiated atmosphere of Roman life and laid the foundations of a dignified and fearless manhood in a chaste, patient, and honourable youth. His first tutor was Fronto, who, though a pedant and a rhetorician, thoroughly won the boy-prince to a love of study, of purity, and of truth, and remained his friend for life.   In the letters that passed between Marcus and Fronto in after years a side of the emperor's character comes out which is apt to be lost sight of amidst the cares of empire and the abstractions of philosophy.   One of these letters gives so clear an account of the manner in which a young Roman of steady habits spent his day in the country, and lets us so clearly see how unchanging the greater part of human life is, that I may quote it in full:

"I slept late this morning on account of my cold, but it is better.   From five in the morning till nine I partly read Cato on Agriculture and partly wrote, not quite such rubbish as yesterday.   Then I greeted my father, and then soothed my throat with honey water without absolutely gargling.   Then I attended my father as he offered sacrifice.   Then to breakfast.

What do you think I ate? Only a little bread, though I saw the others devouring beans, onions, and sardines! Then we went out to the vintage and got hot and merry, but left a few grapes still hanging, as the old poet says, "atop on the topmost bough." At noon we got home again, and I worked a little, but it was not much good. Then I chatted a long time with my mother as she sat on her bed. My conversation consisted of, "What do you suppose my Fronto is doing at this moment?" to which she answered, "And my Gratia, what is she doing?" and then I, "And our little birdie, Gratia the less?" And while we were talking and quarrelling as to which of us loved you all the best, the gong sounded, which meant that my father had gone to the bath. So we bathed and dined in the oil-press room. I don't mean that we bathed in the oil-press room, but we bathed and then dined and amused ourselves with listening to the peasants' banter. And now that I am in my own room again, before I roll over and snore I am fulfilling my promise and giving an account of my day to my dear tutor. And if I could love him better than I do I would consent to *miss* him even more than I miss him now. Take care of yourself, my best and dearest Fronto, wherever you are. The fact is that I love you, and you are far away."[1]

Another letter gives us an equally pleasant glimpse of a Roman domestic interior: "The weather is bad and I feel uncomfortable, but

[1] Myers' translation.

when my little girls are well, the sun shines and my pains disappear." Fronto on his part sends kind messages to the children, "kisses their fat little toes and tiny hands"; and records how well rewarded he had been for visiting the country house of Aurelius, since he was met on the slippery hill road by two of the children, one munching a piece of fine white bread such as a king's son might eat, says the rhetorician, and the other tackling a hard black crust, fit for the child of a philosopher.

But a new tutor brought into the lad's mind thoughts that changed the boy into a man. Rusticus, a Stoic philosopher, first taught him to think, to look at things, not at words: "From Rusticus I received the impression that my *character* required improvement and discipline; and from him I learned not to be led astray to sophistic emulation, nor to delivering little hortatory orations, nor to showing myself off as a man who practises much discipline, or does benevolent acts in order to make a display; and to abstain from rhetoric and poetry and fine writing; and to write my letters with simplicity; and to read carefully and not to be satisfied with a superficial understanding of a book." To Rusticus also he was indebted for a copy of the discourses of Epictetus, of which he might have said, as our own Southey said, "I carried Epictetus in my pocket till my very heart was ingrained with it, as a pig's bones become red by feeding him upon madder." Epictetus was a slave; but thought is as levelling as love, and the future emperor, happily for himself and for us, sat at the feet of the slave and learned how to live a free man, superior to all earthly conditions, moved solely from within, his own master, daunted by nothing, allured by nothing.

But it was in his predecessor in the empire, his adopted father Antoninus, that his natural virtue found its most valuable stimulus. Antoninus was a man of pure and simple tastes; able to enjoy the pleasures of life, but equally able to do without them; not curious, as his nephew tells us, about what he ate or wore, but showing that it was possible to live in a palace without show, without guards, without display and pomp, simple without affectation, never indulging in love of novelty or in petty and mean thoughts—living as a private person, and yet not shirking any of the responsibilities and duties of empire nor forgetting the magnificence that on public occasions befits a ruler. And what seems to have impressed Marcus more than anything else was that amidst the constant pressure of affairs of state, his uncle was always self-possessed and always had leisure —to use his own expression, he never "carried anything to the sweating point," was never fussy and excited, never harsh, violent, or implacable. To be a reproduction of his uncle would have seemed to him a great attainment, as may be gathered from this little address he makes to his own soul: "Take care that thou art not made into a Caesar, that thou art not dyed with this dye; for such things happen. Keep thyself then simple, good, pure, serious, free from affectation, a friend of justice, a worshipper of the gods, kind, affectionate, strenuous in all proper acts. Strive to continue to be such as philosophy wished to make thee. Reverence the gods, and help men. Short is life. There is only one fruit of this terrene life, a pious disposition and social acts. Do everything as a disciple of Antoninus" (vi. 30). An emperor who continually reminded himself that "even in a palace life may be lived well" (v. 16), might be expected to exert a salutary influence on the manners of his time: and yet such were the excesses and enormities that formed the every-day life of the Romans that the good Ruler could but turn away in abhorrence, exclaiming, "Come quick, O Death, lest I too should become like them" (ix. 13).

The result of this training was a reign which went far to justify the saying of Plato, that those states only would be truly happy which were governed by philosophers. Here at last was a ruler who scorned the dissolute pleasure-seeking of a Nero or a Domitian, and, to use his own words, "found nothing better in life than justice, truth, temperance, fortitude"; who, instead of gloomily secluding himself like a Tiberius in fear and hatred of his subjects, would live as on a mountain and desired "nothing needing walls and curtains," but imitated the Pythagoreans in taking the naked and shining heavenly bodies as his models, and reminded himself that "there is no veil over a star." The errors and weaknesses which might have been expected to betray the philosopher, when called to govern so wide an empire, he instinctively avoided. Not only did he head the imperial legions and commit himself to all the hardships of the Danubian frontier with the daring and endurance of the first Caesar, but he clearly perceived the limitation of philosophy, and how impossible it was to make men good by compulsion, or to bring the actual state into the condition of an ideal commonwealth. "How idle," he says, "are all these poor people who are playing the philosopher in politics. . . . Do

not expect Plato's republic, but be content if the
smallest thing goes on well in your hands. For
who can change men's principles? And without
a change of principles, if you change men's conduct, you have only the slavish service of men
who groan while they pretend to obey" (ix. 29).
Yet his own idea of government must have been
as utopian as any. "I have received," he says,
"the idea of a polity in which there is the same
law for all, a polity administered with regard to
equal rights and equal freedom of speech, and the
idea of a kingly government which respects most
of all the rights of the governed" (i. 14).

It is, however, not as Emperor of Rome, but
as author of the *Meditations*, that he has become
endeared to all thoughtful men. Not by his
prowess among the marshes of the Danube, not
by his stemming for a year or two the resistless
tide of northern barbarism, but by the jottings
he set down in his commonplace book, as he lay
solitary in his tent at night, has he become one
of the truest benefactors of mankind. Men of
various types have found true spiritual encouragement in the little notebook, which bears no mark
of having been intended for publication, and
which has been so little cared for in style that
it is often unintelligible. Cardinal Barberini

translates it and dedicates his work to his soul "to make it redder than his own purple at the sight of this Gentile's virtues." Richter, greatest of German humorists, tells us "what swimming belts and cork-waistcoats for the deepest floods he possessed in the *Meditations* of Antoninus." It is one of the great books of the world, a kind of Stoic's Bible, full of reality and helpfulness. Some books are for the shelves, others for the table; this is for constant companionship. There is no beauty of style, but you miss that as little as you miss it in your friend's eager talk: and the thoughts penned 1700 years ago in the wastes of Sarmatia are as little obsolete as water or sunshine.

For in this volume Marcus presents us not with a speculative philosophy, but rather with detached thoughts regarding conduct. There is in the book no systematic discussion or prolonged treatment of any subject; but only such jottings as a very busy but keenly observant and profoundly reflective man could make. It is easy to gather from these scraps the kind of character he accepted as his ideal, and the principles by which he considered human life should be regulated. There are also many considerations urged which should induce men to live well; indeed the book is very much the definite enunciation of the considerations he habitually urged upon himself—it is the reflex of his own spiritual attitude. No one with this book in his hand could be much at a loss regarding conduct or practical ethics: and no one can use it without seeing the reasonableness of virtue and being drawn into a more stimulating sympathy with goodness; but the authority which ethics derive from forming an organic part of a philosophical system is not possessed by the ethics of Aurelius. Matthew Arnold says that in his character, " beautiful as it is, there is something melancholy, circumscribed, ineffectual." I would say this rather of his book than of his character. It lacks root in a defensible scheme of the universe.

The character he aimed at may readily be gathered from almost any page of his book. For example, "Let the God within thee be the guardian of a living being; masculine, adult, political, and a Roman, and a Ruler; who has taken up his post in life as one that awaits with readiness the signal that shall summon him away. Labour not unwillingly, nor without regard to the common interest, nor without due consideration. . . . Such a man, who delays no longer to strive to be among the best, is as a priest and servant of the gods, obeying that God who is in himself enshrined, who renders him unsoiled of pleasure, unharmed by any pain, untouched by insult, feeling no wrong, a wrestler in the noblest struggle, which is, that by no passion he be over-thrown; dyed to the depth in justice, and with his whole heart welcoming whatsoever cometh to him and is ordained" (iii. 5 and 4).   Again: "Every moment think steadily as a Roman and a man, to do what thou hast in hand with perfect and simple dignity and feeling of affection, and freedom and justice"; "When thou hast assumed these names—good, modest, true, rational, equal-minded, magnanimous—take care that thou dost not change these names; and, if thou shouldest lose them, quickly return to them. If thou main-tainest thyself in possession of these names with-out desiring that others should call thee by them, thou wilt be another being, and wilt enter on another life. For to continue to be such as thou hast hitherto been, and to be torn in pieces and defiled in such a life is the character of a very stupid man, and one overfond of his life, and like those half-devoured fighters with wild beasts, who though covered with wounds and gore still beg to be kept till the following day, though they will be exposed in the same state to the claws and bites. Therefore fix thyself in the possession of these few names: and if thou art able to abide in them, abide as if thou wast removed to the Happy Islands."

One of the most stimulating qualities in the ethics of Aurelius is his insistance on the possibility of virtue in all circumstances. "Thou sayest, 'Men cannot admire the sharpness of thy wits.' Be it so; but there are many other things of which thou canst not say, 'I am not by nature formed for these things.' Show those qualities then which are in thy power—sincerity, gravity, endurance of labour, aversion to pleasure, contentment with thy portion and with few things, benevolence, frankness, no love of superfluity, freedom from trifling, magnanimity. Dost thou not see how many qualities thou art at once able to exhibit, as to which there is no excuse of natural incapacity and unfitness, and yet thou still remainest voluntarily below the mark? Or art thou compelled, through being defectively furnished by nature, to murmur, and to be mean, and to flatter, and to find fault with thy poor body, and to try to please men, and to make great display, and to be so restless in thy mind? No indeed; but thou mightest have been delivered from these things long ago." In a similar strain : "Thou hast not leisure to read. But thou hast leisure to check arrogance : thou hast leisure to be superior to pleasure and pain : thou hast leisure to be superior to love of fame, and not to be vexed at stupid and ungrateful people " (viii. 8). In difficult circumstances and temptations he saw only additional material for virtue, as in wood heaped on the flame the fire finds only fuel. He apprehended that virtue lay not in circumstances, but in one's self. "Look within. Within is the fountain of good, and it will ever bubble up, if thou wilt ever dig." Even the opposition of men whom he tried to benefit was not to prevent him from continuing to act benevolently and for their good. "Suppose that men kill thee, cut thee in pieces, curse thee. What can these things do to prevent thy soul from remaining pure, wise, sober, just ? For instance, if a man should stand by a limpid pure spring and curse it, the spring does not cease sending up good water ; and if he should cast clay into it or filth, it will speedily disperse them and wash them out, and will not be at all polluted. How then shalt thou possess a perpetual fountain ? By forming thyself humbly to freedom conjoined with benevolence, simplicity, and modesty " (viii. 51).

The firmness with which he held that good

must be done for its own sake becomes particularly striking when he shows that virtue is its own reward. "One man when he has done a service to another is ready to set it down to his account as a favour conferred. Another is not ready to do this, but still in his own mind he thinks of the man as his debtor, and he knows what he has done. A third in a manner does not even know what he has done, but he is like a vine which has produced grapes and seeks for nothing more after it has once produced its proper fruit. As a horse when he has run, a dog when he has caught the game, a bee when it has made its honey, so a man when he has done a good act does not call out for others to come and see, but he goes on to another act as a vine goes on to produce again the grapes in season. Must a man then be one of these who in a manner act thus without observing it? Yes." Again: "What more dost thou want when thou hast done a man a service? Art thou not content that thou hast done something conformable to thy nature, and dost thou seek to be paid for it, just as if the eye demanded recompense for seeing or the feet for walking?"

No profounder words have been uttered by pagan morality. They enounce two truths which lie at the very basis of ethics and yet are rarely apprehended: first, that a man cannot be called good until he produces good actions as naturally, uniformly, and perfectly as a tree produces fruit; and second, that the reward of virtue is to be virtuous. He who has grasped these two truths has got past the stumbling-stones that prevent so many from advancing in the knowledge and practice of virtue. The first truth is equivalent to the demand that it is the man that is to be good, and not only his actions: and the most radical scepticism cannot question the statement that a chief, if not the chief, end of man is to be as good a man as possible. There may be a question as to what is the best kind of man; but that men should aim at being the best kind cannot be questioned. All creation, as evolution shows us, groans and travails after perfection; and if men are to be at all they should be the best possible. This is one of the immovable data of all ethics since Aristotle. Again, the reward of the pursuit of virtue is the attainment of it. The reward of the care of health is to be healthy; the reward of courage and purity in boyhood is to be courageous and pure in manhood. The one inalienable reward of all virtue is to be virtuous, to have attained man's chief end.

It is interesting to see how Marcus disposes of

other incentives to virtue. What charm could fame have for a man whose reflections so often take a cast like this? "Consider the times of Vespasian. You see people marrying, bringing up children, sick, dying, warring, feasting, trafficking, cultivating the ground, flattering, plotting, wishing some one to die, grumbling about the present, loving, heaping up wealth, thirsting for consulship and kingly power. Well then, that life of those people no longer exists at all. Pass to the times of Trajan; all is the same. Their life too is gone. . . . For all things soon pass away and become a mere tale, and complete oblivion soon buries them. . . . And what is even an eternal fame? A mere nothing. What then is that for which we ought to employ our serious pains? This one thing, thoughts just and acts social and words which never lie, and a disposition which gladly accepts all that happens."

Neither had the hope of actual and conscious reward in a life to come any influence with him. Indeed he again and again candidly owns he does not know whether there is any future at all for men. In the prospect of death he comforts himself, not with the hope of happiness beyond, but by the certainty that "death is according to nature, and nothing is evil which is according to nature" (ii. 17). "Death," he says, "is such as generation is, a mystery of nature ; a composition out of the same elements and a decomposition into the same ; and altogether not a thing of which any man should be ashamed" (iv. 5). "The universal nature, out of the universal substance as if it were wax, now moulds a horse, and when it has broken this up, it uses the material for a tree, then for a man, then for something else : and each of these things subsists for a very short time. But it is no hardship for the vessel to be broken up, just as there was none in its being fastened together" (vii. 23). "Is any man afraid of change ? Why, what can take place without change ? Canst thou take a warm bath unless the firewood undergoes a change ? Can anything that is useful be accomplished without change ? Dost thou not see then that for thyself also to change is just the same and equally necessary for the universal nature ?" (vii. 18). "Thou hast existed as part of a whole ; thou wilt be absorbed into that which gave thee birth, or rather in virtue of a change of state, thou wilt be taken back into its Generative Principle." "Do not act as if you had thousands of years to live. Death hangs over thee : while thou livest, while thou mayest, be good" (iv. 17).

Even when his own instincts bid him hope, he prepares his mind for the other alternative and falls back, as always, on his fundamental belief that all things are wisely ordered : "How can it be that the gods, having ordered all things rightly and with good-will towards men, have overlooked this thing alone ; that some men, virtuous indeed, who have as it were made many a covenant with heaven, and through holy deeds and worship have had closest communion with the divine, that these men, when once they are dead, should not live again, but be extinguished for ever ? Yet if this be so, be sure that if it ought to have been otherwise the gods would have done it. For were it just, it would also be possible ; were it according to nature, nature would have it so."

In these passages we touch again and again the radical idea of his philosophy, that all things form one whole which is wisely ordered, and that each part finds its good in ministering to the good of the whole. "Consider," he says, " that for whatever purpose each thing has been constituted, for *that* it has been constituted and towards that it is carried, and its *end* is in that towards which it is carried, and where the end is there also is the advantage and the good of each thing. Now the good for the reasonable man is society." Again : "If thou didst ever see a hand cut off, or a foot, or a head lying anywhere apart from the rest of the body, such does a man make himself as far as he can who is not content with what happens and separates himself from others or does anything selfish. If you have detached yourself from the natural unity—for you were made by *nature* a part, but now *you* have cut *yourself* off—yet in your case there is this beautiful provision, that it is in your power again to unite yourself" (vii. 34). "The soul of man does violence to itself, first of all when it becomes an abscess or tumour on the universe. For to be vexed at anything which happens is a separation of ourselves from nature. . . . In the next place, the soul does violence to itself when it turns away from any man, or even moves towards him with the intention of injuring him" (ii. 16). This belief of the unity of things, of all being one whole, he allowed to guide him to the grand qualities of goodwill to men and perfect resignation. "Men exist," he says, "for the sake of one another. Teach them then, or bear with them." "It is a satisfaction to a man to do the proper works of a man. Now it is a proper work of a man to be benevolent to his own kind." "It is peculiar to man to love even those who do wrong. And this actually is the case, if when they do wrong it occurs to thee that they are kinsmen." And nothing could be more absolute than his resignation or contentment with everything which happens: "All things are harmonious to me which are harmonious to thee, O Universe. Nothing is for me too early or too late which is in due time for thee. All is fruit to me which thy seasons, O Nature, bear. From thee are all things and in thee all, and all return to thee. The poet says, 'Dear city of Cecrops': shall I not say 'Dear city of God'? "

This then is his creed: Nature is wise and beneficent: whether all things are governed by providence or by atoms, that is, by personal intelligence or by the natural and inevitable properties of matter, he does not know, but he is sure that all things are well and wisely ordered. Take the place therefore nature assigns you; be the best you can, and do the best you can, and go when called. If you ask him what we are to make of the distresses of life, of disease, of the loss of friends, of the disappointments and failures that pursue us and make life seem dreary and vain; he will tell you that these things are but the shavings in the carpenter's shop, the necessary waste and refuse thrown off in the production of the great end. The eye should not too regretfully rest on these things, but should be fixed on the great work positively accomplished by the world. What each man has to do is to maintain himself in loving harmony with other men and with the course of nature, and in all matters to do his best for the furtherance of what is good, not moaning over personal pain and loss, and not distressing himself about a future he cannot penetrate and matters regarding which he has no certain information.

This scheme of thought and belief, of which I have tried to give you an inkling, has been said to be "a kind of common creed of wise men, from which all other views may well seem mere deflections on the side of an unwarranted credulity or of an exaggerated despair. Here, it may not unreasonably be urged, is the moral backbone of all universal religions" (Myers, p. 204). Of the manner in which a man should carry himself in life a truer picture can scarcely be drawn. A character is sketched which commends itself to every educated conscience, and the broad lines of duty are laid down with unmistakable clearness. There is no introduction of any doubtful sanctions; no demand is made for a belief that cannot be yielded.   Attention is fixed upon what is certain, and morality is based on conscience alone. That is to say, we find here the scheme of thought which is so anxiously desiderated by many at the present day—a scheme in which duty and human life shall stand upon their own feet, and in which we shall not first of all be asked to believe in things unseen and supernatural.   Is not this scheme of the Emperor's sufficient, and why should we puzzle ourselves any more about miracles and immortality and a personal God?

The question is answered as soon as put.   The craving for a scheme of life which shall be independent of all that is beyond common knowledge is stayed as we read these earnest yet saddening pages.   Every reader is infallibly drawn to admire and love this soul that is boldly pioneering through the jungle and cutting a path for others while forcing his own way through.   But as you watch him you feel on the point of crying out to him that already the true path is found and cleared.   For through all his manly cheeriness and courage you see the expression of settled melancholy on his face.   It is the admirable but most pitiable courage of the captain that stands to the last on the bridge giving his orders steadily while he knows that the ship is going down beneath his feet. You admire, and love, and learn from him, as you admire the blind man who rapidly threads his way through the crowd, but you cannot but think how pitiful it is that when light is there he should not enjoy it.

For, after all, his scheme of thought and belief is the offspring of his individual character, and lacks that basis in reason which would fit it for propagation among men of all kinds. He himself had strength enough to live a manly and unselfish life, in the faith that all things are wisely ordered, and that he was set in this world to do his best. But if any one asked him *why* he believed and acted thus, he had no answer. Nay, he himself clearly saw the pettiness and paltriness of human life; he found it, to use his own strong expression, "mere dirt and darkness" (v. 10), and wished himself out of it. What then was the inducement to do one's best for such a world? Was it for the world's sake? Why labour for a race which is continually in a state of flux, one generation of fools and greedy cowards giving place to another generation of the same? Was it for his own sake? What was the inducement—to sacrifice pleasure to strive and sweat and toil to attain a character ever eluding the grasp, and even at the last only shining before him as an unattained ideal? Hope was entirely awanting in his scheme, and without hope for the race and for the individual, most men, though happily not all, will prefer and will defend the Epicurean motto, "Let us eat and drink, for to-morrow we die."

In fine, the element of belief which our modern philosophers struggle to discard is that very element the absence of which proved fatal to the ethics of Marcus. His system stands, like his own statue, beautiful, perfect, but cold and ineffective as marble. And that which it lacked to give it life was the belief that there is an unseen spiritual world and a life beyond the grave. Spasmodic efforts will always be made to find the meaning and reason of human life within itself; but all such efforts fail. You might as well seek the reason of the earth's orbit and of all the changes that pass in the earth's climate in itself and with no reference to anything beyond.

It is idle to ask men to live for virtue's sake, if at the same time you tell them they must die before they attain it; and it is idle to bid men labour for the improvement of the race, if the race is a mere flux of insignificant ephemera like themselves. Summon men to strive after virtue on the understanding that they have eternity before them to attain and to enjoy it, and they will feel the incentive. Tell them that the race for which they labour lives eternally in God, and they cannot set before them a surer or more animating hope. Let them know that the ills of life are the ills of school, not of home; that these ills work for us lasting good in a life that is to be; and in *that* there seems reason and encouragement. But if these beliefs be discarded, then not only is life an insoluble mystery, but even the morality which has grown out of these beliefs loses its nourishment and becomes a bloodless, passionless, and feeble ghost. We must learn a higher thing than the Stoic's resignation, the Christian hope: we must learn a more fervid enthusiasm for humanity than a procession of decaying generations can inspire; we must feel our feet firmer on existence than a mere contentment with an inscrutable law of nature can fix them. We must learn to pass through the manly helpfulness of the Stoic emperor to the height at which the modern moralist says:

" We men, who in our morn of youth defied
    The elements, must vanish—be it so !

Enough, if something from our hands have power
To live and act and serve the future hour,
And if as toward the silent tomb we go,
Through love, through hope, and faith's trans-
  cendent dower
We feel that we are greater than we know."

THE END

Printed by R. & R. CLARK, *Edinburgh*

9 783743 382008